D0960260

## Praise for *Lies She Told*

"Holahan spins a suffocating double nightmare that provides compelling support for her heroine's rueful article of faith: 'To be a writer is to be a life thief.'"

—*Kirkus* starred review

"*Lies She Told* had me questioning my own sanity, biting my cuticles well into the night, and jumping at the sound of my cat snacking in the kitchen. The best kind of suspense writer, Holahan will keep readers slightly off balance all the way through the book. Author and character so completely overlap, it makes the reader wonder if art is imitating life or life is imitating art. An excellent and compelling psychological read!"

—Susan Crawford, bestselling author of *The Pocket Wife* and *The Other Widow*

"Wow. I could not turn the pages fast enough! Intricate, intense, and completely sinister—the talented Cate Holahan keeps you guessing until the final disturbing page."

—Hank Phillippi Ryan, Agatha, Anthony, and Mary Higgins Clark Award–winning author of *Say No More*

"This was a thriller I couldn't put down. Cate Holahan expertly constructs two parallel stories connected in unexpected ways with a twist that left me thinking about the characters long after I turned the final page. Bravo!"

—Rena Olsen, author of *The Girl Before*

"Brilliantly conceived, chillingly conveyed, *Lies She Told* is a mind-bender of a novel within a novel, with a story that is both gut-wrenching and compulsively readable. Cate Holahan is one of the best psychological suspense writers out there, and she's only getting better. Read her."

—Brad Parks, Shamus, Nero, and Lefty Award–winning author of *Say Nothing*

# LIES SHE TOLD

ALSO BY CATE HOLAHAN:

*The Widower's Wife*

*Dark Turns*

# LIES SHE TOLD

Cate Holahan

CROOKED
LANE

NEW YORK

Copyright © 2017 by Cate Holahan

All rights reserved.

Published in the United States by Crooked Lane Books, an imprint of The Quick Brown Fox & Company LLC.

Crooked Lane Books and its logo are trademarks of The Quick Brown Fox & Company LLC.

Library of Congress Catalog-in-Publication data available upon request.

ISBN (hardcover): 978-1-68331-295-6
ISBN (ePub): 978-1-68331-296-3
ISBN (ePDF): 978-1-68331-298-7

Cover design by Melanie Sun
Book design by Jennifer Canzone

Printed in the United States.

www.crookedlanebooks.com

Crooked Lane Books
34 West 27th St., 10th Floor
New York, NY 10001

First edition: September 2017

10 9 8 7 6 5 4 3 2 1

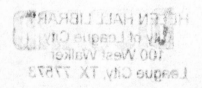

*For Brett*

*"You fill everything." —Pablo Neruda*

It is hard to believe that a man is telling the truth when you know that you would lie if you were in his place.

—Henry Louis Mencken, *A Little Book in C Major*

I don't know this man. Fault lines carve his cheeks from his gaping mouth. His brow bulges above narrowed eyes. This man is capable of violence.

"Did you think I wouldn't find out?" Spittle hits my face as he screams. Fingers tighten around my biceps. My bare heels leave the hardwood. He's lifting me to his level so that there's no escape, no choice but to witness his pain. "Did you think I wouldn't read it?"

I feel my lips part, my jaw drop, but the sheer volume of his voice silences me. His grip loosens enough for my feet to again feel the floor.

"Answer me." He whispers this time, the hiss of a kettle before the boil.

"I didn't do anything." Tears drown my words.

"Why, Liza? Tell me why he had to die." His speech is measured. I wish he would swear, call me names. If he were out of control, I could calm him down, negotiate, maybe even convince him that everything has been a misunderstanding. But he's resolved. His questions are rhetorical. There's a gun on the dining table.

"Please." Sobs fold me in half. I press my hand to the wall, seeking leverage to stand. "I don't know."

He yanks my arm, forcing me from the corner. My knee slams against the jutting edge of the bed as he pulls me toward the oak writing desk and open laptop. The offending document lies on the screen. I'm pushed down into the desk chair and rolled forward.

"You expect me to believe this is a coincidence?" His index finger jabs the monitor.

"It's a story," I plead. "It's only a story."

Though I catch the hand in my peripheral vision, I can't calculate the trajectory fast enough. It lands on the laptop, flinging it across the desk and onto the floor. Parts rattle. The bottom panel breaks off and skitters across the hardwood.

"Liar." He turns my chair, wresting my attention from the ruined computer. A fist rises toward my face. He's been building up to this. I shut my eyes. "You're a fucking liar."

I don't protest. He's right. Blurring fact and fantasy is my trade. I am a con artist. A prevaricator. I make up stories.

So why does he think this one is real?

# Part I

The most dangerous untruths are truths slightly distorted.
—Georg Christoph Lichtenberg, *Notebook H*

# LIZA

He's tracking my time. Every ten seconds, Trevor's dark eyes dart to the digital clock on his computer screen, a driver checking his rearview. My pitch has not impressed. He has more important things to attend to, authors who bring in more money. My work is not worth these valuable minutes.

He doesn't say any of this, of course. Our decade-long relationship has made his thoughts apparent. I read them in the lines crinkling his brow as he sits across from me in his office chair, scratching his goatee while the air conditioner's hiss recalls the reputational damage wrought by my latest book, *Accused Woman*. Not my best work, to say the least. Critics dubbed the protagonist "Sandra Dee on diazepam." She lacked *agency*, they said. Too many things happened *to* her. Really, she was too like me to be likeable. My former psychiatrist, Dr. Sally Sertradine, suggested similar failings.

"An affair?" Finally, he speaks . . . barely. A true Brit, Trevor drops the ending *r*. His accent mocks me, as though my idea has so offended him that even his critique doesn't require clear articulation.

He removes the wire-framed glasses previously perched on the wide bridge of his nose, sets them on his mouse pad, and walks to his window. Before him lies a landscape of penthouse terraces. In Manhattan, success is determined by view. Trevor's placement, high above even the city's wealthy, is a reminder of his importance relative to my own, of the weight his opinion should carry as opposed to mine.

"There's hardly a new way to do an affair."

"Well, I think of it as a classic revenge story." My voice cracks as I make my case. Dr. Sally also said I regress into adolescence at the first whiff of confrontation. The hormones are making things worse. "I think romantic suspense readers want—"

"Right. What *they* want." He faces me and nods. Trevor talks with his head the way Italians speak with hand gestures. The angle of his chin conveys his amusement or displeasure. "You must give your audience what they're craving. Readers are done with love triangles and tortured consciences. Consider what Hollywood is buying: stories about pushing sexual taboos and psychological manipulation. People want to play mind games in the bedroom, eh?"

A forty-two-year-old guy is telling me, a thirty-five-year-old woman smack in the middle of my target audience demographic, what my peers want in the sack. Sad fact is, I should probably take notes. For the past year, David and I have only bothered with intercourse when my basal temp kicks up. Trevor is recently divorced and inarguably attractive: a Bronze Age Rodin of a man. Women must be, as he'd say, "queuing" up.

He snaps to an unknown rhythm. Suddenly, his eyes brighten like he's figured out the step. "How about something with psychiatrists? Does he love her or is he messing with her mind?"

I could name four books involving twisted therapists that graced the bestseller lists in the past two years. But doing so would just support Trevor's suggestion. He isn't claiming that his idea is original, only that it's "on trend." Trends sell, whether writers like them or not.

Trevor mistakes my silence as serious consideration. "Think Hannibal Lecter without the horror. The sociopathic doctor meets a young Clarice, and she falls—"

"I don't know, Trev. Transference? Is that—"

"Trans?" He wrinkles his nose, offended by my attempt to slip esoteric knowledge into our conversation. Trevor often laments this about me. He complains that I bog down my books with details: how a gun shoots, how police detect trace amounts of blood, DNA lingo fit for a biologist. For *Accused Woman*, I attended a week-long writer's workshop at the police academy in Queens so I could get down every detail of the way a gun discharges and how detectives investigate. I even bought my own handgun: a Ruger SR22, touted by experts as the most affordable semiautomatic for women. My aim is horrible.

"Transference happens when a person projects unresolved feelings about their past onto people in their present, like a patient transferring romantic emotions onto their psychi—"

Trevor's full lips press flat against his teeth.

"It's not important. Forget it." My voice sounds small. Somehow, I've neared forty without gaining the surety that's supposed to come with middle age. I cough and try to add heft to my tone. The act clenches my stomach, intensifying the persistent queasiness that I've suffered for weeks. "What if, by the time the book comes out, interest in psychiatrists has waned?"

Trevor gives a *What-you-gonna-do?* shrug. "Well, think about it. And send me an outline before you go too deep into anything."

The request spurs me from my seat quicker than a cattle prod. Not once in my career has Trevor demanded anything more than a rough idea and a finished draft. Now he needs a chapter-by-chapter breakdown? The suddenness of my movement topples the chair onto Trevor's floor. I recoil at the spectacle of its four legs sticking in the air like a poisoned cockroach. I promised myself I'd stay calm.

I right the seat and stand behind it, head lowered. My temples throb their early warning alarm for a migraine. "That's really not how I work. I let the characters dictate the action." My tone is apologetic. *Sorry, Trev. I'm not good enough to write an outline.* That's what he thinks I'm saying.

"Maybe it's worth a try. New methods can lead to new results."

"If I could just write through a draft—"

"Liza, come on. You're a fast writer. An outline's no big deal for you."

"A draft barely takes longer. I'll spend twelve hours a day writing. Fourteen—"

"You've got the MWO conference coming up."

"I'm only staying through my panel." Nerves add unnecessary vibrato to my voice. "Hey, if you like the story, then we're both happy. If not, I'll start over." I force a laugh. "I'll even throw in a psychiatrist."

He runs his hand through his grown-out buzz cut. The longer hairstyle is new, postdivorce. It makes him look younger.

"Please, Trev." I'm actually begging. "I think this idea could have legs. Let me run with it. Give me one month. Thirty days."

Trevor reclaims his glasses and places them on his face. The spectacles magnify the teardrop shape of his eyes as he checks in with his computer clock. "All right." His head shakes in disagreement with his words. "You have until September fifteenth. One month. I can't give you any more than that."

He crosses the room, passing his bookcase of edited award winners. The Wall of Fame. I have a novel on there, though it's long been bumped from the center shelves. The door opens, inviting in the pattering of computer keys and one-sided phone conversations. Trevor smiles as he holds it. I try to mirror his expression, as though he's being chivalrous rather than kicking me out.

As I pass him, he gives my shoulder a supportive squeeze, reminding me that we're still friends, regardless of business. "Hey. I meant to ask, how's the search going?"

His expression is appropriately pained. In the beginning, everyone inquired with overacted enthusiasm, as though it was possible that we'd find Nick unharmed, wandering the streets tripping on acid, too busy admiring the pretty colors of the New York City lights to realize that he'd been staring at them for days. Nick didn't use hallucinogens to David's knowledge, but there was always a first time. An offer in a club by someone cute. Younger. Nick wouldn't have dared seem not "with it." He prided himself on hanging out with models and misfits, the artsy types that applauded themselves for gentrifying the Brooklyn neighborhoods where even hipsters feared to tread.

"I read that the police are watching the water." My throat goes dry. "Warm weather speeds decomposition. If he ended up in the East River, his body is likely to float to the surface."

Trevor winces. Once again, I've provided too much information for him. He's surprised that I would be this clinical. But it's been a month. We all know Nick is dead at this point. Well, nearly all of us.

"Give my best to David, eh? Tell him I'm sorry about his law partner."

I have a desire to scratch the bridge of my nose. Thinking too hard about Nick makes me itchy. "I will. It's been difficult for him. Nick was the best man at our wedding."

Trevor offers a weak smile. "Sorry for you as well, then."

"Oh. Thanks." The words come out flat. Accepting condolences on behalf of Nick Landau is as uncomfortable as constipation on a car ride. Twelve years married to his closest friend, yet I knew him about as well as the public knows A-list celebrities. I could tell police what he looked like, where he'd worked, the general area where he'd lived. But that's it, really. Truth is, Nick never liked me much.

# Chapter 1

Bᴀꜱᴛᴀʀᴅ. Hɪꜱ ɴᴏꜱᴇ ɪꜱ ʙᴜʀɪᴇᴅ in her long neck, his vision blurred by a cascade of black hair and the restaurant's mood lighting. He doesn't see me. I see him, though, despite the dying light outside and the dimness beyond the picture window. Despite the fact that I'm standing across the street from the Italian eatery where he took me just last week—me with my hair flowing like the woman's whose lips now part as my husband brings his mouth to her ear.

Bitch. I recognize her. She testified for him four months ago, hiding her beauty behind her butch blue police uniform, her hair yanked into that severe, standard-issue bun. The hairstyle had emphasized her humped nose, making it overwhelm her face. I hadn't judged her pretty enough to grab my husband's attention, to compete with me, given my circumstances. I'd failed to consider her chest, covered by a bulky button-down, or the way candlelight might soften her features. I'd failed to consider that my husband might cheat while I carried his child.

A black-clad hostess collects Jake and his date. She leads them from the bar perpendicular to the window to a table pressed beside the glass. My spouse is sat with his back to the street so that his eyes remain on the prettied-up woman in the skintight cocktail dress, white with black piping on the sides to fake an hourglass silhouette.

"Excuse me."

A hand drops onto my shoulder. Heavy. Warm. I whirl around, clutching the baby carrier buckled to my torso.

"Is everything all right?"

A slight woman stands beside me in a power suit. Her strained smile deepens the marionette lines around her mouth but fails to form any crow's-feet. She must see my smudged mascara, applied earlier in the hopes of surprising my husband or at least avoiding embarrassment in front of Battery Park's well-heeled stroller mafia.

I swipe beneath my eyes with my knuckles. "Yes. Everything's fine. I'm—"

"So hard being a new mom." She gestures to the tiny hat peeking above the BabyBjörn.

I look at my child for the first time in God knows how many minutes. She squirms in the carrier, arms and legs flailing like a flipped beetle. Her face is nearly the same color as the deep-pink bonnet atop her head. Her navy eyes are squeezed tight from the force of her howling. How long has she been awake? How long has she been squealing like this, with me zeroed in on her father, everything around me blurring into slow-motion light?

My surroundings sharpen as I picture myself from this stranger's perspective. I've been standing on the edge of the sidewalk beside a busy street, seemingly staring at nothing while my baby screams. This woman fears I suffer from postpartum depression. People are wary of new moms in Manhattan. They know we're all shut away in small apartments made tinier by ubiquitous baby gear, our walls closing in while our husbands continue working late as though no one waits at home.

I'd been waiting tonight. But the evening was so warm and the sunset, poisoned with air pollution, such a pretty shade of salmon. Why not go for a walk? And then, as my child continued to sleep against my chest, why not head uptown twelve more blocks to Jake's office? Why not pass that restaurant we went to last

Thursday with the delicious grilled octopus and see about grabbing a table in the backyard garden?

Ignorance is bliss. If only I'd stayed home.

I sway side to side, failing to soothe my child or convince this woman that I don't intend to step into oncoming traffic. "I have two kids, myself," the stranger volunteers. "Boys. Six and Eight. Such a handful." She smiles wryly, inviting me to vent, and introduces herself.

The name doesn't register. With all the thoughts running through my brain, I can barely recall my own. Her expression tenses as she waits for my response. "Um. Beth." I force an *I'm okay* smile. The effort squeezes more tears from my eyes.

"And what about this little one?"

I smile harder. "Victoria."

"Beautiful name for a beautiful girl."

My baby's complexion reddens into an overripe tomato. Her toothless mouth opens wider. Motion is poor medicine for hunger. I pull down the scoop neck of my tank so that her cheek may rest on my bare skin. Instinctively, she roots for my breasts, both of which sense her presence and swell with a searing rush of fluid. The woman watches all this. Her expression relaxes into something more friendly.

"Victoria is for victorious," I explain. "We had trouble conceiving. She's our . . ." My voice catches. Will there be an "our" after tonight? Not if I confront Jake like this: him, enjoying appetizers with his lover, and me, makeup a mess, shouting about broken promises while an infant howls in my arms. I will be the shrew, overwhelmed by the baby at my bosom, uninterested in sex, dressed for a spin class that hasn't happened in months. This other woman, meanwhile, will remain the sexy thing in a body-sucking sheath.

The stranger's smile has faded as she's waited for me to finish my thought. I cough. "Vicky's my little miracle."

That sells it. She gives my upper arm a supportive *we girls got to stick together* pat and continues down the street. Victoria starts fussing again. I pull a nipple beyond my top's neckline, and she latches immediately. I twist my head as I nurse, spying on the happy couple, trying to remain in the shadows and simultaneously project my pain through the restaurant's window. I want Jake to sense me without seeing me, just as I can feel him when he enters a room, recognize his presence by his scent, the length of his stride, the shape of his head as he approaches a restaurant with his hand spread on the small of a stranger's back.

After an eternity, Victoria releases my nipple, exposing my breast to the warm air. I adjust my shirt, and she settles against my sternum. Her lids lower. A satiated smile curls the sides of her mouth. Love, painful as a contraction, rips through my chest as I marvel at her chubby cheeks and double chin—the bond between Jake and I made flesh. *Our* victory.

Again, I turn my full attention to the restaurant. The waiter stands beside their table, a black leather folder in his outstretched hand. They've split an appetizer rather than shared a meal. Perhaps my staring has served a purpose. My husband realizes his mistake. He's calling this whole thing off. His biggest indiscretion will prove to be a misplaced hand and inappropriate whispering.

I retreat from the curb in anticipation of his solo exit. Jake passes cash to the waiter and then offers his hand to the woman, helping her stand from the bistro chair. I count the seconds until he releases her fingers. One. Two. Three Mississippi. She matches his stride out the restaurant, hip brushing his side.

There's laughter as the door opens. Hers. He's amusing her. It's been months since he's made an effort to do the same with me. They walk up the street. I follow on the other side, weaving around the downtown tourists with my head tilted to the sidewalk. Vicky's socked feet strike my stomach. My walk is too bouncy. I could wake her.

As I slow my stride, an illegally parked Ford Taurus flashes welcome on the opposite corner. A door opens. The officer slides into the driver's seat.

*Come on, Jake. Say good night. Say good-bye.*

He glances behind him, sensing me at last, perhaps.

*Say good night. Say good-bye.*

My husband walks around to the passenger's side. I look away, fearful that he'll see me. When I look up, Jake is no longer on the road. A blue police light flashes on the Ford's dashboard as it speeds off in the opposite direction.

An internal voice tries to calm me. Maybe everything I have seen has an explanation. They *are* coworkers, of sorts. They were talking shop, had too much to drink. Maybe they're flirting, not fucking. Maybe they're headed back to the office.

Maybe I already know the truth.

I turn around, sniffling and swollen, imagining my husband's thick hands cupping this woman's sides, his fingertips brushing back her dark hair, his voice telling her she's beautiful, exciting, enticing—so much more so than boring Beth, his overtired wife.

The traffic light turns. Cars race to beat the next red signal. Their headlights form halos in the darkening sky. For the briefest moment, I consider stepping off the curb.

# LIZA

I stare at the white screen, hands arched above the keyboard, a pianist waiting for a cue. Voices crescendo from Eighty-Sixth Street through the open window above my desk. Horns blare, traffic jammed on the FDR Drive. The target length for a romantic suspense story is eighty thousand words. To make my deadline, I must write 50 percent more than my daily average.

I've gotten as far as chapter two and a carriage return. Beth, my protagonist, has happened upon her cheating husband. A mild nausea gnaws at my gut as I consider how I'd handle her predicament in my life. Given my nonconfrontational personality, I'd probably try ignoring the affair at first and keep playing the happy wife, hoping that my husband would soon outgrow his "midlife crisis." Eventually, though, my lack of acting skills would show. I'd become sad and withdrawn each time David came home late, until he stopped wanting to come home at all. Ultimately, he'd leave for good, and I'd be left huddled beneath unwashed covers, unable to drag myself to the shower. I'd probably pity-eat to the point where my clothes wouldn't fit. Friends— Christine, mostly—would demand that I "get back out there," dragging me to "hot spots" in the city sure to nuke whatever dignity I'd managed to maintain during the divorce. I recall a makeover intervention that she'd staged when we were fifteen. She'd insisted we slather on eye shadow and sneak into some seaside dive sure to make me forget about my dad. "We need to toast to his departure, not get depressed about it," she'd said. "Let's make the tourists serve us for a change!" I'd ended up puking behind a dumpster while Chris held my hair. Not the night that she'd envisioned.

A shudder crawls from one shoulder to the other as the bittersweet memory is replaced with the bilious image of me back at the meat market, flaunting my depression weight gain before men my age who are too busy salivating at twenty-year-olds to notice. Meanwhile, David—the man upon whom I'd bestowed my own twenties—would be busy making beautiful babies with his surely fertile husband-stealing bimbo.

I shake the sickening thought from my head and breathe deeply. David is not cheating on me. He's stressed about his missing friend. That's all.

I drum my fingers on the black keys, not hard enough to type anything. What will be my opening line this time? For a suspense writer, even one who fills her pages with licentious liaisons, the first sentence of every chapter is like an AA meeting. It demands the immediate confession of a problem by a specific someone. *My name is Liza, and I'm a . . .* I obviously know Beth's issue, though I don't yet know how to solve it. We'll figure it out together, two friends fumbling toward a solution. My main characters are more extensions of my social circle than figments of my imagination. Each is fleshed out with characteristics of myself or my loved ones, endowed with unwritten pasts stitched together from my own experiences and the secrets of those closest to me. These embezzled backstories dictate my characters' actions as much as my own personal history decides my emotional responses. I don't invent my characters. I steal them from my surroundings. To be a writer is to be a life thief. Every day, I rob myself blind.

A door slams. I look behind me into the short hallway leading past the bathroom, trying to discern whether the bang was in my apartment or the neighboring unit. Footsteps answer my question. I check the time as I log off. Ten o'clock. Dinner has been staling on the stove for the past forty minutes.

I exit the bedroom and peer around the wall into the living/dining room, spying on my spouse. I do this often now, watching him from a distance, trying to ascertain his mood before engaging. Since Nick's disappearance, he's toggled between stages one through three of grief: tearful shock, frantic denial, and raging anger. I never know whether I should settle down for a silent night of him staring into space or brace myself for an endless rant against the inept police who still can't figure out how his friend and law partner "fell off the motherfucking map."

David stands in the dining area. His suit jacket hangs from one of four chairs surrounding a round glass table. It looks slept in. My husband came of age in the midnineties, when men were waxing philosophical about shampoo. He prides himself on his bespoke suits, and his vanity is filled with retinoid creams. The state of his blazer is a very bad sign.

He gazes out the French doors leading onto our Juliet balcony, hands shoved in the pockets of his pinstriped pants. The traffic noise is louder in the living area. One of the doors must be cracked. Though the apartment lacks central air, we never open them wide. A squat, seventy-five-year-old railing is the only thing preventing our potted Ficus from falling eight stories to the street below.

"Hey, you." I drape my arms over his shoulders and punctuate my statement with a peck below his ear. He pats my hand against his chest before pulling away. There are no words.

As much as I'd like to fault Nick's disappearance for his silence, our conversations have been dwindling for the past six months. It started, I think, with a case: a ten-million-dollar wrongful death suit against the state of New York, filed on behalf of the heartbroken mother of a high school senior who committed suicide after four years of merciless bullying. Nick had always been a strict constructionist with regard to attorney/client privilege, but the publicity surrounding the case had made David follow suit for the first time. Overnight, every question about David's day became a threatened violation of his professional ethics. Now I don't ask.

A dozen years together has eliminated any pressure to cough up a few sentences for politeness' sake. Our relationship has discarded formalities like my spouse's scalp has shed hair. All that's left of David's once Richard Gere–worthy mane are buzzed salt-and-pepper sides and a receding widow's peak. He overcompensates with a permanent five-o'clock shadow, which I find sexy, albeit sandpapery.

His shoulders rise with each breath. I monitor their tempo, wait for the rhythm to pause. "You hungry?"

He grunts something affirmative. I walk through to the kitchen and turn on the gas burner beneath my room temperature pasta dish. "How are you?"

He responds, though not loud enough for me to make out the words. I think he's said, "Oh, you know."

I grab two plates from the cupboard and a pronged spoon, which I use to dish out some of my reheated concoction. While David keeps mulling over the view, I shut off the range, grab utensils, and balance the plates on my forearm like a diner waitress. I slide his dinner in front of the seat draped with his wrinkled suit jacket and set my place beside him. His briefcase claims my chair. As I move it to the floor, I spy a stack of papers slipped into the back pocket. They're stuffed vertically into the flap so that half of an enlarged photo sticks out.

## Have You Seen This Man?

David has used Nick's headshot from the firm's website. The image doesn't do justice to the dead. Nick was handsome, though not in a generic, Hollywood way. He had wavy black hair that he wore to the nape of his neck and a Roman nose made more prominent by his narrow face. Deep-set eyes. Thin lips. Static images emphasize the angularity of his features. To appreciate Nick's beauty, one had to see him in action: smiling, frowning, posing. He had a roguish quality, a swaggering confidence that he possessed despite, or maybe because of, his small stature. Nick couldn't have been taller than five foot six; I towered over him at five foot nine. But like an actor, he commanded a room with his presence and orator's voice, delivered with a Mississippi twang and a side of biting wit. Friends of mine who didn't find him attractive on first sight would be falling all over him by the end of a night.

I put David's briefcase on the floor by his jacket and ask if he'd like wine, mostly to draw his attention to the table. He mumbles, "No thanks," and pulls back the chair. As soon as he sits, he begins shoveling pasta into his mouth, the first stage of ignoring me. I interrupt his eating before his eyes glaze over. "I have an appointment tomorrow."

David's chewing slows. I decide to interpret his deliberate mastication as a flicker of interest.

"Dr. Frankel will check on the cysts and the scarring. Last week she told me that the synthetic hormones seem to be helping other women in the trial . . ."

David shoves another forkful in his mouth.

"I want to ask her about the migraines too. I know I've had them before, and it's common for them to get worse with the hormones, but they've been really increasing in frequency . . ."

Though I'm not hungry, I take a bite of penne for fellowship and wait for David to speak. Maybe I shouldn't expect it, but I'd like a little empathy, perhaps an apologetic sorry that the drugs have me in a state of constant hangover. David meets my gaze and stabs at his pasta.

I put down my utensil and rub my temples for emphasis. "Aspirin always worked for me. Now it doesn't even help most of the time."

"Then stop with the drugs." He points at my left forearm with his fork, indicating the implant.

Though most people wouldn't notice, a trained eye would see six raised lines, each about an inch long, spaced equally apart like a flesh-colored bar code or scarred brand. Beneath each track mark is a needle filled with one month of fertility hormones. Two are already spent.

"No one is making you take them," David continues.

Tears, on a hair trigger since the new hormones, flood my vision. I flutter my lashes at the ceiling. David considers crying a female form of manipulation.

He shrugs. "I was ready to call it after the Clomid failed. But then you wanted this experimental thing . . ."

My pulse throbs in my temples and my teeth. The doctor's visit should have been a safe discussion, even a welcome one. David, after all, had encouraged me to take the fertility hormones after a year of single-line pregnancy tests and the endometriosis diagnosis. He'd known how desperately I wanted to have *our* baby, to raise a little person derived from our union, endowed, perhaps, with my creativity and his dark hair or blessed with his studiousness and my bone structure. And he'd wanted our baby too. He'd often mused about watching our genes flourish under a progressive parenting style, so unlike the authoritarian structure with which he'd been raised. How could he give up on our child? Over pasta?

My legs are trembling. Adrenaline urges me to run, to escape to the bathroom, where I can turn on the shower and dissolve into a sobbing mess. I place my palms flat on the glass table and breathe. I will not flee. I will not lose control. David doesn't mean it. This is Nick's fault. Stress from his partner's disappearance has overwhelmed him to the point of—temporary—surrender.

"Honey, I know your friend is gone and—"

"Missing."

"And I know it's not the best time to do this. But each day that I age decreases our chances of conception. I'm doing what I can, and I need you to do your part too. We need to make time for—"

He pushes back from the table and reaches for the briefcase.

"What are you doing?"

"I'm not having this conversation."

"It's not even a conversation! I was telling you about my appointment. It's been a month, Dave. Our life can't remain on hold indefinitely while we—"

"On hold?" He slaps the table and stands. Ceramic rattles against the glass surface. I wince as a knife clatters to the floor. "You think life has been on hold? In addition to my own case-load, I have all of Nick's work falling on top of me. It's impossible to get a continuance for everything. And the police are doing nothing to find him! I don't know whether he had a mental breakdown and is hiding out somewhere or if he was the victim of a hate crime—"

I pat the air, trying to calm him and myself. Yelling will push him out the door. "Why would Nick be the victim of a hate crime?"

David throws up his hands. "Why? How can you ask that?"

"Well, he's a white male. I don't see—"

He gestures to the side of the room, appealing to an invisible jury. "We won a ten-million-dollar suit on behalf of a transgender teen that held public institutions accountable for allowing toxic environments for LGBT people. Our names were in the paper. The firm has been inundated with hate mail ever since. At least two people have threatened to kill us if their daughters ever have to use a bathroom with a transitioning girl. It's a two-second web search to find our pictures. For all we know, someone stalked Nick to his apartment and is holding him hostage. But the police are doing nothing!"

I misjudged his mood. Grief stage three is not the time to bring up infertility issues. "Please sit. Let's just have dinner." I reach out toward him. "I'm not your enemy here."

His look casts doubt on my statement. Still, he collects the knife from the floor and settles back into the seat. He palms his fork and stabs his pasta until each prong is overloaded with noodles.

"I know you're under a lot of pressure. Maybe we should get away for the weekend. The house is free."

David's nose flares at the affected way I refer to the Hamptons place. *The house* is nothing more than my childhood home, a cedar-shingled two-bedroom, one-and-a-half bath in Montauk, on the water. It *is* worth a significant chunk of change, however. Whatever I think about my father, I must concede that the man knew real estate.

"Why didn't you get a renter?" He points at me with his loaded fork. "August is prime time."

"I got that insane offer from the trader who only wanted mid-June to the first week of August. What he paid alone will cover taxes and upkeep for the entire year, so we didn't need another guest." I proffer a smile. "I thought we might enjoy it."

"You should have put it on one of the short-term B and B sites."

David's frown saps whatever was left of my appetite. Though his salary has always covered our expenses with plenty to spare, things have been tighter since my books stopped making any significant financial contribution. The fertility treatments haven't helped our bottom line, either.

"Well, I didn't so . . ."

David jams the food into his mouth. "I can't commit to a vacation right now."

Talking with his mouth full is an act David only performs for present company. I should probably take his lack of basic social skills around me as evidence of a solid marriage. He's so secure that there's no need for basic courtesies. Still, I long for the days when he felt I was worthy of a conversation that didn't involve the view of chewed particles.

"You go." A fleck of basil lodges between his teeth. "The quiet will help your writing, and you can hang out with Christine."

A familiar tension twists in my temples. As much as I'd love to see my best friend, the whole point of staying at the house is for David and me to be together, away from the distraction of his job or Nick's disappearance. Also, I hate sleeping in my childhood home by myself. It makes me inexplicably anxious. Perhaps something about the crash of the sea outside, like a persistent knock on the door by someone intent on coming in. Or maybe the way the wind whistles through the rafters at night. All I know is, when I'm there alone, the house feels angry. The presence of other people purges the bad energy.

"I don't need quiet to write. I want you there."

David's eyes roll. Though he knows I dislike staying solo at the beach house, he thinks I'm insane for it. Montauk, as he so often insists, is one of the safest places on the planet.

"I mean if you're really concerned that you have a bull's-eye on your back because of that case, don't you think it would be good to get out of the city?" I walk behind his chair. He bristles as my palms land on his shoulders. I massage his neck for a beat before hugging him from behind. Once, he'd lean into me as I did this. But something has shattered between us, something invisible that I sense deep within me, the way a broken bone detects coming rain.

"Come on, David. We need this. Your trial will start next month, and I'm leaving for the MWO conference Sunday. I won't see you. We won't get to try . . ."

He exhales, a long, drawn-out sigh, something from anger-management therapy or yoga classes. "I have Nick's cases."

Again, the conversation has returned to Nick. The missing man sits in the center of a corn maze, and I keep getting turned around trying to find the exit. Nick. Nick. Nick.

When Nick and David met in law school, it was as though my fiancé had found a long-lost twin. Here was a man who could relate to his fundamentalist upbringing and his conflicting desire to challenge the rules he saw as unfair. Someone who understood—unlike his single mom–raised, New York–bred progressive wife—how it felt to be a Southerner surrounded by Northeasterners. As long as what happened to Nick remains a mystery, David will think of nothing else. The month that's passed hasn't dulled the pain of his friend's disappearance. A year could go by and David would probably still be focused on him, holding out hope that the man he considered a brother might turn out to be alive and well.

I drop my chin onto David's shoulder. "Hey, the police academy in Flushing is on the way to Montauk. I could talk to my contacts from that writers' police workshop. This one cop, Sergeant Mark Perez, was a twenty-year veteran. He might know something about violent crime in Nick's neighborhood, or someone who can tell us something."

David reaches up and pats my cheek. "Thank you." He exhales, an audible surrender. "Maybe I will try to get away for a couple days. I could come out Friday and Saturday, get back to work on Sunday."

I kiss his neck and thank him. Two days. Intercourse, maybe twice a day. Between two hundred million and five hundred million sperm per ejaculation. Seven or so ripe eggs in my ovaries ready for fertilization. All I need is one to stick to my uterine wall. The odds seem in my favor.

David seems to sense where my mind is. He sighs again and tells me how tired he is from "everything."

I decide not to push my luck. "I better get back to my book."

I scrape my dinner into the garbage and then put the plate in the dishwasher. Afterward, I grab David's jacket with a promise to toss it with the rest of the dry cleaning, like I always do. It smells of his sweat and cologne, a mossy, musky mix that I recognize as his signature.

My open laptop waits for me on the bedroom desk. I sit on the rolling chair and stare, again, at the near-blank page. What is Beth's main problem this chapter? What does she want? Her husband to renounce the other woman, beg her forgiveness, and tearfully renew his pledge to be faithful, for starters. But that's not happening this chapter. Maybe it won't happen at all. I swirl my finger atop the trackpad. What does Trevor want? A troubled ingenue falling under the spell of her Jungian therapist as he interprets her dreams?

Before my better self can block the image, I see my editor lording over a leather couch. The light from a reading lamp reflects off the sweat beads on his bare brown chest. The image lingers like a hot flash. I force it back into the trash bin of my memories and rejected fantasies, blinking until I regain focus on the glowing screen in front of me. I press the keys.

# Chapter 2

I LIE ATOP THE SHEETS, covered in darkness. Waiting. Dreading. Victoria sleeps in the crib crammed between the wall and our queen bed, breath whistling from her tiny nose. A breeze slips through the cracked window. It blurs the central air's hum with the sounds of the river and music—loud booty-shaking baby-waking music. Party boats. Each time one rounds the island, choppy calypso invades the room, destroying the tense quiet. Interrupting my focus.

The clock sits on the nightstand, casting a green glow into the space like a searchlight: 10:00 PM. When I was little, a public service announcement would sound at this same hour, moments after my dad settled down with his bottle of Bushmills to gripe at the evening news. *It's 10:00 PM. Do you know where your children are?* I'd be hiding beneath the blanket in my room. My mother would be upstairs in her bed, probably doing the same thing. The man of the house was to be avoided when drunk. Avoided period.

*It's 10:00 PM. Do you know where your husband is?*

The click of the deadbolt answers. A drawn-out groan announces the door opening. The pertinent question is no longer where is my husband, but where has he been. I know what he'll say if I ask: the office. He's already left me a voice mail attesting to it. *Hey, hon, I'll be home late. Trying to make headway on an upcoming case so I don't have to work on the weekend. No need to wait up. You need your rest.*

Work is the safe excuse. Murder trials can require a hundred-hour workweek. There's no homicide case on Jake's docket, to my knowledge, but how would I know one is not in the offing? And he is working on that case of the wealthy socialite who injured a bunch of people backing her car out of a restaurant. Why wouldn't I believe it's taking up more time? More important, why would I ever question his stated whereabouts? Before maternity leave, I accepted such excuses without a murmur. Most of the time, I was the one giving them.

I peel myself off the bed. My full-coverage cotton panties, the mom version of tighty-whities, reflect the moonlight from the window. The same glow lands on my bare breasts. Typically, my toplessness would be an invitation for a quiet quickie. Tonight, it's due to a lack of clean nursing bras. I bet that bitch didn't wear a bra under her dress.

I hold myself extra straight as I creep from the room and shut the door behind me. Five weeks postpartum and my belly is almost back to normal, though I must tense to keep my lower abdominals from rounding. Whatever excuse Jake has made for his behavior, he can't point to his wife's weight gain.

He hangs his suit jacket in the foyer closet, the door obscuring my presence in the living area. Somehow, he doesn't feel me feet from him. Perhaps his mind is miles away—with her. The door shuts as if in slow motion. I trace the curve of his buttocks in the light-gray suit pants, the side of his leg. I examine his arm, sleeve rolled up to his muscular bicep, his thick neck rising to his barely there beard and balding head, shaved tight so that the hair loss on the crown appears to be a choice rather than a consequence of nearing forty.

He sees me as he shuts the door and startles, stepping back toward the exit as though the woman before him is an intruder. "Beth!" He smiles, pretending he's not disappointed by my presence. Only a corner of his thin top lip ticks up. His eyes fail to crinkle at the corners. Some things you can't fake. "I didn't realize you were up. Did you get my message?"

A demilune console table is pressed against the wall to my left. Without looking, I can see the two photos atop it in their heavy pewter frames. The first is of Jake and me on our wedding day. I'm hugging him while he laughs. I'd interpreted his mirth as happiness. Now I see it as mockery. He knew that I had no idea what I was getting into.

I grab the frame and hurl it at him, a pitcher trying to bean a batter crowding the base. My aim is sure, but he's too fast. He yanks his body out of the way, head diving from the projectile, shoulders following suit. The frame grazes his dangling forearm before slamming into the front door. Glass shatters. Not in a spray, but in two neat shivs.

"What are you doing?" he sputters. "What's wrong with you?"

"Oh, what's wrong with me?" I grab for the other photo.

The image stops me. A few-hours-old Victoria sleeps on my half-covered breast, wearing the pink-and-blue-striped hat that St. Luke's slaps on all newborns. I am gazing at my photographer husband, a closed-lipped smile on my face that seems to shout, *We did it. Here she is. Our victory.*

My distraction is to Jake's advantage. Before I realize what is happening, his hands are around my wrists. He pulls me toward him as I struggle to wrest free while hissing insults.

"Baby, stop it. Stop." He doesn't yell. Either he's guessed that Victoria is asleep in the neighboring room from my whispered epithets or he's remembered that she goes down around ten. He leads me to the couch, fingers still locked around my wrists like handcuffs. When he sits, he pulls me onto the cushion with him. "Tell me what's wrong."

My response burns, bile in my throat. I am feverish with the effort of not shouting. "Where were you, really?" The words slam against gritted teeth. "Where were you while I've been here caring for our baby?"

He blinks. For a moment, I swear the pink drains from his face. The blood quickly returns, flushing his neck. "At work," he speaks slowly, examining my face. "As I told you in my message."

The bald-faced lie should inflame my rage. But he's looking at me with those intense eyes, blazing as a summer sky. They open so wide it seems his soul could slip out. He has honest eyes. I'd thought so the moment we met in that courtroom. I remember the way he looked at me as I loitered beside the prosecutor's desk. Him, a handsome young lawyer on his first murder trial. Me, a new recruit to the paper's law-and-order desk, struggling to project enough confidence to believably ask him hard questions. His brow had wrinkled at the sight of the press pass hanging from my neck like tacky statement jewelry. Then he'd seen my face, and those baby blues had sparkled like December birthstones. He'd looked at me and grinned, as though he'd been waiting his whole life for me to show up beside him in some airless courtroom. Now that I'd arrived, we would escape and be happy.

And I'm bawling. Tears cascade down my face. Convulsions shake my body and twist my mouth into grotesque shapes. Fluid fills my nose. I cry so hard I start coughing. I'm drowning.

He holds me to his side, cooing like a mourning dove. "What is it? You can tell me." The concern in his tone sounds so real. Yet how could it be? How could he care at all about me and lie to my face?

I gasp, unable to speak without screaming. His arms wrap around my back. When I shudder, he pulls me into him and rubs his hands over my spine, as though I've caught a chill that he can soothe with body heat and friction. My nose presses against his white button-down. I inhale in short bursts, trying to compose myself. At the same time, I sniff his clothes. What does she smell like? Jasmine? Linen? Sex?

The green scent of his deodorant soap and the mossy perfume of his aftershave assail my nostrils. He's applied this recently.

Liberally. I push back and stare at the bulge bobbing in his neck. No trace of a sheen at his collar, despite the hot day. If he stunk of this woman, I could convince myself that they'd hung out, maybe necked a bit in the car, at worst had a one-night fling that he'd fled in a shameful daze. But he's made an effort to clean up. An experienced cheater move. How long has this been going on?

He brushes my long bangs off my forehead, tucking the limp hair behind my ear. Part of me wants nothing more than to close my eyes and erase the memory of hours earlier. Him, me, and baby makes three. This is all I want. I hate myself that this is all I want.

"Is it Vicky?"

The mention of our daughter encourages me to get it together. I can't have a breakdown. I have a baby to care for. I inhale and exhale. Breathe. I need to breathe.

"Is it being cooped up all day in the house without anyone to talk to? You feel lonely." He rubs my back as though I've been ill. He's the sick one. How can he comfort me after trying to destroy me with his selfishness? He strokes my hair. "You know, a lot of women go through this after birth. Moodiness. Depression. Anger. You were on those drugs before we conceived. Everything is probably out of whack."

His audacity is a blast of hot air, evaporating my distress. He thinks he's so slick that I can't have any upsetting suspicions. I'm irrationally angry because he came home late. It's the crazy hormones. He continues watching me, expression sincere as a begging puppy. I have an urge to poke my fingers through his sockets and scratch out his eyes. It would be a public service—keep them from tricking anyone else.

"You should talk to someone. We have free sessions with a psychiatrist through the health insurance. I can give you numbers."

Without my tears, I feel brittle and empty. All I can do is gawp and blink. Why do I love this man?

"What do you think?"

Do I even know him?

"You want the number?"

*I don't need a shrink; I need not to be married to a lying scumbag.* The insult freezes on my tongue. Any argument will end with me shouting and him storming out. He'll call me nuts, claim he never left the office. I'm delusional, he'll say. I imagined it. New York City has eight million people. He's sure to have a doppelgänger somewhere.

"Should I make an appointment?"

I should have confronted him at the restaurant. Better to have embarrassed myself than to have my accusations dismissed as postpartum hallucinations.

"I don't know." My voice creaks like a broken hinge.

"Tomorrow." Again, he brushes my hair behind my ear. Fingers rub my head. He's petting me. "I'll book tomorrow." He yawns, a jaw-dropping expression that he covers with his hand. "I have to get to bed. Early morning."

He stands and stares at me, waiting for me to follow. My hands are barbells in my lap. My stomach glistens from fallen tears. One drop has settled around my still distended belly button.

He kisses the side of my head. "I'll give you a minute."

I grit my teeth. *A minute? You'd promised me a lifetime.*

# LIZA

The gynecologist chair is a modernized medieval torture device, coated with vinyl and topped with wax paper. Every time I'm in it, bare butt falling off the edge of the seat, legs spread in metal stirrups, I believe medicine has not come much further than the days of leeches. I'm wrong, of course. Researchers grow entire human organs from a smattering of microscopic stem cells. Babies are conceived in glass cylinders and installed in willing hosts. Yet none of these advances are aiding me.

My doctor, Angela Frankel, enters with her practiced empathetic expression. Brows flat, mouth set in a line, eyes swimming with sympathy. I've watched her with other people, seen a smile light her face as she calls in couple after couple who will leave twenty minutes later twittering about genders and genetics. Her mouth has never curled when inviting me into her office.

She takes the chart from a clear bin affixed to the door and asks after David. I excuse his absence as work related, refusing to admit the looming truth. David is done. He can't deal with the specialists, hospitals, and clinics anymore. He's finished with slathering scar solution on laparoscopy incisions in my belly and hearing me belch carbon dioxide. Done with ejaculating into sterile plastic containers destined for petri dishes.

My doctor grabs a rolling stool from beneath a desk supporting a model uterus. The sculpture is propped on a metal stem like a carnivorous slipper orchid. It stands beside a tower of urine collection cups. In my mind, the other rooms have better knick-knacks: model wombs split like walnut shells to reveal developing babies and gestational growth charts comparing average fetal sizes to common fruits. I'm always seen in room B.

The snap of latex gloves focuses my attention back on my physician. Casters rumble across the tile floor, coming to rest somewhere between my legs. A gloved hand grabs for a long wand attached to a small monitor. The device is about the size of an electric toothbrush, only thicker, with a bulbous tip. I hear the embarrassing squirt of lubricant before the internal ultrasound disappears below my paper dress. Pressure fills my pelvis.

"How are you feeling?"

This question is one of those standard doctor diagnostic tools. She doesn't expect a real answer unless I'm in serious trouble. I am to complain only if it's time for the epidural.

"All right. Thanks for asking." I force a smile, unintentionally tensing my body in the process and worsening my discomfort. "How are you?"

I pull myself up on my elbows to see her response. Between my legs is a wild mass of corkscrew curls, cut short to keep strands out of her eyes. She's not looking at my face. "Okay. Just relax," she says.

I slurp air through clenched teeth. How am I supposed to relax with someone puttering around my womb, poised to certify my female handicap? No fertile ground here. I miss my last shrink. If only she could appear like the insurance agent in a State Farm commercial. It would be nice to have someone sympathize with the torture of wanting something so much that your cells ache. I haven't seen Dr. Sally in nearly a year. Fertility treatments aren't covered by insurance, and good psychiatrists also expect cash up front. My last book advance didn't cover two out-of-pocket specialists.

My fertility doctor stares at the monitor as she moves the wand around. I shut my eyes, unable to bare the familiar black void on the screen without clenching every muscle. "Well, the good news is there are fewer fibroids this time around, so the progesterone is helping." A sharp pain radiates in my hips as the device probes further. "And the ovaries have multiple ripe follicles."

Before I knew better, the mention of "ripe" in connection with my female parts got me excited. The adjective brought to mind plump apple trees, limbs bending from the weight of swollen fruit ready to fall from the branches and accept a worm. I soon learned that in hard fertility cases, like mine, the follicles are rarely the problem. God, it turns out, is a pessimist. Instead of giving women five hundred or so follicles—one for each month of the forty-some-odd years that the average female is fertile—he starts us all off at puberty with more than four hundred thousand. Each follicle is capable of producing an ovum, so nearly all women have enough eggs for a hen house. Thanks to the drugs, I have half a dozen ready for market in any given month. If all my fertile eggs managed to hang on to the walls of my scarred uterus, I'd birth a litter.

All at once, the pressure releases. I remove my feet from the stirrups and scoot back into a more modest position on the examination chair. "If the fibroids continue to decrease, do you think in vitro could be an option? Maybe we could remove some of the eggs, fertilize them, and force them to implant?" My voice squeaks. Despair is awful, but hope can hurt worse. At least with despair, the cycle of destruction is complete. Hope is the Novocain shot before the surgery.

Dr. Frankel takes a short breath. "We aren't there yet."

I wipe the napkin sleeve of my gown against my lids before the tears can fall. My OB-GYN must be so sick of seeing me cry. God knows I'm disgusted with doing it.

"There's still a chance that an egg might implant naturally." She stresses the word "chance." There's a chance of winning a casino jackpot, too, but few people stake their future on it.

The casters roll to my right. I look up to see Dr. Frankel with her gloves off and an open laptop resting on her thighs. Since starting this experimental trial, our visits always end with her taking notes for the study. "So tell me, how are you doing emotionally?"

"Okay." I force another smile. "I try to save all my tears for this office."

She gives me a knowing look. "How are the mood swings?"

"Swing" isn't the right word in my case. My emotions don't vacillate between happy and sad like a pianist alternating between major and minor scales. They're stuck in a discordant chord. For the past six weeks at least, my days have started with a vague sense of foreboding. Throughout the day, my anxiety tends to intensify. Mild confrontations and disagreements have morphed from being uncomfortable to utterly panic inducing, leaving me unable to calm myself down.

Admitting all this, however, could prompt Dr. Frankel to remove me from the trial. People with histories of depression or anxiety were barred from participating because psychiatric medications would complicate results. As I didn't have a pill-treated mental problem, I'd signed up. But I'd also conveniently failed to mention that Dr. Sally had been pushing antianxiety meds for over a year, which I'd refused to take due to the increased risk of preterm birth.

"I'm fine. If this works, I'm sure I'll be the happiest person on earth."

She smiles at me, teeth pearly as a promise. "So how about physical side effects? Any nausea, cramping, headaches, migraines, or hot flashes?"

This, I know, is safe to confess. Everyone feels premenopausal on fertility drugs. "All of the above."

"How often?"

"The low-grade nausea is pretty constant, though it's slightly worse in the mornings. The headaches tend to hit me more at night. I've always had occasional migraines, but they've definitely gotten worse with meds."

She nods while typing as though what I've said confirms some research thesis. "Some people have reported haziness or forgetfulness since taking the drugs. Have you experienced any such symptoms?"

I wrack my brain for recent instances of absentmindedness: leaving the oven on, maybe, or misplacing a dry cleaning ticket. Have I parked the car in the past couple months and failed to remember the cross streets? Nothing comes to mind. Being a writer requires a certain attention to detail. I take many mental photographs.

Dr. Frankel looks up from her computer. "So any memory loss?"

The joke is a lay-up, and I want to show her that I am not always this weeping mess, that I've kept a sense of humor. "Memory loss? Nope. Not that I can recall."

She smirks at me. Apparently, she's heard this one too often to fake a giggle. "Okay, then." She rolls her eyes, showing that she's not amused by my corny sense of humor. "See you next week. Same joke. Same time."

I force a chortle at her awkward attempt at a competing one-liner. She takes her computer and tells me that I can get dressed. Her secretary out front will make the appointment for next week.

It's not until the door shuts that it occurs to me: I might have delivered that punch line before.

# Chapter 3

I ROLL THE STROLLER BACK and forth outside the office of Dr. T. Williams, never moving it farther than ten feet from the door. A small speaker sits at the base of his locked entrance, pumping a baby-soothing static into the narrow hallway. Vicky sleeps, motionless, in her bassinet.

Now that she's down, I wish his door would open. It's uncomfortable hovering outside a plaque bearing the abbreviations "MD PsyD." I could run into another mom, some woman who will recognize me later at the park and wonder aloud, "Is she crazy?" And I'm not. Damn it. I'm not. Though every moment that passes with me standing outside a shrink's office drives me increasingly insane. Why am I even here? This doctor can't help me. He can't patch my marriage. He doesn't even know there's anything wrong with my marriage. I'm sure when Jake booked the appointment, he said it was because I needed antidepressants.

I won't take drugs. Something horrible has happened, and I feel appropriately awful. I don't want to medicate away my legitimate feelings or deal with any side effects. Yet here I am, still, because I have no one else to talk to. I can't share this with my friends. They'd spout girl-power mantras. *Kick him to the curb, Beth!* They'd rebuke me for staying, thinking only of the indignity of being cheated on. I know, though, that the real humiliations would start after the divorce finalized. Jake, doted on in his girlfriend's sex den. Me, crammed in a small condo, working long hours to pay Vicky's sitter, spending every second outside the office playing mom *and* dad in a desperate attempt to give our baby a "normal" childhood.

No. I've made up my mind. I don't want to leave him. I want this other woman to go away, stop messing with my hard-earned life. And I want my husband to feel very, very sorry.

The door opens. A girl exits wearing an NYU sweatshirt and sunglasses. She passes me, staring at her shoes, as though she were schlepping back to her apartment Sunday morning in Saturday night's cocktail dress. I direct my attention into Vicky's carriage, fussing with the blanket at the base of her tiny feet.

A deep voice calls me inside. I push the stroller in first, chasing it with apologies. "I'm sorry. We don't have a nanny, and my husband is at work. She's asleep. I hope you don't—"

The sight of the doctor stops my speech. He stands in the middle of the room, a hand outstretched, back hunched to lessen the impact of his imposing height. He's easily over six feet tall, with a muscular body that his thin summer sweater can't hide. Handsome isn't an accurate description for the man. He has a face that could sell cologne: skin the color of roasted coffee beans, full lips, high cheekbones, and large brown eyes. As if things weren't bad enough. I'll be confessing my humiliation to a Ralph Lauren model.

"It's a little unorthodox," he says, dropping the doubled consonant in "little" so that the word sounds gentler than I'm used to. I guess that his faint accent hails from the West Indies. There's a slight Caribbean ring in the way he stresses his syllables.

"But that's all right." His mouth stretches into a wide smile. "I can't imagine it's easy finding a sitter for only an hour."

"Thank you." I feel my face flush. I'm hot, though the air is going, and I'm wearing a cap-sleeve dress, one of my few former work outfits that still appears business appropriate on my swollen chest.

He extends a hand. I shake, starstruck for a moment. He gestures to the love seat behind me.

There's a sweet, comforting scent in the air, like the smell of old books, though I don't see any. The couch is a gray leather, worn lighter in the center. That's where I'm supposed to sit in this medical office that's been camouflaged as a living room so that I'll delve into dark secrets.

The doctor sits, back to the window. A blackout shade has been pulled low for privacy, though sunlight breaks in from the sides. Most of the light rains down from bulbs embedded in the ceiling. One beam reflects off a tasteful black-and-white print of a tree. In the photograph, the sun breaks through clouds, creating an angelic glow above the branches.

"It stood out at an art fair. You like it?"

"'Only God can make a tree,'" I say, quoting the famous Joyce Kilmer poem.

He nods. "I see you made this beautiful child recently . . ."

Cue segue to discussion of postpartum depression. I perch on the edge of the couch. "Um, I think I should clear something up. I'm not here because of Victoria."

The doctor's face remains relaxed. "Well, what brings you here today?"

"My husband is having an affair."

I expect him to raise an eyebrow or squint, do something to show that he now understands why a perfectly sensible person is in his office. Instead, he nods, conveying only that he comprehends the meaning of my words.

"I saw him and a woman at a restaurant. He didn't see me. They were flirting, sitting really close. He held her hand."

Dr. Williams's mouth pinches on one side. "I can understand that being very hurtful."

The statement is too careful. I want him to side with me, tell me my husband is a jerk and I don't deserve that kind of treatment.

His lack of indignation indicates that he's reserving judgment. Maybe he wonders whether my husband is fleeing a paranoid, jealous type that stalks his every move.

"I wasn't spying on him. I'm not like that. It happened by accident. I was out walking the baby and thought I'd surprise him at work. I passed a restaurant near his office, and he was in there with her."

"Is this the first time you believe he's been unfaithful?"

"I don't know."

"You've thought he was unfaithful before?"

"No. I always thought he was happy." My voice cracks as I lament my own naïveté. I try to cover it with a fake laugh. "Clearly, though, I'm not that observant."

He winces at my self-criticism. "Well, it could be that this is his first time. And," he says, leaning forward, resting his elbows on his thighs, "here's the big secret about cheating. Most people who do it aren't unhappy in their marriage. Usually, they're unhappy with themselves."

The statement sounds like a shrink platitude. The third-person equivalent of "it's not you, it's me." I don't buy it. Jake's job is intense, but he enjoys it. And he wanted to be a father. I must be doing something, or not doing something, that is driving him away. Or *she's* doing something that I've never thought of.

"So how are you handling this?"

"I'm here."

"Does he know that you know?" His expression is blank, nonjudgmental. His big eyes say, *You can trust me*. I've fallen for that before.

"Look. I know I'm supposed to be a feminist and rage against him. Tell him that I will not stand for this. He can leave. I'll do it all on my own. Take care of the baby, of myself, of our finances." I gesture to the carriage. "But she's not even six weeks old, and I had this idea of her life, you know? It involved two parents."

"Well, she can have two parents whether or not you stay with your spouse." He tilts his head and gives me a weak smile. "In my line of work, you see plenty of separated couples. As long as both adults agree to be part of their kids' lives, the children will have both parents."

*Until someone gets a job offer several states away or remarries or has children with someone else.* I close my eyes to keep them from rolling. "That wasn't my experience."

"Your parents aren't still together?"

"Like half of America's."

"When did they separate?"

A familiar anger wells within me. Questions about my childhood pick at old wounds. I can't handle them while licking fresh ones. "Does it matter?"

"It can."

"I'm sorry, I just really didn't come here to talk about my youth. I'm here to discuss my husband."

He sits back in the chair and bestows a kind smile, showing he doesn't take offense to my snippiness. "Of course. What do you want to tell me about him?"

I picture Jake's clear-blue eyes. The way he rubbed my back last night, playing the supportive spouse after sleeping with another woman. The smell of his freshly washed skin. "We can start with him being a lying psychopathic shit."

"And yet you're thinking of staying with him."

"For Vicky."

"Only Vicky?"

An image of Jake's face on a recent dinner date flickers into view. He's laughing. I can always crack him up. For a moment, I think I might start crying again, but I've used up my supply of salt water. The prior night has left me with an emotional hangover. There's nothing left in me except bile. "I don't know," I say finally. "Maybe that's why I'm here."

Dr. Williams scratches at the side of his goatee and nods for me to continue. I lack the energy. Instead, I unlock the stroller and pull it toward me so that I can be cheered by my baby. She lies inside, button nose and bald head. The sight threatens more dry sobs. She resembles her father.

I direct my attention to my lap. The air conditioner hisses. Children play outside. High-pitched conversations and squeals penetrate the window. I try to pick out words. Identify street sounds. Anything not to feel.

"What do you think would happen if you left?"

"She'd win."

The doctor opens a palm and gestures to me. "She . . . the other woman?"

"Yes."

"What would she win?"

"My life."

"Your life is your husband?"

"My life is my family. Me, my husband, and Vicky."

"If your husband cheats throughout your marriage, would that still be a good life?"

He's lobbing questions too fast, a tennis machine on an expert-level setting. I can't volley this. I raise my hand as if to block another inquiry from flying at my face. "I don't know." A weak answer. How pathetic I must look to a man like him. I cover my face with my hands and lament my life. Respected journalism career, beautiful baby, loving husband: it was all a sham with a charlatan at its center. And yet, I want nothing more than to return to the mirage, to stick my finger down my throat and spit up the red pill. But I can't. He's been seen. I'll never forget what Jake is really capable of, who he really is. I'll never erase his lover's face.

Something soft brushes against my forearm. I lower my palms, revealing my psychiatrist's outstretched hand. A tissue waves between his fingers like a surrender flag.

For a moment, I'm offended. I'm not crying. Then I realize that it's a way for him to get my hands away from my face. "Sorry," I say.

"No need to be sorry. You're dealing with a serious betrayal. Feeling upset is natural."

I twist the tissue with both hands. "Is it natural to want them to just die?"

He cocks his head to his shoulder and offers a noncommittal shrug.

The digital clock on his desk shows three minutes till. Somehow, an hour has passed. Sadness has slowed my mental processes. The questions that had seemed to fire at me were, in all likelihood, offered after minutes of mulling over my thoughts. Dr. Williams follows my eyeline. "We'll talk again?" His voice rises in a question. Jake's only made the one appointment.

Despite everything I think about this doctor's inability to help me, I find myself nodding.

"How about next Friday?" He walks to a closed laptop on his desk and opens it. A calendar is on the screen. "Does this time work?"

"I don't really have a napping schedule for Vicky."

"Is there another time that is better? Usually, I recommend once a week, but seeing as how something pretty traumatic has happened, I think it would be best to come a bit more frequently at first."

I look at my newborn, pupils moving beneath thin eyelids. She sleeps most of the day now, waking up only to feed and briefly play before her next nap. The pediatrician blamed a six-week growth spurt. She'd said it often lasts until two months. "Okay. This is good."

He hits a few keys on his computer and informs me that I'll get an e-mail confirmation. I sniffle a thank you. Part of me wishes I could come sooner. How will I stomach my husband in the interim? What will I do with the time in between?

# LIZA

I sit alone in David's office, rereading my last chapter while I wait for him to return from wherever and head out to the Hamptons with me. His only court appearance was a change of venue motion that he'd said would wrap up around two. The time on my laptop reads quarter to four.

At least the space is conducive to editing. It's quiet. Dark. David keeps the blackout shades lowered, preventing me from amusing myself by peering into the windows of neighboring buildings. His sparse furnishings don't tempt distraction, either. The roll-arm leather couch is standard fare, the kind decorating a million NYC bachelor pads. His oak desk is devoid of photos or mementos, as are the wooden bookshelves filled with bound legal volumes. Nothing in David's office hints that there is someone he may be thinking of besides the law and his client. I assume the lack of personalization is to assure visitors that confidences are kept inside these wood-paneled walls, things David won't even tell his wife.

The doorknob jiggles. I save my document and then e-mail it to myself for good measure. Relying on my hard drive alone is not good enough. I learned that a few years ago after a computer virus hijacked all my processing power to send pornographic spam. By the time the Geek Squad had successfully deleted the malware and returned my machine, I'd lost weeks of work.

David's secretary, Cameron, enters with a steaming mug of coffee. Amazonian gams scissor beneath a pasted-on pencil skirt as she approaches David's desk. Her blonde hair bounces above her ample chest. Cameron should really play a secretary on television rather than be one. She has that hot-cheerleader-got-a-job thing going for her. Part of me wishes that David had a less attractive administrative assistant. All the thinking about affairs has made me wary of pretty women in close proximity to my spouse.

She smiles at me like I'm a professional photographer as she sets the cup on the desk. I am about to engage in some polite conversation when she begs off to man the phones. "Things are so busy with Nick gone," she explains.

As she opens the door, I spy my spouse hovering in the hallway. He still wears a dark suit jacket and pants, court attire, rather than the khakis I'd expect for a ride to the Hamptons. I hear Cameron announce me, followed by something from him in a lower tone. Something unintelligible. She shuts the door behind her.

Beth's voice whispers in my mind. *Maybe they're flirting, not fucking. Maybe you already know.* I blink at my screen and try to focus on the last paragraph of Beth's psychiatrist visit. There's no reason for me to be suspicious of David and Cameron. More than likely, he is sharing details about a case that I can't overhear without him violating his attorney-client privilege. Cameron would be covered under the exception for law firm staff. He's meeting with her in the hallway with the door closed because I'm in his office.

Though I tell myself all this, I still lift my butt from the couch and peer through the frosted glass window in David's door. The fuzzy image of a blonde stands beside my husband's distinct shape. Their outlines don't overlap. He steps toward the door. Quickly, I drop back onto the couch cushion and pull the computer onto my lap. My snooping is silly. I don't want him to catch me doing it.

*Jake wouldn't touch another woman if he knew that I was watching*, Beth says . . .

David enters the room and shuts the door. I jostle the laptop back into a front pocket of my navy travel duffel, as though I've only now stopped working, and slip the bag's strap over my shoulder. "Ready to go?"

A frown draws down David's face. I know this expression. It precedes disappointment—usually mine. "I can't come out this weekend. I have a motion on one of Nick's cases."

"You just found out?"

"I'm sorry. I should have called before." It's a lawyer's answer. David is not admitting that this information is recent. He's implying that he learned it today by suggesting that his mistake was not notifying me earlier this afternoon as opposed to belatedly changing his mind. He gestures to my travel bag. "You should go, though. You're all packed, and I'm going to be stuck here all weekend."

"Can't you write it Sunday? I'll be off to the conference then."

"I need to prepare. I can't pull legal arguments out of thin air." David gestures to his shelves. "I need my reference books."

"And this was sprung on you this morning?"

David presses his lips together, annoyed with me for asking the same question in a more direct manner. His lack of affirmative response is all the confirmation I need. He was never actually planning on coming with me to the Hamptons. The agreement was a war tactic, meant to disarm me when I was on my home turf. Now I'm on his.

I think of my belly, bloated with hormones and swollen follicles. My ripe eggs will rot inside me. There aren't enough fertility drugs in the world to fix a husband refusing to bed his wife.

*Maybe that's because he's sleeping with someone else.* I want to shout at Beth to stop projecting her story onto my own. I slump back into the couch and press my thumb and forefinger to my eyelids, trying to forestall the hot, disappointed tears I feel building behind them.

"What do you want me to do, huh?" David's tone is not apologetic. "Nick's cases are more complicated than I thought. I can't wing it. If the firm is to continue, I need his clients to stick with me. Let me tell you, we won't be able to keep the apartment if my business is cut in half, unless we sell the summer house, which you don't want to do."

He's right on all counts. My flailing career certainly can't pay our mortgage, and I won't sell my house. Some force—maybe my mother's spirit or simply the memory of her—will not let me part with the place.

With no counterargument to David's case, I wallow in a mental image. I'm lying on our mattress, doubled over with cramps from passing multiple unfertilized eggs at once. No doubt this month will end the same way.

"Some of Nick's clients are big names worth a lot of money to us. I can't just Google some facts and win cases." This last statement is a dig at me. David often quips that my job is searching random information on the Internet.

I rub my eyes until my vision clears enough to see David standing beside his desk, not yet sure enough in his victory to sit. "I guess I'll go home and wait for you," I mumble.

David's hands land on his hips. "Oh. So quid pro quo, huh? I don't do what you want, because I need to work, and you forget about the favor of asking your policeman friend for information on Nick's case." He throws up his hands and strides to his desk. "Honestly, Liza, sometimes I can't believe you're this selfish."

I bite my lip to keep my eyes from watering, again. "I want to have a life with you, David. A family. Why am I the villain for that?"

Rather than answer, he settles into his rotating desk chair. As he does, I realize that I made a mistake before. His office isn't bereft of photos. There, on the counter, is a stack of new posters. Each one bears multiple images of Nick, apparently nabbed from Facebook. Instead of Nick staring straight at the camera with a confident, lawyer look, he's laughing with friends at a table, smoking a cigarette beside a brick wall, pointing to a bar sign. These are flattering photos.

"I need to work." He turns his desk chair to his computer screen, dismissing me. Part of me wants to slap him so hard that the seat spins back around to face me. Another part wants to leap into his lap and kiss him until he has no choice but to acknowledge the intimacy that I'm rightfully entitled to as his wife. My fear won't allow either of those sides to show their faces, though. I'll never win an argument with David.

"Okay. I'll go to the house," I say quietly. "I'll stop in Flushing on the way."

I leave the door open as I exit, praying that he might change his mind. The hope persists until I'm through the midtown tunnel. As I watch the brake lights shine in the artificial darkness, miles below the East River, I realize that he is not going to surprise me in the Hamptons. He's staying in New York, waiting for whatever the cops will dredge from the water.

*

A summer Friday afternoon is the worst time to drive to Long Island. The financial set clears out of the city as soon as the markets shut down at four. Everyone else who can afford a rental gets on the road even earlier. By four thirty, the traffic on I-495 is as thick and sluggish as cold gravy. It continues consolidating as it travels deeper into the heart of Queens, cholesterol-filled blood forcing itself through narrowing veins. We all know it's only a matter of time before it stops completely.

I get trapped in bumper to bumper near Corona Park, where the Grand Central Parkway intersects New York's main east–west artery. Part of me wants to sit in traffic and forget about the police academy to spite my spouse. The other part of me knows visiting my contact is the sole reason that I am in this mess of cars in the first place. I have to help David find out what happened to Nick so that we can move on with our lives once and for all.

I escape the gridlock by heading north. Traffic is still heavy, but it's moving. Within five minutes, I'm sailing on the Whitestone Expressway. Another three minutes and I'm pulling into the home of NYPD's new recruits.

The two-year-old building still shines like a new nickel. Skinny maples line the parking lot, their trunks the size of my thin arms. Very young trees are cheaper to plant, but I prefer to think these saplings were chosen for their metaphorical qualities. Like the men and women inside, they yearn to mature over long lives into something solid and powerful.

I smile and think of Beth. That line would never emerge from her lips. She's no romantic. At least, not anymore.

I park in the stadium-sized lot in front of the facility and make my way to a massive portico. Its rectangular shape reminds of a giant metal detector. Walking under it, my keys don't feel as though they belong in my jeans' pocket. Glass doors lie on the other side. I pull one back and enter a wide open space that resembles a hotel entrance rather than a police station. The whole building smells faintly of glass cleaner and gunpowder, though the latter scent may be from my memories of the in-house shooting range.

I'd forgotten the size of this place. It was a mistake thinking that I could barge in and talk to an instructor who had me in class for a mere week. Sergeant Perez must train hundreds of real officers responsible for public lives, let alone writers trying to get fictional details right in shootout scenes. Why would he remember me?

For a moment, I think about leaving without approaching the annoyed-looking female officer manning the visitors' desk. I could always tell David that I couldn't locate my contact. Of course, then I wouldn't get to be the hero wife who helps her husband move on from his friend's death and is rewarded with regular sex and a healthy full-term infant.

The desk officer's full cheeks and bright eyes make me guess that she's no older than twenty-two. Still, she watches me approach with the clinical gaze of a seasoned detective. My tentative walk and sheepish expression do not do me any favors. By the time I reach the desk, she's staring at me as though I've come to sell her magazine subscriptions. She demands my name in the gruff manner that I imagine she'd use to dole out loitering tickets. I provide it and my license, along with a rushed explanation of my purpose at the academy and my history with Sergeant Perez. "He said I could call him when I graduated, but since I was in the neighborhood, I thought I'd stop by."

Her look suggests that she has not decided whether or not I'm a mental patient. Even with the jury out, though, she plugs Sergeant Perez's name into a field on her computer screen and calls up his extension. A man picks up on the third ring.

The officer doesn't do me any favors with her introduction. She explains that she has "a woman here" who "says she is from a writers' workshop" and "claims that you know her." She covers the handset and rolls her eyes up at me. "What did you say your name was?"

"Liza Cole. I'm an author." Her eyes don't show any recognition, but I don't expect them to. While I've written half a dozen thrillers, only one of them had the kind of success capable of making me a household name—and that was years ago. I clear my throat. "I wrote *Drowned Secrets*."

The woman's narrowed eyes open. "Oh. I know that book. My mom read it. It's about the kid whose dad—"

"Yup. That's it," I deliberately interrupt.

"Wasn't it turned into a movie or something?"

"They still play it on Lifetime."

Now convinced I'm not insane, the woman repeats what I've said to the sergeant and tells me he'll be right down. I thank her and step away from the booth to lean against the glass wall. The last thing I want is to discuss my first novel and—to date—my only bestseller. That plot is not the stuff of polite discourse.

Sergeant Perez emerges from an elevator moments later. He looks exactly the same as he did a year ago: a fade haircut and a Tom Selleck mustache, along with an easy smile that must have short-listed him for a teaching position.

"Liza Cole," he says. "Working on a new murder mystery?"

"Something like that." I extend my hand. "It's actually a real case."

His chin pulls back into his neck as he shakes. "I can't talk about cases on the record without approval."

"I'm not writing about it. It's a personal matter." His look becomes even more skeptical. "I don't know if you've read any of the articles about a missing lawyer? Nick Landau."

The sergeant's thick black eyebrows rise into *V*s. "The guy that won that big judgment against the city?"

I hesitate before nodding yes. Police are paid out of municipal coffers. It's possible that David and Nick's lawsuit didn't win them any friends on the force. "Nick was—" I clear my throat. There's no evidence that Nick deserves the past tense—at least, not yet. "Nick *is* a partner in my husband's law firm, and he *was* the best man at our wedding. My husband is pretty distraught. He doesn't know what to tell clients. He's also afraid that Nick may have been targeted because of the lawsuit and that he could be in danger himself."

"Do you think your husband is in danger?"

My mouth opens, but no sound emerges. I realize that I've never seriously considered the answer. I'd always assumed that Nick's disappearance/death had been related to his party lifestyle or the rough neighborhood in Brooklyn where he insisted upon living. But I didn't know about the hate mail until last night. Maybe some nut job *had* done something horrible to Nick. Or someone who'd lost their job over the suit—a teacher at the kid's school, maybe—decided to seek revenge. Such things happen in thrillers because they first make headlines.

"If Nick's disappearance is related to the lawsuit in any way, I guess it's possible," I say. "I also think it's plausible that he was the victim of a mugging or a drug deal gone wrong."

Sergeant Perez scratches the side of his mustache. I may have made a mistake bringing drugs into the mix. Now he's wondering whether I do coke on the weekends.

"Nick wasn't really settled down like me and my husband. He hung with a young crowd and liked to party, and he lived in a higher-crime neighborhood in Brooklyn."

The sergeant puffs his cheeks and exhales. Drugs and bad neighborhoods are deadly combinations. "I'll look into it. Give me your number and I'll get back to you in a few days."

Relieved tears suddenly blur my vision. David will be so pleased and impressed when I tell him that I have a sergeant looking into Nick's disappearance. He'll apologize for calling me selfish and want to make up for his distant, cold attitude. I might not lose out on my chance to get pregnant this month after all.

"Thank you," I manage. "It means a lot to my family."

Sergeant Perez pats my arm like a friend. "Hey, don't mention it." He winks. "And if I were David, I wouldn't be so nervous with you around. Your aim has really improved since class."

I struggle to understand the joke. My aim? Did my last book have a detail about shooting that made it seem like I'd learned how to properly point a handgun?

The sergeant picks up on my confusion. "I saw you at the academy range the other day. Maybe a month ago."

He must have seen someone who resembled me. I have long dark hair. Dark eyes. Olive skin. Pretty much any thin, medium-height Latina, Mediterranean, or Middle Eastern woman could pass for me from a distance.

"You hit the target straight in the heart."

His chest swells as he smiles at me. It makes him proud to think that his one-week course turned a wordsmith that had never held a gun before into a marksman. He may even have agreed to help with Nick's case because he believes I was a good student.

I thank him again, my face growing hot with my lie of omission. The truth is, I haven't been to the range in a year.

# Chapter 4

HER FIRST NAME IS COLLEEN. I mentally repeat it as I watch her exit a Chinatown dumpling shop and return to her unmarked police car. What you having for lunch, Officer Colleen? Not going to chase that speeder, Officer Colleen? Trying to make sure you get off early to see your boyfriend, Officer?

She is parked on the corner of Mulberry and Mosco, close to one of five massive basketball courts. To some of the five-hundred-dollar-sneaker-sporting players, the woman with a baby carriage pacing the narrow lawn between the blacktops must seem odd. But it's Manhattan, so no one pays me any attention. This town encourages natives to leave eccentrics alone. Pay little mind to the woman shunning the relative quiet of the pedestrian path who, apparently, prefers that her baby nap to the sweet sounds of squeaking rubber soles, male grunting, and dropped f-bombs.

Officer Colleen hasn't noticed me watching her despite the twenty minutes she's spent in the car. She sits in her vehicle, alone, paper box on the dashboard, chopsticks in hand. A dumpling pops in her mouth. She taps the sticks against the container side as she chews, drumming out whatever happy beat is playing in her head. I ask the Universe to let the *shumai* stick in her airway.

It is not healthy watching her like this. Yet I have to. I need to understand what my husband sees in this woman. There's the body, of course. So unlike mine. Petite and rectangular, whereas I am tall and pear-shaped. But Jake would need more than beauty to be swayed from my side. He'd need a brain. Would she be smart enough to do what I did to track her down? Could she guess that her husband's e-mail and Facebook passwords were the same as the shared Amazon Prime login? Would she know to search both his e-mail and archived chats for conversations around the date of the case in which his lover had been a key witness and then zero in on the messages from the female cops? And after finding a seemingly innocent note from one of these officers revealing a personal e-mail address, would she then have the wherewithal to search for and read through all the deleted messages from that address? Would she note the increasing familiarity in her husband's salutation—"Colleen," then "Hi, Collie," then "Col, I can't get you out of my mind"—and trace the progression of their banter from flirty jokes to innuendo to outright sexting? Would she read the message sent this morning, the other woman lamenting her daily schedule and hinting at how happy she would be if a certain someone surprised her during her lunch break, and then go to that very locale?

I don't think so. Though, obviously, I'm biased.

Officer Colleen is dumb enough to think that Jake will leave me. That's clear in the way she gushes about how "precious" and "beautiful" Vicky is in their conversations, leaving out any mention of mommy. She's implying with her selective effusiveness that she'd be a good stepmother. She'd love his daughter. He doesn't need the wife-who-must-not-be-named.

But he does. He does. Jake—he is Jake, despite the infantile diminutives scattered throughout her messages (Jakey, DJ, Boo)—wants his pie and whipped cream. If he planned on trading me in, he wouldn't have hired a babysitter for all those Saturday date nights after seeing her for a quickie Friday afternoon. He wouldn't have gushed about how much he loves me hours after she'd been sending him racy photos. He wouldn't have bought me a new dress after giving her a silk scarf. And he wouldn't now be standing her up for lunch.

She eats her last dumpling and closes the container. Her car door opens. She saunters over to a garbage bin on the corner and tosses in the paper box. No recycling for that policewoman there. No. Rules don't apply to her. Screw the planet and everyone else on it.

A cry comes from the carriage. Victoria stirs in her seat, mouth opening and closing for food. That's my exit cue. Though I might be invisible now, everyone will notice me when I feed my child. I don't have the baby carrier to block prying eyes from my exposed nipple.

I push the stroller away from the courts toward a manicured lawn surrounded by two-foot-high fences. There will be benches alongside the grass. I can nurse there and then play with my baby. The day is beautiful, despite the scenery. Warm, with enough clouds to provide scattered shade.

Before I get out of eyeshot, I cast one more hateful glance toward the police car. She's checking her phone, probably texting the man who refused to take the hint. My husband.

I'll see you soon, Officer Colleen.

# LIZA

I pull up to the house's gravel driveway before sunset, take a deep breath, and turn inside. My old Mercedes rumbles over the white pebbles that have hid in my sandals since I learned to walk, coming to a stop at the side door and the concrete step that my mom chipped with an iron garden shovel. The house never changes. It sits at the end of a narrow lane, tucked behind a hedge of cherry laurel bushes and flowering weigela. Even the grayed exterior is as it has always been, despite last year's long-overdue siding repair. Montauk's salt air soon weathers any exposed wood, so no new shingle bears cedar's true color for long.

I've resisted all attempts to modernize this two-story bungalow, ignoring realtors' promises that they could rent the property for a fortune if only I renovated the kitchen or tacked on an extra bath. Overseeing contractors has always seemed too daunting. Moreover, I have no desire to sift through the house's contents, weighing what I should discard of my past, dredging up memories of my father's alcoholism and my mom's constant struggle with it, a battle that ultimately ended in his storming out and her body surrendering to cancer before my twenty-fifth birthday. I'm content to leave the house alone, a sentinel of my memories— especially those I'd rather forget.

I take two steps at a time, avoiding the chip in the stair, and key into the side door. My muscles tense as it opens. It's disconcerting, returning to the well-preserved scene of my youth, knowing that it lives on without me, hinting at my secrets to strange summer guests. My old bedroom, painted lavender when I was eleven, now hosts the children of affluent visitors. The kitchen's ancient white fridge, stocked with local vegetables when I was a kid, is typically bare now save for half-carved blocks of stinky cheeses. Occasionally, a recorked bottle of white wine chills in the door.

I check for free booze as I inspect the house. A two-thirds-full bottle of rosé wastes away in the fridge's lower shelf. I twist off the cap and swig it as I search for anything else out of place. The wooden table in the dining room bears a new permanent watermark from the condensation on someone's glass. No one besides me would notice. The dining table shows so many circular stains from years of coaster-shunning guests that they appear like old knots.

I pass through the living room to the sliding doors at the back of the house. The pool glitters beyond the glass, a blue topaz in a wooden setting. It has always felt like mine, even though my father built it for himself. He'd taken up swimming during a months-long period of sobriety and had decided that he deserved a lap pool. Mom hadn't wanted it. The money, she'd argued, should go to my college fund. But no one could tell Don Cole how to spend his cash, and his real estate business was doing well at the time.

In retrospect, it's one of the few arguments that I'm happy she lost. As I take in the scenery, I recall kissing Jack Maley on the deck at thirteen, sunbathing with Christine on summer weekends, an alfresco dinner during which David complimented my mother's bone structure, aware that she'd become self-conscious since losing her hair.

It was on this very deck that I first fell for David. I can see him now, sitting upright on the lounge chair, hands folded in his lap, impeccably groomed with his Princeton haircut and golf shirt, earnestly telling my mom about his intent to defend people victimized by the system. He'd tried so hard. As if I'd needed any convincing to be with him. I'd decided to sleep with him the moment he'd approached me in the Columbia law library. He'd walked over to the checkout counter, seemingly another handsome prep-school product without a work-study tuition subsidy. But instead of shoving his book across to me as though his parents were personally paying for my English degree, he'd blushed and asked in his soft Texas twang about the novel in my hand. John Gardner's *Grendel*. I still remember.

My nostalgia fails to create any warm fuzzy feelings. Instead, I become aware of a gnawing emptiness in my gut, a space demanding to be filled. I swallow the remaining wine and walk back around to the driveway. My navy duffel is in the trunk. The satchel is heavy, stuffed with my clothes for the upcoming conference and assorted marketing materials: pens, bookmarks, folders. I sling the bag over my shoulder and lumber back through the side door, across the house and up the steps into my old room. Taking over the master alone seems wrong. David's presence grants me permission to use the grown-up spaces.

My old bedroom is stuffy, filled with hot air that has floated through the floorboards. Breathing is difficult. I squeeze around the bed and turn the painted white knob locking the window. The shutters open inward, revealing the twinkling water beyond. My body relaxes as I inhale the fresh air. I've always felt more at home outside this house.

A buzzing interrupts my moment of Zen. I unzip the front compartment of my bag and grab the source. Trevor's name lights up the cell's screen. It's unlike him to reach out so soon after a meeting. Is he trying to renegotiate our agreement?

I can't take another confrontation after the one with David. Best to let him leave a message. I'll call back after I tell my husband about Sergeant Perez and am feeling better.

As I return the phone to the bag, my thumb hits the accept button. "Hello, Liza?" I fumble with the handset and attempt a breezy I-wasn't-trying-to-forward-you-to-voice-mail greeting.

"How are you?" He sounds like he wants to know, not as though he's making polite conversation before reneging on a handshake agreement, but the British accent impairs my judgment. Everything Trevor says in his deep-throated London sing-song sounds either frank or sexy. Hollywood's fault. The Queen's English is the sole language of the upper crust, spies, and suave car thieves.

"I'm okay. What's up?"

"Marketing would like to know when everyone is getting in and out of the conference."

I've been holding my breath. I release it with a long sigh. The emptying of my lungs restores the buzz that I'd been working on moments earlier. "Courtney e-mailed me the flight itinerary a few weeks ago. I can forward the message."

"That'd be great. Normally, I'd ask her, but she's out today."

"Give me a minute." I rifle through my bag for my laptop, feeling suddenly resentful that the couple days I have not to think about the conference are in fact being taken up by the conference. I'm dreading this trip. Conferences are fun for the famous—authors sure to win an award or who have sold so many books that such things don't matter. Those of us on the midlist must spend the whole time hustling, trying to gain the attention of more successful scribes and the few book enthusiasts who bother to attend.

My computer hides beneath a weekend's worth of folded clothes. I pull it out and open my e-mail. The itinerary is in my in-box along with half a dozen messages from me to myself containing attachments of my latest manuscript.

I click on the flight info. "Looks like Sunday morning, arrival 11:10 AM."

"I'm in then too. How will you come from the airport?"

"Guessing a cab. To be honest, I haven't decided." I'm tempted to add that I've been busy thinking about Beth's character arc and writing, but I don't.

"We can share a taxi to the hotel. You're booked in the block at the Sheraton, right?"

"That'd be great." My high pitch rings false. There was a time when I'd take Trevor's offer as nothing more than a favor for a friend and colleague. But since my so-so streak of novels post–*Drowned Secrets* and my downright disappointing last book, I wonder whether he wants to break some bad news in person. I grip the bed's worn coverlet and muster the courage to ask a direct question. "Trev, if there is something you want to tell me, I'd rather know beforehand—"

"No. Nothing. Liza, you really worry too much."

"Expect the worst and you won't be surprised."

Trevor chuckles. "Suspense writers." I can picture him shaking his head. "Speaking of suspense, how is the work coming?"

My hold loosens on the bedspread. "Okay, I think."

"Did you give any more thought to what I'd said about the—"

"Shrink?"

"Well, at least adding some psychological tension to the romantic scenes."

I mimic his accent. "You worry too much, love. I promise to have some proper naughty bits in the shagging scenes. Everything will be tickety-boo." As soon as the words escape, I realize that my mockery could be considered rude rather than "cheeky." The wine is blurring the difference.

Trevor laughs. "I don't say 'tickety-boo.' Otherwise, not bad."

I exhale in relief. Pissing off your editor is never a good idea. "But not great?"

"You require practice. It's good that we have this conference ahead of us. A few drinks in . . ." He makes a clicking noise with his tongue. "I might break out the cockney."

"Oh. I'd love that."

"I bet."

Are we flirting, or is the wine making me imagine things?

"All right," Trevor says. "I'll let you get back to it. Looking forward to the conference."

Suddenly, so am I.

*

The house has nothing to eat. After writing for an hour, my stomach announces this fact with all the subtlety of a whoopee cushion. I head out to the car at twilight, intent on hitting up the market down the main road before it gets too dark to drive without my distance glasses. While stopped at a red light, I shoot Christine a text that I'm headed to Blue Horse Grocery. As the store only exists in Montauk, the short message serves as an announcement that I'm in town and an invitation. Chris doesn't need me to ask her to dinner.

She hasn't returned my text by the time I turn into the store parking lot. I assume she has plans and consider purchasing a prepared dinner salad. It'd be great to drop a couple pounds before my dog-and-pony show. As I exit my car, my phone beeps. Four words sit on my screen: "Great minds think alike."

She's standing with her back to me as I enter, perusing the wine selection. I'd recognize my best friend's red hair and finely freckled arms anywhere. The girl doesn't tan as much as she becomes pop art. A happiness that I didn't realize I was missing swells inside me. Same ol' Chris. To me, she'll always be the sixth-grade ginger I befriended twenty-four years ago, albeit with some cross-hatching around the eyes and new elevens between her brows. The former she earned from a sunglasses-less childhood. The latter was inflicted by a recent divorce.

She turns to me as the door jangles shut. My name rings out like an accusation. "Liza Cole! What's on the menu?"

I grab a wire basket from a stack against the door and slip into the first aisle. A slab of weathered wood is bolted to the wall, punched full of holes like an old-time switchboard. Wine bottles protrude from each space. "What would you like? David's not with me. Work has ruined another romantic weekend."

Chris examines a label and then, murmuring approval, withdraws the bottle with a flourish. "Who needs those?" She smirks, betraying her sarcasm.

I hug her, peering into the basket dangling from her forearm as we embrace. A bottle of Pinot Noir, a bottle of sparkling white wine, and a Riesling already sit in her cart. She drinks more now that George is gone.

"I'm alone as well." She wrinkles her nose. "The bastard gets Emma for nearly the whole summer. They're taking her camping this week."

The trip sounds like a fun father-daughter bonding excursion. A good dad thing to do. But Chris doesn't want to hear me praise the man who ran off with her twenty-six-year-old au pair. "Camping? Doesn't he know preteen girls need cell service?"

Chris fails to turn her smile into a believable grimace. "She's going to hate it, right?"

"Well, the campfire stories will be scary." I imitate a strong German accent. "Vonce upon a time, dere was a succubus—"

"And she's telling this story! Ahhh." Chris laughs. Laughter is the only vaccine for crying. You shed a few tears instead of a thousand.

As Chris has the wine covered, I move on to the fresh produce aisle. The crudité components are bestsellers and thus in a metal shelf at the front. Baby carrots, heads of broccoli, bell peppers, grape tomatoes. I grab all these along with some vegetable dip.

Chris pouts. "We're not rabbits."

"I need to lose five pounds."

"You do not." She leans back and assesses my figure. "You're what? A size four?"

I pat my belly, rounded from the preparation for a nonexistent zygote.

She lowers her voice. "Being too thin makes it harder to conceive."

I try not to bristle. Chris means well, though she's under the mistaken impression that home remedies and old wives' tales can cure infertility. Every time I see her, she's gushing about a new vitamin supplement or sex position that some questionable study has linked to improved conception rates.

"What are you in the mood to eat?"

Chris places a bright radish into my cart. "For your salad." She pinches my waist. "I'm relieved that you're here. Honestly, I couldn't have made it through another dinner alone with my parents." She tilts her head toward her basket. "My mother's antiquated dating advice demands too much medication."

I wince for her. "What's her latest suggestion?"

"Christian Mingle."

I snort and continue to the fresh fish display. "Doesn't she know you're looking for a Jewish doctor?"

Chris elbows me in the side. "Anything other than a Scots-Irish prosecutor from Pennsylvania. Come to think of it? No lawyers at all. George has poisoned the well." She turns her attention to the glass-eyed whole fish in the display. "How is David?"

I shrug. "He ditched our romantic weekend."

"Well, people can't be romantic all the time." She elbows my side. "Lest we forget, you had the lighthouse."

Tears burn behind my eyes, no doubt triggered by the hormones. I force a laugh, as though they're fueled by mirth rather than melancholy. "That was a while ago."

I could never forget the lighthouse.

*

Montauk is home to the oldest lighthouse in New York State, a pristine white cylinder sitting on a bluff overlooking the Block Island Sound, surrounded by scraggly sea grasses and sheared rocks. Chris and I would hitchhike to it as teenagers, grabbing rides from the young moneyed set who rolled into town every summer with their foreign sports cars and January bank bonuses. Someone was always happy to give a couple of jailbait locals a ride to a secluded state park, especially if you hinted that the Atlantic Ocean wouldn't be the best part of the view. I loved it there. For ten dollars and a pair of burning thighs, I could press my nose to the glass in the lantern room and watch the ocean stretch to the horizon before falling off the edge of the world. After my father left, I would imagine that's what had happened to him. The cartographers had lied. The world was flat and he'd gone over.

Chris must have told David it was my favorite place. One winter break, long after the summer crowds had abandoned their beach houses, he asked if I wanted to go for a drive. He had this cherry-red Ford F-150 that his dad had gifted him for high school graduation. David wasn't a pickup type of guy, but the bed of the vehicle had been big enough to cart all his belongings from Texas to Manhattan. I think he loved that truck for that. It had let him leave without a trace.

I climbed into the cab without any idea where we were going except that it would be colder than the city. David had told me to wear gloves and my down jacket, the one I thought made me look like a roll of Rapid Fill packaging. He'd put on a black ski jacket and cargo pants. The pants should have tipped me off—he'd needed pockets.

We drove for three hours listening to Sigur Rós's lead singer wail in his unique mix of Icelandic scat, the voice drifting in and out of the piano riffs like a warm wind, each too nervous to interrupt much. By the time we arrived at the lighthouse, it was well past midnight. I'd never seen the park after dark. The building and grounds closed at sunset, and the park rangers policed it strictly in the summer. Without a car, I'd never been able to come past high season.

Millions of stars speckled the sky. They stretched across the landscape in glowing waves, an endless school of phosphorescent algae swirling in a black ocean. Looking through the truck's moonroof, I could understand how ancient explorers had navigated at night and named constellations after animals. Finally, there were enough pinpoints of light to trace the lines.

David asked that I stay inside the truck while he took things out of the bed. I listened to him banging around the back, trying to guess the reason for this whole surprise trip by the flashes of him in the headlights with bulky items tucked beneath his arms. I waited with the heater on full blast until he tapped the passenger window with the butt of a flashlight. He grasped my hand and led me over the snow-dusted grasses to a narrow strip of sand. There on the rocky beach, he'd laid out a plaid blanket. Massive hurricane lanterns weighed down the corners, each containing glowing candles. At the edge of the blanket, there was a basket with wine and a pyre of driftwood.

The wind ripped through my coat. David noticed my shivering and hurried us over to the woodpile. From one of his bulky pants pockets, he produced a lighter. Newspaper beneath the logs immediately glowed red and yellow. David wrapped his arms around me as we waited for the driftwood to catch.

I'd never seen anything so beautiful. The red and yellow flames from the paper gave way to an electric blue with purple tips. Driftwood, David explained, burns differently than white oak or pine. Something about being soaked in salt water gives the flame electric colors.

"Did you learn that in Boy Scouts?" I asked.

"A friend taught me in high school," he said. "He called them rainbow fires."

"They look like flowers."

David proposed that evening. I needed to remove a glove to put on the ring, and my hand didn't fit back inside with it on. But I didn't care. After saying yes, all I wanted to do was lean into my future husband and watch my diamond sparkle in the purple flames beneath the stars.

*

Chris snaps her fingers in front of my face, calling me out of my daydream. She knows that I didn't hear her continued condemnation of her mother's antiquated dating advice because I also haven't noticed the fishmonger in front of us. They're both pointing to a deep-pink salmon with narrow bands of white fat between the meat. Wild caught. Expensive. Delicious, especially when grilled with a hint of lemon.

"That looks great," I say.

She taps the glass. "My treat. The last client loved the living room so much, she hired me to finish the entire house. God, what they pay! I wonder why I ever was a journalist."

"You thought you had a higher calling."

"Hell with that."

"The house is the one on Washington Drive, right?"

"Giant pool. Overlooking the beach. Hedge fund guy."

Chris explains to the fishmonger that she wants a pound of the wild Alaskan and "not the tail piece." He cuts and weighs it on a flat scale facing us, then waits for Chris to give him the go-ahead when it comes up a few ounces heavy. As he folds white paper over it, I ask if Mr. Hedge Fund and his wife have any single friends.

"He's much older. I doubt it." She winks. "But hey, what about David?"

The hairs stand up on my arms as though my body has just noticed that the seafood aisle is several degrees colder than the front of the store. "What do you mean?"

"Any law school buddies as hot as Nick?"

I remember the photos on the missing poster. What does David hope to accomplish by tacking those along the river? He can't honestly think that someone is going to pass by a flier and think, *Hey, I know that guy. He's been begging on a street corner, telling everyone he can't remember his name.* Is he hoping that someone will come forward with information about where Nick might have been that night? Where his body might be? Is he simply trying to seem helpful to police so they'll work the case harder?

"Ranking Dave's friends one through ten?" Chris teases. "I'll take seven or above."

"No. I . . ." My skin itches as though I've seen a bug crawling on someone nearby. "Nick was the only really handsome one."

Chris slams her palm against her forehead. "Shit. I'm such an idiot. I'm sorry. I forgot. I mean, I didn't forget, I know he's missing. I didn't think before I spoke."

The grocer interrupts with the wrapped fish and an instruction to have a wonderful evening. I thank him as Chris places the salmon atop her wine collection. "Maybe that's why I can't get a man," she says as soon as the grocer is out of earshot. "Foot-in-mouth disease."

"Don't beat yourself up. I forget he's gone sometimes too." It's a lie. David won't let me forget Nick for a second.

"Such a shame." Chris looks into her basket of bottles, probably wishing she could uncork one of them in the store. "I'd hoped maybe one day . . ." She laughs. "But I wasn't Nick's type."

I think back to his last girlfriend. She'd had a blonde pixie cut that had accentuated her big blue eyes but made her square jaw appear even more masculine. I remember telling David that she couldn't quite pull off the Linda Evangelista look. He said I was being catty.

"Ugh. I hate being single. Every man pushing forty is still fishing in the fry pond. I should have lined up my next relationship in my twenties, when I was still married. If only I'd known." She looks up at the store's paneled ceiling. "Whoever said 'cheaters never prosper' didn't date."

For a moment, I think she might cry. There's little I can offer for solace. Truth is, the real world isn't fair. George, the philandering husband, got the girl, while my friend had to explain to her daughter why Daddy and Mommy "grew apart." The faithful often find themselves blindsided. They don't suspect anything because they can't imagine doing something so awful themselves.

I drape my free arm over her shoulders. "Oh, Chris. If only life was one of my novels. George wouldn't have survived the second act."

# Chapter 5

Dr. Williams opens the door as I'm wheeling the stroller down his narrow hallway. Seeing the bassinet shade pulled all the way down, he holds up a finger and ducks back into the room. He must hit a dimmer switch. When he welcomes me inside, the office is the shade of an unlit room on a cloudy day.

He settles on his chair and gestures to the couch. "How are you?"

It sounds as though he cares. I blame the mild accent. The way his intonation rises and falls with every other syllable causes him to stress the word "you," as though the fact of my existence is particularly important. Dr. Williams's body language also helps: head cocked, tilted so his ear is inclined toward me.

My butt lands on the leather couch. I pull the carriage protectively in front of my legs. "As well as can be expected, I guess."

"Three days ago, you hadn't confronted your husband. Has that changed?"

The answer is humiliating. I examine the pattern on the rug beneath his feet. It's a busy oriental style with rings of red-and-beige flowers, something that belongs beneath grandma's dining table. It doesn't fit with the minimalist decor.

His suede oxfords shift. The hem of his khaki pants hits his ankles, showing a sliver of brown leg. He's paired a striped white shirt with the slacks today. Fine blue lines trace the curve of his pectorals. His chest rises and falls slowly, as though the good doctor is deliberately smoothing out his breathing.

"I tried," I say. "I kind of set it up so that I might catch him in the act. But it didn't work out."

"He might lie even if you catch him red-handed. People often continue to be untruthful in the face of overwhelming evidence. They'll lie to themselves, convince themselves that they didn't do anything really wrong . . ."

He trails off, and for a brief moment, his pupils follow suit. Breaking eye contact isn't something shrinks really do. I consider that he's tired of listening to women wailing over their husbands' affairs. I'm tired of doing it.

"I'm sorry. I don't want to talk about Jake. I don't even want to look at him. Every time he's come home this week, I've pretended to be tired and gone into my room with Vicky." I run my hands through my hair. The strands feel slimy. When was the last time I washed and blow-dried? When was my last shower? What must this man think of me? "I can't. I . . . I'll talk about anything else."

"All right, then." He smiles. "Let's talk about you. Why do you think confronting him is so difficult?"

The question stings. It suggests that I am doing something abnormal. Does he think accusing a spouse of sleeping around is easy? That it won't be crushing to hear the man I love admit that he is bored with me, that he wanted something more than I could provide? I try to quench my building anger by looking at my baby. Vicky's pupils move behind her thin eyelids. There's a red splotch on one, a broken blood vessel from birth. I'm good at recognizing when a thin vein has burst under the skin. Growing up, my skin was dotted with finger-sized red blotches.

I feel Dr. Williams staring, urging me to speak. The leather couch is tufted. I poke at the button hole nearest my thigh, looking for lint. An agonizing minute passes. Isn't he supposed to be giving me practical advice to make me feel better?

"Do you think confrontation is difficult for you in general?"

I meet his gaze, letting my smirk convey the simmering fury. Confrontation is not difficult for me. I'd just rather go into it with all the necessary ammunition. "No. I don't."

"When you were younger, did you find it easy to speak up for yourself? To talk to your dad?"

"This is when I'm supposed to tell you about my childhood damage, huh?"

"Well, yes, if you think your childhood is a reason that you're reluctant to talk to your husband."

"Aren't childhood patterns the reason we do everything?"

"Sometimes people do things as adults because they're repeating models with which they've become accustomed." He leans back in his chair with a shrug as if nothing I say will bother him. "We humans are a strange lot. We tend to prefer familiarity and predictability over nearly everything. We repeat what we've seen, even when we know it's a mistake."

He gives me a weak smile, a peace offering. The look robs me of my rage. I mimic his shrug. "My father was an alcoholic with a temper," I sigh. "But that's not Jake."

"What is Jake?"

I remember him when we'd first started trying for a baby. Doting on me. Always asking if I needed anything, if the hormones were making me sick, fixing a water-and-toast breakfast on the days when the smell of everything made me hurl. Preparing pancakes on the better mornings. I don't know what Jake is.

A tear tumbles down my cheek. I swat at it like a mosquito has landed on my face and then resume picking the lint from the tufted couch. Again, the white tissue materializes out of nowhere, the dove up the doctor's sleeve. I hate that he is so prepared for me weeping.

"This is really humiliating, you know? I mean, I don't even know your first name and I'm confessing all my secrets."

His sympathetic grimace morphs into surprise. "I apologize. I thought you would have seen it on the website—"

"No. Jake booked you. I only see the T. abbreviation on your plaque."

"Geez. I'm . . ." He shakes his head, admonishing himself. "Tyler. It's Tyler."

The tissue still hangs between his fingers. I take it. "Beth." I manage a little puff of air out my nostrils. "We have to stop meeting like this, Tyler."

A cry sounds from the basinet. I peer inside and see Vicky's dark-blue blinking eyes. Her mouth opens with a kitten's yowl. She pulls her chin in toward her neck and screws up her face. A sound, air slowly escaping a balloon, comes from the carriage. Someone is pooping. I laugh. "Sounds like time's up."

Tyler glances at the clock. Technically, our session can go another fifteen minutes, but I doubt he wants me changing a diaper in his office. "Do you want next Wednesday again? Same time? Wednesdays and Fridays?"

Two meetings and all I've managed to do is mortify myself in front of a painfully handsome person. Where's the value in that? I stand beside Vicky's stroller and flip the handheld break lock. "I'm sorry. Thank you for talking to me. But it's not helping."

He grimaces.

I instantly hate myself. The stress of Jake's affair has afflicted me with foot-in-mouth disease. I've become incapable of tact. "It's not you. I'm sure you're a very good psychiatrist. I just have to talk to Jake."

His full mouth parts, as though he's about to protest. Something about the way I'm avoiding eye contact—or perhaps the increasing volume of Vicky's tooting—stops him. He nods, stands, and extends his hand.

"I understand that you feel that way right now. I'm here if you change your mind." His grasp is strong and warm. This is the first thing he's done to make me feel better.

"Good luck, Beth."

"Thank you, Tyler. I'll need it."

# LIZA

Fresh fish doesn't smell. The fragrance wafting from the grill is all citrus and salt. I shut off the gas and don my mother's ancient paisley oven mitts to cart the foil-wrapped salmon to the deck table. Chris sits on a cushioned stool beside an uncorked bottle of Pinot. We already polished off the prosecco, though I cut my two glasses with orange juice and she drank her two straight.

She pushes a carrot into the veggie dip and then wags it at me like a slimed finger. "Can you believe that? I 'made him do it.' Oh, I 'only care about Emma.' Well, maybe I wouldn't have needed to focus so much on our child if that bitch had done her job and not been busy bedding her boss. The audacity, right? Telling me that I'm too busy with our kid when he's been fucking her sitter."

I've heard Chris recount this conversation before. It's her favorite story to share when she drinks, though not because she relishes the telling of it. Dr. Sally once told me that the mind has two ways of dealing with trauma. One is to bury it deep within the subconscious, building up walls of gray matter so thick that our waking brain never senses the event itself, though it dictates our knee-jerk reactions. The second way is to fixate on the injury, burning every detail into our mind in an effort to avoid similar circumstances in the future. Chris's brain has done the latter with the final argument of her marriage. She never wants to have it again, so she can't help but repeat it.

I place the salmon on a waiting plate and peel back the foil. Chris pauses her "George the Donkey" tale long enough to compliment me on dinner before picking right back up where she left off. "I tell you, he was lucky that he told me in Manhattan and not out here, where I could have grabbed my Dad's gun from the cabinet. I really might have shot him. I don't even think anyone would have faulted me for it." She chuckles. "Biggest regret of my marriage, that the frame I threw missed his face."

I murmur something affirmative as I dish out a salmon portion onto Chris's paper plate. We should eat fast. The night air is chillier than I'd anticipated, and the citronella candles flickering on the table are providing more light than heat. If David were here, we could stay out. He would build a fire in the pit at the end of the pool. Not a flower fire, though. We learned later that the colors came from metal salts soaked into the ocean-bleached wood. Burning them gives off carcinogens.

Chris grabs a fork in one hand and then swaps it for the wine glass. "Cheers."

I drop the knife for something to clink. The wine splashes up to the rim of my glass as I tap it against Chris's goblet. She takes a long sip and shakes her head. "I'm going on and on and I haven't even asked about you. How are the fertility treatments?"

"I started that new one two months ago." I dish the fish onto my plate. "I've seen a reduction in some of the uterine scarring."

"It's a pill?"

"It's an implant." I place my elbow on the table and angle my arm toward her, showing the raised lines on the inside of my bicep. Chris's fair eyebrows retreat to her scalp. As much as she wants me to get pregnant, I know she hates my taking hormones. On more than one occasion, she's cautioned about unforeseen side effects. Though she hasn't suggested it, I think Chris would rather I hire a doula to chant incantations while dripping honey over my belly than pump my system full of synthetic gland secretions. The former might not work, but at least I wouldn't suffer morning sickness for months and then fail.

Chris's nose wrinkles with disgust. "I've never seen that before."

"The treatment is still experimental."

She snarls. "Does it hurt?"

"I can feel it under there, but it's not a big deal." I take a forkful of fish. Smokey lemon flavors coat my tongue. I'm not bad on the grill. David would be impressed. When he finally returns my calls, I can brag about my courage at the academy and my cooking skills.

"What are the side effects?"

I swallow and pick up my wine. "Bloating. Moodiness. Nausea. Forgetfulness. Headaches." I raise the glass in jest. "Hangover-type symptoms."

A frown pulls down one side of Chris's mouth. I've had migraines since I can remember so I'm used to working through the blinding pain and hours of incessant throbbing. Chris is not as able to withstand even a slight headache. When she went on Zoloft during the height of her divorce, she complained endlessly of pounding in her temples. *I don't know how you bear these things, Lizzie. My brain is about to explode.*

I sip my wine and return my attention to the pale-pink fish on my plate. Wild salmon may be extinct in ten years. Sea lice, prevalent in fish farms, are killing the juveniles before they can properly breed. There's no getting around procreation problems.

"Forgetfulness." The candlelight hides the lines in Chris's forehead, but I can tell her brow is lowered. "You mean like blackouts? Waking up and not knowing where you are or how you got there?"

I eye Christine's wine glass, already near empty even though she refilled it minutes ago. Drinking like she is could make a person familiar with blackouts. "Nothing that bad."

"What have you forgotten recently?"

"I don't know. Stories I've told." She stares at me like I'm withholding key details. "I told my gyno a joke the other day that, judging from her reaction, I'd probably made before."

"That's it?"

I shrug. "As far as I know."

She settles back into her chair and brushes her red hair behind her right ear. This is her nervous tic. She has tucked her copper locks behind her ears since I can remember. If she is really on about something, she'll twist the hair.

"What's wrong? You okay?"

"Yeah." A visible shudder undermines her assurance. She reaches across the table and puts her hand over my own. "I worry about you, Liza."

The gesture is almost parental. Christine has always been protective of me, but I must be giving off some really helpless vibe for her to go into full-fledged mom mode. Is it that obvious that I'm a weepy wreck from the hormones? I force a smile, embarrassed that I've caused my friend such concern. As if she didn't have enough on her mind juggling the dating scene and a new job while her daughter spends the summer with the woman who stole her husband.

"I'm fine. Really."

Her gaze travels from my face to the pool. In the darkness, the water resembles a creased black sheet. The switch for the lights is by the grill. I never flip it, though. Makes the pool eerie.

"You need to be very, very careful with drugs that stress out your body and your brain, Lizzie." She faces me again, as though looking at the pool has given her new resolve to act as my lifeguard. "Anything messing with your memory *and* your moods could have a major impact on your health, particularly in your case."

I feel a rush of anxiety followed by pressure in my ears, a hyperawareness of the soreness in my jaw. These are the precursors to a stress headache. I sip my wine, trying to stave off the migraine. "What do you mean?"

Chris twists her hair. I'd intended the question to sound casual, but it shot out as upset as I feel. It's easy for Christine to say that a side effect is too much to bear—she has a twelve-year-old daughter. She can't know what she'd actually put up with if a doctor pulled her into a "counseling room" and said that, in all likelihood, she'd never, ever be a mother.

"I mean the mind is a carefully calibrated piece of equipment. You put something out of whack, and next thing you know, you're irrationally stressed or unable to cope. You could really damage yourself, Lizzie. *And* it's not like you don't have a history with depression. With everything that happened in high school, don't you think you're tempting fate a bit? There's got to be another treatment out there that doesn't impact your brain. You don't want—"

I put down my glass. It hits the table more roughly than I'd intended, cutting Chris off with a crack and splattering wine onto the glass surface. "I'm sorry. I don't want to talk about this anymore. Okay?"

"But—"

"I want a baby. You can't understand because you have Emma. And you can't tell me she's not worth a thousand Georges and you wouldn't suffer anything to be with her, even him sneaking around with the sitter." My voice is trembling as though I might burst into tears. I breathe and speak slower. "I'll be fine."

Again, Chris sweeps her hair behind her ear. She looks at me like I'm a kid about to go off to college. There are things she's warned me about, the look says, but sometimes you can't learn until you suffer the consequences.

I take a long gulp of wine. The act works like a placebo, easing the pressure in my head even though the alcohol can't have hit yet. "I'm working on a new book."

Chris's shoulders sag. "What about?"

"An affair."

She snorts. "Well, I guess you have the right friend for research. Lucky you."

I consider Chris. Sunset hair, honey-colored eyes. Brassy personality. "She's not you. She's a mousey brunette who slowly becomes a murderer."

Chris gives me her classic not-amused smirk, perfected during her teenage years. She doesn't believe me. I guess I wouldn't either if I were her. I've fleshed out characters with her features before. Why wouldn't I base an affair story off of her experience? She's told me enough.

"In what world would you be mousey?"

She gulps down the rest of her drink and smacks her lips together. "Appearance is a detail."

# Chapter 6

I DRESS TO KILL. A skintight sheath, fished from the back of my closet, is glued to my figure, or rather to the full-coverage Spanx cinching my postpartum body into my prepregnancy shape. My hair is blown out, the way I used to wear it before my morning routine included sponge bathing an infant. I've applied makeup: lipstick *and* eyeliner. If I'm going to confront Jake about breaking his marriage vows, I need to resemble the woman to whom he said, "I do."

I push the stroller through the glass doors of a squat, square courthouse building and head for a hallway lined with ancient Otis elevators. When I press the call button, there is a metallic shriek behind the wall reminiscent of the sounds heard through subway grates. A bell rings. I wheel the stroller inside, barely fitting it between a pair of suited men and the elevator operator, an employee from a different era who eyes my nonwork attire as though I may be an undercover operative before asking what floor I need.

The doors open to a marble hallway. I roll the stroller over the hard stone, past the windowless room in which Jake's secretary, Martha, works, squeezed between an oak desk and file cabinets. I like the woman. She's an aging spitfire who couldn't care less what people think of her. Last time I came here, she'd dyed her chin-length bob a silvery blue befitting a unicorn's mane. She'd quipped that the color was closer to her natural gray than any of the Clairol shades.

Maria's door is always open, probably because any normal person would suffer claustrophobia with it closed. As I pass, she ducks her head out like a cautious anchovy and waves me over.

"Hey, Beth. How are you? Did you bring Victoria?" Maria's hands open and close. "I want to see how big she's grown."

I push the carriage over to her door and peel back the sunshade. "She's sleeping." I'm stating the obvious. On a normal day, I'd relish chatting with the woman. Not today, though. "Is Jake in?"

Maria's smile twists into a bothered expression, deepening the frown line on the side of her mouth. "You know, I think he might be . . ." She points to the phone on her desk. "Let me call him for you."

Something about her behavior sets off my new infidelity detector. Maybe it's how she pretends not to know what he's doing or how she retreats into the room with tiny footsteps, as if tiptoeing. Perhaps it's how she reaches for the receiver without pausing to sit down.

I rotate the stroller and head down the hallway. "No worries. I'll just pop my head in."

"Beth."

The sound of my name doesn't pause my march to Jake's door. It has a window encased in the wood, his full name etched into the glass. Through it, I see him seated in his office chair. A uniformed officer sits on the lip of his desk, leaning toward him.

I throw open the door with such force that it bangs against the outside wall. I feel nothing as I enter. Instead of communicating my feelings about the presence of my husband's lover, my mind dispassionately imparts logistics. Officer Colleen is six feet away from me. Her gun is on her holster. The carriage is to my left.

"Beth!" Jake bolts upright and rounds the desk. "I wasn't expecting you."

The officer turns toward me, unpainted lips in a pursed smile. Her face is tinged with color, as though she's blushing.

"Officer, this is my wife." Jake stands between us, angled to the side, leaving open my route to shoving her onto the thin carpet and breaking the bumped bridge of her nose. She's smaller than me but undoubtedly more athletic. Stronger. Still, I'll have surprise. Her guard is down. She's trying to seem friendly. She doesn't know that I know.

"Honey, this is Colleen." The term of endearment confuses me. I glance at Jake. The same red hue that colored his girlfriend's skin tone transfers to him, darkening his tight smile.

The woman extends her hand. I blink at it in awe. She's sleeping with my spouse and still has the gall to shake?

I face Jake. "I need to talk to you."

His face scrunches with concern. "Is something wrong?"

I stare at Colleen. Her hand falls from the air onto her hips, inches away from her holster. "I was heading out anyway." She walks behind my husband, shoulder nearly to the wall. It's as wide a berth as she can give me.

"You'll e-mail with that arrest report?" Jake shouts after her. She pauses, one foot already in the hall. Her expression is first puzzled and then furious. He is pretending that their meeting was professional, for my benefit. A man poised to dump his wife for his mistress wouldn't play such games. She grunts something affirmative and strides out the open door. It slams with a bang that rivals my own moments before and the noise wakes Vicky. She starts crying, sounding that little baby alert, part yell, part meow.

"Heavy door." Jake scoops her from the bassinet, cupping her head to his chest and supporting her back with his open palm. His weight shifts from side to side. Immediately, she starts to settle down, safe now from the noise that startled her to consciousness.

The reddish hue fades from my vision. My husband is a decent father. Doesn't my baby deserve her dad?

"We need to talk." The urgency has left my tone.

"Everything all right?"

"I'm going to leave Vicky with my mom in Jersey for the night."

"Are you feeling like you can't take care of her?"

The anger returns like a reversed tide. This must be how he's excusing the affair. *My wife became depressed after the baby. I needed attention.* I look at his handsome face and regret that the picture frame missed his nose. "We need to talk."

He stops swaying and lowers Vicky from his chest into a cradle position before placing her in the stroller. A proud smile sneaks on his face. The sight of it threatens to weaken me. Anger is a lifeline to courage. I grasp for it by picturing Colleen's face.

"I'll get back by seven," I say. "You'll be home. We can talk then."

"Sure. Well . . ." He looks up at me, smile no longer genuine. "Uh, I have some work that I was thinking might keep me."

*I bet.* "This is important. You're not on trial. I need you home at seven."

"You don't want to give me a clue as to what this is about?"

"Seven, Jake." I say it in a seething whisper. "I need you home at seven." I lean into the stroller and tuck a blanket around Vicky's legs. As I do, Jake dips his head in and kisses the side of my face.

"I love you two," he whispers. "You know that?"

My fight vanishes. The only choice now is to flee. I wrest my head away from his warm lips and grasp the stroller handle. "Seven. Okay? I'll see you at seven."

# LIZA

I wake with blood in my mouth. At first, I think the metallic flavor is a phantom taste left from my nightmare. In my sleep, I'd been floating above a mortally wounded Colleen, an omniscient narrator ready to read my character her last rights. She'd writhed below me, hands cupping a hole in her gut. The liquid pooling around her had appeared black in the darkness, motor oil from a busted gasket.

My hand reveals that the cut is not in my imagination. A wet mark shines on the finger that I dragged across my lower lip. There are dark splotches that must be dried blood. I peel the sheets from my sweat-drenched body and roll from the bed, making my way from memory into the pitch-black hallway and toward the bathroom. Once inside, I close the door behind me and flick on the buzzing overhead light. The woman in the vanity has crazy hair and a raised welt from where a front tooth pierced flesh. I must rub my eyes to recognize myself.

I grab a washcloth from beside the sink, wet it, and press it to my mouth. Reality still feels ephemeral. Am I nursing a real wound or still asleep, facedown on a drool-drenched pillow?

By the time my bottom lip stops oozing, I'm wide awake. I return to my room and remove my charging laptop from the nightstand. I may not be ready to kill Colleen, but I can picture Beth's next move: dropping the kid off with her mother. I cannot have her confront Jake again with a stage whisper.

*

I finish the chapter as day breaks through the shutters. The light casts an alternating pattern of sun and shadow on the knotted pine floor, like a still shot of the view outside a moving subway. My mind feels slow. I'd like nothing more than to pull the covers over my head and get a few more hours of shut-eye. Doing so, however, would negate my early morning progress. I'll need a few all-nighters to make my deadline as it is.

Still, my brain requires carbohydrates, and my body could use a shower. A musky odor, like the smell of a dog's neck, fills the room. There's only one place it could be coming from.

I return to the bathroom and step into the shower. When I was a child, sliding glass doors above the tub had walled off the area, turning it into a mini-steam room. My mother swapped them for opaque plastic curtains before I turned ten, presumably so I could brush my teeth in the sole upstairs bathroom without watching her shave. Seeing your parents naked is only appropriate when you don't have a sense of why "private parts" should be private.

Water sputters from the shower head. Though I have the dial turned to the hottest setting, the temperature is lukewarm at best, a consequence of the forty-year-old plumbing system. It's amazing that people pay as much as they do to rent this place.

As I scrub my body, I think of my mother, of the way her energy still permeates the house during the day, buttressing the rafters no matter how rotted the wood may be. If only I'd inherited some of her strength. Her fight. She would have no problem making this month's deadline while on fertility treatments. A woman who can work in an office all day and then do all the cleaning, cooking, and child-rearing at night while her husband goes out drinking and womanizing would not be so easily overwhelmed by synthetic hormones. She certainly wouldn't be near tears all the time.

Despite everything my father did, I can only vaguely recall her crying once. I don't remember what for. Probably he'd hit her. She'd done her best to send me upstairs when she'd sensed an argument would get ugly, but it was hard for her to correctly gauge it all the time. He'd come home drunk a lot, looking for a fight or a fuck—neither of which she'd ever wanted to give him. Either he was going to get violent or go looking elsewhere. How could she always guess right?

As I rinse, I try to understand why I'd become so depressed after my dad left. I should have been grateful. Maybe kids always want both parents around—even when one is a terror. Or maybe I had more good memories back then. I only have one now: a time when I'd stayed home sick from school and he'd lounged on the couch with me all day watching movies. He'd even let me rent an R-rated teen flick all the older kids had been chatting about six months earlier because of some nudity and the suggestion of sex. My mom had barred me from watching it, but Dad had said that she was being overprotective "about nothing." I'd gone back to junior high the following day as the coolest eighth grader ever.

After I shower, I head into the kitchen for cereal, only to remember that I forgot to buy any at the store the night before. Christine's presence had distracted me from my mental grocery list. I return upstairs to my phone and send her a text. "Nothing in the pantry. Breakfast?"

Her reply appears almost instantaneously. "Meet you @ Crow on a Roof. Nine."

I head back to my room. As I climb the stairs, my stomach protests waiting three hours to eat, grumbling and groaning louder than any creaky floorboard. I have a feeling it will make me pay for this later. Already, I am more queasy than usual. By the time I reconstitute my office setup—sitting on the mattress with my computer in my lap and phone by my side—my lower abdomen is in full revolt. Each of my unfertilized eggs seems to have grown limbs and is throwing a tantrum, kicking and clawing at my muscles and vital organs. I run to the toilet with my hand over my mouth. Fish, cured in stomach acids, burns in my throat and my belly. When I see porcelain, I'm not sure which end belongs over the bowl.

When everything is out, I wipe down the bathroom surfaces with bleach left beneath the sink, pausing every few seconds to catch my breath. The smell of so much chlorine turns my stomach, but it's preferable to the stench of sick. The bleach will also disinfect the room on the off chance that the hormones aren't responsible for my illness. A spritz of standard bleach obliterates nearly everything: E. coli, salmonella, viruses. It will even unravel DNA. The only thing it can't destroy is blood.

When I finish, I shower for a second time, brush my teeth, and head back to my room. Feeling clean helps, but a heavy metal drummer still plays in my head, thumping on the bass and slamming his sticks into the hi-hat to maintain the ringing between my ears. I stumble over to the bed, weak-kneed, and curl up in fetal position on the mattress. Sleep doesn't ask my permission.

*

The phone's vibration startles me awake. I swat blindly around the mattress, trying to find the handset without opening my eyes. Around the third slap, I remember my breakfast date with Christine and add vision to the search. Chris is good about giving me a five-minute grace period. The waiter is probably telling her that he needs the table.

The phone lies beneath a pillow. "Chris?" My voice sounds skinned.

"Liza, are you on your—Wait, are you okay?"

"Alcohol and fertility drugs don't mix."

"Say no more. I'll grab you an egg sandwich to go."

You choose your friends, not your family. Christine is the best sister an only child could ever want. She arrives twenty minutes later with a white paper bag from the restaurant, coffee, and a bottle of aspirin. Love and appreciation overwhelm me so that all I can do in return is offer a sniffling hug.

She pats my back. "What are best friends for?"

My gratitude gives way to guilt as I watch her set up breakfast on the dining table, grabbing plates and glasses from kitchen cupboards as if she owns the place. If Chris had disappeared, I'd be wallpapering Montauk with posters and pestering the police daily. David is doing the same for his friend. I've been selfish to expect him to snap out of it and start paying me attention after only a month.

I sit at the place that Chris has set for me. A fried egg sandwich with a thick medallion of ham between two croissants rests in the center of a plate surrounded by a glass of water, two aspirins, and a large black coffee.

I swallow the pills first and drink the water. Chris nods her approval and then indicates the Starbucks cup with the bacon, egg, and cheese sandwich in her hand. "I always go with coffee first. If your stomach isn't ready to hold anything down, you'd rather find out with liquids."

I pull the paper cup beneath my nose and inhale the steam. The familiar scent calms the throbbing in my skull. The drummer is not playing so much anymore as he is feathering the snare, creating internal white noise.

Chris settles into the chair across from me, her back toward the kitchen. It's the seat she always took growing up. Me on the right, her across, my mom at the head. Even when he lived with us, my father rarely ate dinner with the family.

I tentatively sip the black coffee. A warm, calming sensation spreads through my gut as the liquid goes down. "This is exactly what I needed. Thank you."

"Love you." Chris blows me an air kiss. "Besides, you'd do it for me. In fact, you have done it for me, many times. How many nights did you stay over after the divorce?"

The answer intensifies my shame about David. I spent four days at Christine's house helping her pack George and the nanny's things into boxes. I'd had Chris and Emma over for dinner at least one day a week afterward. Yet I'd wanted David to get over his friend's likely death in a month.

"You're my sister from another mister. I'd do anything for you," she says. Despite her jokey tone, I know she means it. Chris and I have looked out for each other our whole lives. "How are you feeling?"

"Physically or mentally?"

"Both."

"Physically? Much better thanks to you. I don't know what I would do without you." I reach out and squeeze her hand. She smiles at me to accept the compliment and then rolls her eyes at my sappiness.

"And mentally?"

"I feel sick with myself. I've been giving David a lot of grief about still wallowing over Nick and not boarding the baby train. But if David cares about Nick half as much as I adore you, then he's within his rights to crawl into a hole for a year. It's not fair to him."

Chris tucks her hair behind her ears rather than join me in admonishing myself.

I sigh. "It's also not very respectful of Nick. I haven't mourned him at all."

She leans her forearms on the table and looks up at me from beneath a wrinkled brow. "And Nick would have shed a tear over you? Come on. He was cute and charming and very driven . . ." Her honey eyes get a bit soupy at the thought of her once crush. She shakes her head to pull herself out of the daydream. "But we both know he wasn't *that* nice, especially not to you. He always treated you like the girl David had settled for."

"Well, I took away his clubbing buddy."

Chris grimaces. "Most people grow up and get over that. Nick used to call you 'Little Miss Mistake' and say that you were too troubled to have real friends so you made up people to keep you company."

Though I never heard Nick say such things, I can imagine him doing it behind my back, whispering it to one of those milquetoast girls he always brought on group dates that looked like she'd been pulled straight from a Robert Palmer video. I have a harder time picturing him insulting me with Christine in earshot. "When did he say that?"

She sips her coffee, hiding her face behind the mug. "When we went on that date."

I burst out laughing. The reaction is involuntary and not at all rational. Nothing is particularly amusing about my beautiful maid of honor and David's handsome best man trying each other on for size. Yet I find it absurd. "You're kidding. You never went on a date with him."

"I did. A little less than two months ago. I told you about it."

"You did not."

"I did. You don't remember."

I give Chris my best *Really?* look. There is no way that I would forget my closest friend going on an official date with my husband's law partner. She must have glossed it over, acting like she ran into him and they had one of their usual stilted conversations. "Well, give me details."

She scans the table and groans. "Ugh. I need a drink for this story. Where's the bottle we didn't get to?"

Part of me feels that I should tell her that drinking before noon is a sign of alcoholism. But I have zero moral authority to warn her when I was the one who couldn't hold her liquor the prior night. "There's a Riesling in the fridge."

She heads into the kitchen. "It was at the start of the summer, actually." The fridge door opens, hiding Chris's face. "I'd put Emma on a plane to see George a few days earlier and was feeling a bit lonely. So, because the universe tends to steel-boot kick people who are feeling sorry for themselves, I ended up bumping into Nick in the city."

The fridge shuts. Sunlight from the screened back door glints on the green bottle in her hand. Glass clinks as she looks through a cabinet above the dishwasher for a wine glass.

"You're leaving me in suspense," I say.

"You're the last person who can complain about that," she quips, removing a stemless wine glass from the cabinet. "Anyway, Nick was looking GQ as always, so we started talking. Then he asked me what I was doing later . . ."

I try to catch Chris's eye as she says this. I can picture her asking Nick on a date, but not the other way around. After her divorce, she'd asked me to set them up. David had insisted that he wouldn't go for her.

Chris returns to the table with the white wine in her right hand and the rims of two glasses pinched between the fingers of her left. The mere suggestion of alcohol turns my stomach. "I'm never drinking again." I take a massive bite of my sandwich for emphasis.

She shakes her head at me and twists off the cap. "So anyway, Nick takes me to this speakeasy-type place in Brooklyn, one of those bars without an officially marked entrance. I forget the name of it. I *do* remember lots of gold-framed mirrors and red leather booths."

"Stalling."

"Okay. Let me get a drink in me." She pours a taste and takes it like a vodka shot, tilting the glass back until it has disappeared.

"Okay. So I'm in Marie Antoinette's bedroom, hanging on hand-some Nick's bicep, wondering whether it's bad form to sleep with him on the first date given that we've known each other socially for years, and I realize that every single person in the place is gay."

"He took you to a gay bar?"

"Well, it could have been a hipster bar," Chris concedes, pouring herself a real portion. "Or maybe it was a straight bar most of the time and we stumbled in on gay night. So anyway, he acts like the whole thing is completely natural and takes me to a booth. We order drinks." She takes a Pavlovian sip of her wine. "He spends the whole night basically bitching about you in hopes that I would relay the message, which I never did because fuck him, right?"

I'd known Nick wasn't a fan of mine. But the act of taking out my best friend for the sole purpose of trashing me is something out of a mean-high-school-girls movie. "What did he say?"

Chris grimaces. "It doesn't matter."

"I want to know."

"Typical complaining from an insensitive man." She rolls her eyes to show she doesn't take any stock in the forthcoming criticism. "The hormones had made you all emotional and clingy, and David couldn't do the things he needed to because you might fall apart."

"What, like work?"

She shrugs. "Nick said at one point that he brought in all the big-money clients, so maybe he thought David wasn't pulling his fair share because he was busy taking care of you."

If Nick had said such things to Christine, he'd undoubt-edly been saying them to David daily. Was it any wonder now, with Nick's voice ringing in his head, that all David wanted to do was work? That he didn't want me to continue treatments? Nick had probably convinced him that a baby was bad for business.

The drummer in my head starts a new rhythm, something ferocious and tribal like an ancient hula. I drop my forehead into my hands and try to soften the beat. Angry tears spill from the corners of my eyes.

"Hey, don't get upset. Nick was being an ass. I mean, David's his best friend, right? He couldn't shoulder the load for a few months?"

Chris comes around the table and crouches beside my chair. She drapes an arm around my shoulder. "I shouldn't have said anything."

"No. I'm glad you did." I sniff and wipe my eyes with the back of my hand. "And I know it's horrible to say, but I'm glad Nick's gone."

# Chapter 7

I TELL MY MOM THAT Jake and I are having a long-overdue date night. She doesn't believe me. Doubt restrains her smile as she stands in the doorway to the clapboard Cape Cod where I grew up, trying to make direct eye contact after asking how parenthood is treating "you two."

"It'll be good to have time together," I say, pushing Vicky's stroller past her waiting hug. On my shoulder hangs a massive bag stuffed with backup onesies, bottles, and bags of frozen breast milk. I drop it on her plaid couch and then remove the milk pouches as my mother takes her granddaughter from the stroller.

"Hello, Vicky-boo. Are you ready to spend the night with Nana? Huh, baby? Spend the night with Nana?"

I carry the milk through the small dining room into the adjacent kitchen. The floor is black-and-white-checked linoleum, a design so old that it's become fashionable again. My mother has also held onto the retro-chic fridge of my childhood, an ancient white box with an attached freezer a little bigger than a beach bag. I lay my baby's food atop a pack of chicken breasts encased in snow-covered plastic.

"I'm leaving you with forty ounces," I shout as I reenter the living room.

"You look nice. Where are you going?" Though she calls out the question between coos at her granddaughter, I recognize when my mother is fishing. She's searching for clues as to why I asked her last minute to watch Vicky, why I nearly begged that she reschedule her girls' dinner with the neighbor. My urgency would make sense if, say, Jake scored concert tickets.

"You can't defrost the milk in the microwave. It needs to be put in a hot water bath for five minutes, until it reaches room temperature. Microwaving kills all the good nutrients."

"Please, Beth. I know how to heat up breast milk." Again, she tries to make me look at her. "Is anything wrong?"

The little girl inside me wants to bury my face on her tiny shoulder and unload my entire burden. My better self strangles her. I take Vicky from my mom's arms and kiss her forehead. She smiles, or at least gives me an infant's best approximation of one. Her sapphire eyes glitter. Though Vicky's irises are darker than her dad's, her lids have his downturned shape. If we end things tonight, will I ever be able to look at her and not see him?

"Mommy will be back tomorrow," I whisper. "I love you more than life."

A hand lands on my upper arm. The lines on my mom's brow deepen. "Beth, is everything all right?"

I hand her my baby. "I'm sorry. I'm in a hurry. Zipcar charges by the hour."

She searches my face for something more. I gesture to the bag and start detailing everything inside, an attempt to overload her mother-radar. It's not working. I can tell by her erect posture. The way she looks at me rather than at the bag from which I frantically pull out bottles, needlessly explaining how to ensure nipples don't mold.

As I'm heading out the door, she tries one last time. "Are you sure nothing is wrong?"

I throw up my hands. "I'm a new mom."

She gives me a wistful smile, as though that explains everything.

*

It's 6:20 when I enter. For the next half hour, I wait, huddled on our living room couch like a crouching tiger, ready to pounce the moment Jake walks through the door. He calls at seven sharp. I hold my breath as I answer my cell and shut my eyes tight, praying that he'll tell me he's on his way.

"Um . . . Beth."

*Coward.* I want to unleash the word with an onslaught of expletives. I want to scream that I know he's about to lie, that he's not working late, that his girlfriend is pissed off because he was affectionate toward me and that she probably gave him an ultimatum about seeing her tonight. I want to reveal that I know everything. I am not a fool. I am not hormonal. I am not crazy.

"Why aren't you here?"

"It's work. I'm so sorry, hon. This upcoming case is taking so much time, and every time I think I have a handle on it, something new shows up in discovery that changes my whole strategy."

"My mother is watching Vicky."

"I know, babe. But there's no way I'm going to be able to make it home at a reasonable hour. I'll be stuck here all night."

"You said we could talk. Why can't you work late tomorrow?"

"Because I can't," he snaps. "What do you want me to do, huh? I'm needed here. My job pays our bills." Anger is the best cover for guilt. It's an outward feeling that pushes people away, puts others on the defensive, prevents them from demanding apologies.

"You promised."

"Well, I have to break this one. I can't rearrange my work schedule on such short notice. I'll make it up to you soon. We'll go out someplace nice. In the meantime, you should get some rest. I mean, Vicky doesn't let you really sleep. Think of it: without her and me bothering you, you can get a good eight hours for once."

I picture him delivering these lines, eyes flitting to the clock, trying to end the conversation with his wife so as not to be late for his lover. If only lies had substance. They would lodge in his esophagus, an indigestible wad of dirty gum. He would struggle to breathe, hands around his own throat, choking on the last of his untruths.

He keeps blathering on about my need for sleep. Really, him working tonight is doing me a favor, he says. Rest is important for mental health. It's important for my mood. We will have a more productive conversation if I'm no longer exhausted. "I'll be there when you wake up in the morning," he assures me.

A scream curdles in my stomach. I hang up and hurl the phone at the wall. It lands on the floor, saved from smashing by the throw rug and the hard plastic case protecting its back. The lack of destruction frustrates me. I twist my diamond engagement ring off my finger and fling it at the wall. Then, for good measure, I take the wedding band and throw it too. Blood rushes to my head like a brain freeze. I'm going to be sick. I run to the bathroom and hang my head over the toilet. My stomach contracts. Bile and foam pour from my mouth into the bowl, staining the water a rusty orange.

After I finish, I take stock in the mirror. The woman who looks back at me has aged five years. Circles from weeks of sleep deprivation darken beneath her eyes, hollowing out her appearance. A greenish tint mars her coloring. Her dress is splattered with sick. I peel it off and stumble into the shower, turning the dial to its hottest setting. My skin reddens in the water. I scrub myself clean, wash my hair, my face. When I again look in the mirror, I have the skin of a healthy young woman, flushed pink with fury.

I grab my cosmetic bag. Makeup is war paint for women. Jake is about to be very sorry.

# LIZA

David texts me good-bye Sunday. I receive the message while waiting for the ticket machine to spit out my boarding pass. "Have a good conference." With a smoochy face. Not once did he call, despite my messages dangling the prospect of good news from Sergeant Perez and apologizing for our argument. He could have at least acknowledged my calls. Emojis don't exist for what I'd like to write now.

I'm in the midst of penning a passive-aggressive reply when the machine's printer starts clicking. I slip my phone back into my purse. Writing a snitty e-mail to my spouse is no reason to miss a flight.

Fortunately, few people travel so early on a Sunday. My lack of socks is a bigger issue than the line. I toss my sandals on the security conveyor belt and walk, barefoot, through a full body scanner. My feet sweat, mental images of plantar warts and fungus-stained toenails running through my head, as I wait for a hypervigilant TSA official to determine that the metal in my purse is loose change.

I slip back on my sandals while trying to snatch my exposed laptop before another shoeless traveler mistakes it for theirs. Somehow, I stuff my electronics into the front pocket of my carry-on as it careens down the conveyor belt. I hoist it back onto checkered linoleum and wheel it behind me as I weave past a sock-footed family, proud of myself for splurging on a suitcase with multidirectional casters.

When I reach the gate, I am surprised by Trevor's profile. He sits in a chair, right leg crossed over the left, head bowed over a book. I can't see the cover, though I can tell from the size it's not one of mine.

"Trev?" I say his name as a question, on the off chance that some other gorgeous black man with wire-rimmed glasses is reading a massive novel while waiting for a flight to take him to the destination of the world's largest suspense writer's conference. Dark eyes travel to my face. He smiles wide enough to show his top teeth and nods to the empty seat beside him. Judging from all the unoccupied chairs outside our gate, the early flight appears only a third full, though it's possible my fellow travelers are still in the bookstore or braving the line at the single open coffee shop.

I settle into the seat on Trevor's right but move to the far side of the vinyl. Though we're friends, his good looks require a professional distance. Incidental physical contact with a man this attractive always means more.

"I didn't realize we were on the same flight."

"I suppose Courtney booked the whole New York crew on the earliest plane out of here." He laughs. "If it goes down, that will be the end of the imprint."

We talk about what I have planned for the conference: when I'll sign at our publisher's booth, which panel I'm booked on, who will join me on the dais. Marketing only slotted me into one discussion group: "The First Bestseller: Unraveling the Mystery Behind a Debut Blockbuster." I'll need to talk about *Drowned Secrets*. I'm not looking forward to it.

A few minutes into a conversation about a panel that Trevor is moderating—"The Long Run: How to Create Compelling Series Characters"—the stewardess begins "inviting" passengers on the plane. He stands when they announce priority boarding for business-class ticket holders. I remain seated. My ticket is in row 22. Business-class privileges dried up with my last novel's sales.

Trevor steps toward the gate door and then glances over his shoulder with raised eyebrows. "Courtney has you in coach?"

"It's no big deal. I'm narrow." The phrase "beggars can't be choosers" comes to mind, but I can't utter such a hackneyed expression in my editor's presence. I'm fortunate that the publishing house is footing the bill for the trip at all. Many writers pay their own way at these things.

He rubs the back of his neck. "That's too bad. Now I'm stuck finishing that waste of paper I was reading."

I frown out of fellowship for the unknown writer. Trevor never couches his criticism with favorable fluff. Books are either superb or they stink. There's no in-between for him. "Whose is it?"

"Greg Hall's latest. The guy must have a deal where no one is allowed to touch his work. I'm not even halfway in and could have shaved twenty thousand words."

"Well, if you really need the excuse, I'm sure whomever is sitting next to me will gladly switch for your reclining seat with extra leg room."

Trevor doesn't laugh at my joke. Instead, he eyes the queue. A handful of passengers are lined up, though probably not the number needed to fill the front cabin of the massive plane tethered to gate. He grabs his rolling suitcase and points at me with his free hand. "Look after that book for me. Be right back."

Trevor grabs an attendant's attention. He points in my direction twice during the conversation, erasing any doubt as to what he's doing. Embarrassment at my unintended role as an upgrade beggar encourages me to open a blank document on my laptop and pretend to work. I should think of something to say on my panel, though I have little idea what made my first book so much more "believable" and "gripping" than my others. Even after I wrote it, I'd largely faked my way through the bookstore tour. I've always felt as though another version of me penned the novel or that I'd been a conduit for some outside storytelling intelligence that had quickly moved on, leaving me with a bestseller and no concrete idea of how to repeat it.

The story itself wasn't that novel. *Drowned Secrets* told the tale of a young girl whose alcoholic father had been sexually molesting her. The mother finds out one summer and hits him in the back of the head with a shovel beside their pool. He falls in, concussed, and drowns. Later, the mom buries the murder weapon beneath the bushes. There aren't too many twists and turns. No gotcha moments. The perspective, I think, was what hooked the readers. My narrator was Bitsy, the abused twelve-year-old. Reviewers crowed about how I'd really gotten into her head.

Trevor's step has added swagger as he returns. I pick up the Hall novel and hold it out to him, a lead weight in return for his trouble. For the first time I notice the cover: a Southern gothic image of a house with a child waiting on the porch. I wouldn't have wanted to read it before Trevor's scathing review.

"Will you be needing this?"

"I was able to upgrade you, sans charge."

"That never works for me. It's the accent, isn't it?"

He winks. "Gets you Americans every time."

*

The business-class seats are wide and deep. No one tells me not to recline before takeoff or to stow my electronic devices. Instead, the flight attendant assures us that the food service will start as soon as the cabin doors close and asks for cocktail orders.

Remembering how violently three drinks had mixed with my medication, I am about to say, "Nothing for me," when Trevor orders a red wine. I must look shocked by the hour because he clears his throat and says, "Conferences make me a bit nervous. So much selling."

His sentiments so agree with my own that I tell the flight attendant to "please make that two."

As we wait for the drinks, Trevor and I gush over the latest releases from mutual favorite crime writers who, in our humble opinions, deserve all the money they've made. My editor is the only man I've ever met that enjoys fiction as much, if not more, than I do. He's the Calvin Johnson of literary references. It's impossible to make a quote that he won't catch. When the wine appears, conversation moves on from respected writers to overrated hacks. We trade names, hipster teens pitching pebbles at the popular kids. Trevor is mean in his straight-man British monotone. He's always had an uncanny ability to cut with bluntness.

Two minibottles of Barolo arrive that I am sure would never have made it to the back of the plane. As I sip my drink, Trevor turns the conversation to my book. "How is the writing coming?"

He probably wants to hear that I'm a third done. But I can't deliver that line with a straight face. A more responsible person would have declined her editor's offer of first class and sequestered herself in steerage, laptop open on the dining tray. "The setup is taking me a bit longer than I thought."

I glance over Trevor's shoulder into the aisle. The flight attendant's backside sticks into the walkway as she passes a bag of chips to a passenger. If Trevor is going to grill me about my story, I need a clear head. Water not wine.

"I wanted to apologize for being so negative about your idea before."

I stop trying to make eye contact with the airline employee. Trevor looks at me from beneath half-lowered lids. His dark gaze draws me in, like the mouth of a cave. "I think affairs are a sore spot for me after the divorce."

"I always meant to ask what happened with Kyra. But I wasn't sure you wanted to talk about it."

I've already heard the story. Manhattan is a small town of eight million. A friend with a son in Trevor's daughter's pre-K class shared that there'd been a scandal with a mom trading her husband for another parent. The drama had coincided with Trevor's separation.

Trevor scratches his scalp and shifts in his chair. His wounds have not healed. "I'm not sure that I know what happened, really. Maybe she got bored. She started picking at everything, saying I didn't do enough around the house, give her enough attention. My head was always buried in a book." The hand that had fussed with his head falls to his tray table. "Anyway, not long after we separated, she shacked up with one of the dads at Olivia's school."

I try to act surprised, dropping my jaw and shaking my head, mimicking how Trevor performs shock.

"She swears nothing happened beforehand. Still, there's emotional infidelity, isn't there?"

I squeeze Trevor's hard shoulder. The gesture is a common platonic show of support. It's supposed to be safe. But the truth is, I don't feel safe around this man anymore. His confession—or maybe the show of vulnerability—stirs something in my subconscious. It's as though he understands me in a way that no one else has or ever will. Part of me aches to tell him this. The other part of me knows that I've consumed too much wine, am pissed at David, and am on a cocktail of hormones.

"Want me to kill her off in a book?"

Trevor smirks, a devilish half smile that sets fire to his eyes. "Well," he chuckles, "somebody always has to die."

∗

I don't see Trevor after check-in. He has multiple panels to moderate, more famous authors to ply with alcohol. I, on the other hand, am not expected anywhere until my three o'clock slot at the signing table. How to kill the time?

A check-in packet lies on my hotel bed. The spiral-bound book weighs as much as Trevor's maligned novel and includes a twenty-page outline of the various author discussions happening every hour, on the hour, for the next several days. I don't look at it. After a decade, the panel topics are all choppy remixes of the same ol' tunes. Most veteran authors tour the city until called upon for their own promotional activities.

I pull back the long blackout curtains and look outside. The view is of downtown New Orleans, though not the famous French Quarter. That section of town, with its painted buildings and wrought-iron balconies, is too small to host a gathering of MWO's size. The convention hotel is on the waterfront, between the city's main expo center and a warehouse selling Mardi Gras supplies. If I press my head to the glass and look left, I can almost see the Mississippi.

The buildings beyond look far away. Foreboding. The king-sized mattress, on the other hand, appears inviting, made up with bleached-white linens and mint chocolates on the pillows, penned in by the four walls surrounding it and the door to the en suite bathroom. My laptop rests on the nightstand. A pink chaise sits to the right of the bed. I angle it toward the window and grab my computer.

I write for several hours, sobering up from the plane ride all the while. A phone call interrupts me as I am cutting words from a scene where Beth is getting ready to go out. Readers, I've decided, will not care what color lipstick she chooses for her revenge date.

I think David is finally getting back to me and am surprised when I don't recognize the New York number. Likely, a telemarketer has obtained my information. I answer anyway. It could be my gynecologist. "Hello, this is Liza."

"Sergeant Perez. Sorry to phone on a Sunday, but a friend got back to me with some news, and you'd seemed so upset before . . ."

A tingling sensation pricks my fingers, as though they were wet and touching the end of a battery. "Yes. Thank you for calling."

"Your husband reported Mr. Landau missing when he didn't show up for work that Monday and he couldn't get in touch with him. According to the detectives on the case, the last person to report seeing him was a bartender at a local cocktail bar near Mr. Landau's apartment. Some fancy French-styled place."

A mental image of the bar Christine described flashes in my head. I can see the red-cushioned French chairs and gilded mirrors.

"The bartender said that Nick came there that Saturday night with another man. They had several drinks. Apparently, shortly after they left, a woman asked about him. He remembered because she seemed angry and left before finishing her drink."

"Did the bartender see what this woman looked like?" I ask.

"He said she was good-looking."

I think of Nick's exes. They were all attractive women, albeit a bit severe in appearance. Did he break up with the wrong one? "Did she have short hair, by any chance?"

"No. Why?"

"Nick's past girlfriends all had short hair."

"Oh." The sergeant's tone seems surprised.

I realize that, if Nick had dumped this girl, she might have changed her look. Women did that after bad breakups. "Did she have blonde—"

"Unfortunately, I can't provide any more details without compromising the investigation." Sergeant Perez clears his throat. "So as you already agreed to, none of this gets written up. I thought you and your husband would feel better knowing that detectives don't suspect Mr. Landau's disappearance had anything to do with a hate crime or that case against the city. They're leaning toward some kind of romantic spat."

I thank Sergeant Perez and hang up. With the phone still in my hand, I consider calling David. Ultimately, I decide against it. If he can't even deign to return my multiple messages, why should I rush to give him this new information?

My first scheduled appearance is in forty minutes on the first floor. I shower, fix my hair, and change into a navy pencil dress that I hope will transition from day to the nighttime reception. When I examine the reflection in the mirror, I'm disappointed. I look like a side chair upon which someone has hung a promotional tote. The judgment sends me to my makeup bag for red lipstick. Painting my mouth helps. I may still be background furniture, but I now have a decorative pillow.

The exhibition booths are identical long desks covered in printed tablecloths. Behind each are makeshift shelves featuring the latest titles. I notice a kiosk about a hundred feet away that has an electric coffeemaker and giveaway cups. Now *that* will draw a crowd.

The cloth draped over our table is red and printed with this year's book covers. The same curtain is pinned to the wall behind me. Painted milk crate shelves are stacked on either side of the fabric display, showing off the house's latest hardcovers. My new book is there, bottom shelf, where liquor stores keep the rotgut spirits.

In the center of the wall tapestry is the image for the latest from Brad Pickney, my publisher's star author. I could have designed it. Basically, it's a navy background with his name in bold, orange letters. A title is scrawled beneath, along with a tinier subscript announcing that the book is "the latest" in the Trent Cross series. Pickney needs nothing else to sell his work—no image of an attractive man or woman looking off into the distance, no bleakly rendered city or foreboding suburban landscape.

Two gray chairs wait behind the dais. One is for me. The other is for the marketing chaperone who will accompany our house's better known scribes. For me, the second chair will remain occupied by the ghost of sales past. I take a seat, drop my tote, and scan for the swag that my publisher always brings. What do we have? Coffee cups? Stress balls? Five months ago, someone in marketing had asked my opinion on giveaways. I'd suggested plastering a quote from the book on a T-shirt. The woman had thanked me in an unexcited manner. Whatever the team decided on, it wasn't that.

There's nothing save some generic pens. So that's what I have to offer. My signature and some of the bookmarks and business cards that I always bring to these things. I force a smile that I hope could land me a job as an Olive Garden hostess and scan the sparse crowd.

There's a well-dressed man at the other table who reminds me of Nick. They have the same dark hair worn long enough to have a slight curl at the nape. Same deep-set eyes. As I look at him, the room grows fuzzy, like I've moved from a sunlit space into a dim hallway. Suddenly, the overhead lights explode with shocking brightness. My head pounds. I hear phantom traffic sounds followed by an explosion. Instinctively, I press a hand to my left temple. Why is this happening now?

My stomach cramps from the blinding pain. I open my eyes just enough to take in my escape route. The elevators are to the left, a hundred paces beyond this room's exit. I weave around the convention attendees, avoiding people by the placement of their feet on the gray hotel carpet.

By the time I enter my room, the worst of the migraine is over, though my temples still throb the rhythm of my accelerated heartbeat. The suddenness and severity of the headache makes me feel as though I was sucker punched. I want to speak to my husband.

His phone rings five times. I expect to leave a voice mail when an unfamiliar male voice answers.

"Hey. It's Liza. I was calling for my husband."

"I'm sorry. David is meeting with his secretary. May I . . ."

An orange sunset creeps through the hotel window, staining the pale-brown walls with rust streaks. The remnants of the migraine have made me light sensitive. I shade my eyes with a lazy salute and struggle to draw the curtains. Once the room is dark, I regain focus. The man is asking if he can take a message. From the tone of his voice, it's not the first time he has posed the question.

"Sorry, I . . ." Talking hurts. "He's meeting with Cameron?"

"I'll tell him you called."

The man hangs up. I flop on the center of the bed and bury my face in the pillowcase. Why am I suffering a stress migraine? Is it my fear of selling a so-so book? My anger with David for refusing to return my calls? Learning that Nick had been souring David on the idea of a baby? David's desire to work all week? Cameron?

I groan into the fabric. David isn't going to cheat on me with that girl. She's too pretty for him. Too young. He probably spends all day ordering her around: "Take dictation." "Where is my dry cleaning?" "Hang these missing posters." But then, why do I feel so nervous about him in the office? Why the blinding pain in my brain?

My limbs are trembling from the migraine aftershocks and fear of another attack. I always travel with medicine. I dig in my bag for an Excedrin bottle and shake out two pills, swallowing them with bottled water from the minibar.

Afterward, I stumble into the bathroom, vision still blurry from the receding pressure in my head. I splash water on my face, over and over, until my breathing normalizes and the room no longer resembles a club at closing time. Then I flop on the bed and reach for my laptop on the nightstand table.

Deadlines do not stop for migraines. I send the marketing team a quick e-mail explaining that I left my signing early due to "illness" and then open up my most recent document. No more thinking about David or Nick. It's time for Beth to have her revenge.

# Chapter 8

A WARM WIND STROKES MY exposed shoulders as I exit my apartment building onto the street. The park stretches out before me. On nights like this one, couples have picnics on the lawn and illicit intercourse behind the bushes. The city runs the sprinklers around midnight to flush everyone out.

I meander toward Chambers Street and the A train, tottering in the high heels that my feet haven't squeezed into in over a year. The whore's apartment is in Williamsburg, Brooklyn. Jake had her address saved in a Google chat. The conversation, dated more than two months earlier, had caught my attention. They'd been debating "sexual experimentation" in that abstract, pseudointellectual way people have of discussing intercourse when they still haven't seen each other naked. I'd suffered through the whole exchange, figuring it had to end with a meeting place.

I won't go there. Traveling into Brooklyn alone at nine o'clock isn't dangerous. But waiting on a street corner until the wee hours of the morning for my husband and his lover to emerge from her building certainly would be. Moreover, I don't know that they've actually gone to her place. Jake's e-mail and chat history didn't leave clues as to where he intends to take his girlfriend tonight.

Adrenaline carries my anger to every limb. I want to run a marathon or bare-knuckle box. A drink will take the edge off. Finding one in this part of Manhattan, though, is unusually difficult. Like the Upper West Side, the Battery Park area is little more than a suburban breeding ground tucked in the city. Residential buildings, parks, and magnet schools are the draw here, not nightlife. Wine stores and takeout shops are common. Restaurants are rare. Bars have been pretty much exiled.

I pass the brick-and-glass building housing my former shrink on the first floor. What would Tyler think of me right now, dressed up and on the prowl? Would he say I'm having an unhealthy reaction to recent trauma? I imagine his handsome face. Arched eyebrows. Strong, broad nose. Perfectly trimmed goatee. The idea of Tyler distracts me as I reach the casement windows of the neighborhood's only sports bar. Folks in soccer jerseys fill the place. Not what I had in mind, but beggars can't be choosers.

As I head to the entrance, a red-faced man in a crimson jersey comes barreling out of the place, shouting over his shoulder about "gunners blowing." At least, that's what I think I hear. His slurred British accent makes it difficult to tell. The man's thick, swinging arm connects with my side as he passes me, forcing me to hop back with a little yelp. The sound seems to attract him. He turns toward me, blatantly assessing my bedability.

"Hello, love. Well, isn't it my lucky day?" The swinging arm rises and falls over my shoulder. "In there's rubbish. Where are you headed all tarted up?"

I peel from beneath his arm. "I'm sorry. I'm married."

His boozy gaze travels to my left hand, which he grabs and holds up. "No ring." I yank my arm out of his grasp. The man's eyes roll over my dress. He snarls at me. "Lying cunt."

My eyes sting with sudden tears. I back away, stumbling in my heels, despising my husband. Jake should be here, deterring men like this. Instead, I'm alone, left to handle drunken idiots by myself.

"How dare you?" I yell. "You bump into me, don't apologize, eye me like chicken on a rotisserie, and then call me a nasty name when I don't want to go anywhere with you?"

The man dismisses me with a wave.

My body shakes with the force of my fury. "No. Really. Who the fuck do you think you are, asshole?"

He whirls with all the menace of a stuck bull. Red snakes in the whites of his eyes. His nostrils flare. "What did you call me?"

"Asshole."

His hands twitch by his sides. He steps toward me and puts a hand to his ear. "Say again?"

I feign shock. "I'm sorry. I was sure you would have heard that term before. Let me help you. It means a misogynist, selfish prick who thinks other people exist as props in his crappy life. Also known as the place where shit spews out."

"Listen here, bitch—"

The door swings wide and a man exits, tall enough to play center on a basketball court but broad enough for a tight end. He's dark skinned with a neat goatee and an angry frown. Tyler? Does the subconscious send comforting images after being knocked into a concussion by a belligerent drunk? Have I missed a moment?

"Hey, hoss. This here woman is my friend." Tyler's accent is thicker than usual, a kind of singsong British cockney. He's probably been drinking. "You should apologize to her."

The bull glares.

"Now we all saw you bump into her and get grabby." He points to his left while keeping his eyes on my aggressor. "I'm sure there are half a dozen folks with camera phones held up to that window right now. Your best bet is really to say you're sorry and walk away. Anything else, and you'll be in jail facing criminal charges and God knows what else."

The mention of legal action reminds me that my husband is a criminal prosecutor. I open my mouth to share this fact but then see Tyler's strong set jaw and puffed out arms. To hell with Jake.

The bull starts lumbering away. "Fuck you. Fuck her." He turns to the window and puts both middle fingers up. "And fuck Arsenal."

I watch the man shuffle down the street. As he disappears around the corner, my legs start shaking uncontrollably. The fear that I should have felt moments ago when mouthing off to a drunk twice my weight rushes in like blood returning to a cramped extremity.

I look at Tyler as I shiver. "Thank you." Again, tears threaten my eyes. I close them, promising myself that I will not cry. My mascara is not waterproof, and I've looked pathetic in front of this man far too often.

He scratches his head. "Nah, don't mention it. You all right?"

I chuckle. "I could really use a drink."

"Were you meeting someone?"

"No. My mom's watching Vicky." I blink hard, still trying to stave off tears. "It's a beautiful night. I didn't want to spend it alone in the apartment."

"It is real nice out." He smiles. The warmth flows back into the air. I'm reminded that I'm in a twinkling city on a hot summer evening with money in my purse, no parental responsibilities, and no phone for Jake to track me down on. I came out to make the best of all this.

"Well, nice except for that guy," I say.

He gestures to the red jersey outlining his developed pectorals and grins as though he's done something even more spectacular than coming to my rescue. "Arsenal had a good night. That guy had been drinking himself into oblivion over it."

My legs begin to feel normal. I test out a step toward my savior. "May I buy you a drink?"

Tyler bites his lower lip, his eyebrows raise. His head tilts to the side. I can read this expression even though I don't know him well: *That would be a bad idea, don't you think?*

"I owe you one."

"No. You don't. The man was out of line. Anyone would have—"

"Please." I'm directly in front of him now. I've drawn closer, but he's also stepped farther out onto the sidewalk. "It would help me feel more, I don't know, normal."

I catch a small flick of his tongue against his lip as he points down the street. "There's a wine bar down that way." He wrinkles his nose and gestures behind him. "Give me one minute to settle my tab. Too many drunks in there. I don't want to be fighting them off all night."

Was that a compliment? He didn't say "off you," but it was implied. Wasn't it? It's been so long since I've heard genuine flattery that I can't be sure. Jake tells me I'm beautiful, but it's a rote response. "How do I look?" "Beautiful." "Beautiful as always." "You know you're beautiful." I can't believe him. He lies about everything.

Tyler returns with a shy smile. I ask him if I'm spoiling the game. He swears that it was over anyway and fills me in on the history of the bar. Thursday nights are for the expats, particularly the British that the banks are constantly shipping over. The owner, an Irishman, has a satellite dish propped on the back of the building. Tyler spreads his arms, displaying his impressive wingspan. "Thing is bigger than my apartment."

I glance at his hand. There's no ring or visible tan line around the finger, though I'm not positive I'd notice, given his darker complexion. Not that it matters. It's just a drink, and he's only agreed to it because he thinks I'm a fragile soon-to-be-divorced patient who might do something drastic. This is pity date, courtesy of the Hippocratic oath.

I ask him about the game, even though I'm not interested in soccer and only have a vague sense of how it's played. Clearly, he's a fan. He boasts about a Trinidadian "right-back" who plays on Arsenal and came very close to scoring in the recent match. I like hearing him talk. His baritone is deep and comforting, a good voice for his profession. Moreover, it's taking much of my concentration to keep pace with his stride without wrenching my ankle in my stilettos. Instead of looking at him, I'm forced to eye the ground for subway grates.

The wine bar reminds me of the inside of a barrel. The ceiling is wooden with exposed beams that arch toward a line in the center. The floor is cork. It's dark, lit only by electric candles on the tables and three hanging pendant lights above the bar. The counter is a slab of unfinished wood staffed by a young man in a black apron and button-down. Behind him are rows of exposed shelves alternately topped with bottles and bell-shaped glasses of various sizes.

The bar is nearly full. I start toward the only visible free stool, figuring that we'll both hover around it for our drink. Tyler's fingers brush my bicep. He gestures to a table in the corner. "It's seat yourself here."

I follow him and perch on the inside stool, back against a brick wall. He straddles the outside seat, closer to the door, and waves over one of the waitresses. She brings a menu and asks what kind of wine we like. I'm about to say Cabernet but think better of it. Red makes me weepy. Instead, I ask for a dry white. She suggests a sauvignon blanc from New Zealand with herbal, peppery notes, which I say sounds great, though I never taste anything in white wine besides pear and acid. Maybe the postpregnancy senses will change that. When Tyler says he'll have the same, she recommends that we buy the bottle. It's ten dollars more and we'll get two additional glasses for the cost of one.

"Sure." I glance at Tyler to see if his expression disagrees.

He gives a noncommittal shrug. "Good value."

I watch her head off to the bar and then return my attention to Tyler. He's out of place here in his soccer jersey, jeans, and sneakers. But he's so handsome that he makes the button-down set look overdressed.

"What brought you here from Trinidad?"

"Am I from Trinidad?"

"Aren't you?"

"What gave it away?"

The answer is his accent coupled with the nationality of his favorite "footballer." But I smile rather than say any of that. He's playing defense, making me work for small answers so that our conversation stays on the surface. He knows my most humiliating secret. Is it wrong to want to know something real about him in return?

He nods slowly, acknowledging that I've figured out the game. "Ex-wife. She was a general manager at the Hyatt down there and got offered a dream job to run one of the brand's Manhattan hotels. I came with."

The waitress returns with the bottle. She pours a taste in my glass, which I pass to Tyler. "I don't really know wine."

"Not sure that I do either." He sips anyway and then pauses a second before nodding approval. I'm relieved. Rejecting wine is something only royal pains do to look fancy. I would have thought less of him if he'd done anything other than accept it.

She splits half the bottle between our glasses. The wine sparkles in the flickering light of the flameless candle. I raise my glass, viewing Tyler for a moment through its pale-gold filter. He has such a nice complexion, smooth and dark, like a stained piece of oak.

"To you." Our glasses clink. "Thank you for standing up for me."

The drink tastes light and nearly nonalcoholic, though I know it must be at least 12 percent dangerous to classify as wine. I should be careful with this. "Do you like New York better than Trinidad?"

"It's not exactly home."

"Why stay?" I sip my wine to cover the fact that my back has tensed. This is when he'll tell me that he left his wife for another woman who, conveniently, was also living in New York City.

"My daughter is here. She splits the week between me and her mother." I flash back to the conversation in his office about not needing to stay with a cheating spouse for the kids. The advice may have come from personal experience. "And there's the job. I built a pretty decent practice in the past thirteen years. I wouldn't want to abandon my clients and start over."

My muscles relax. "I imagine that would be difficult."

The wine lubricates conversation. We chat easily about the city, our neighborhood, kids, the news. The latter discussion segues into my job covering crime and the courts. I share the highlight reel of my most interesting cases, happy to show off that I was not always a betrayed housewife on maternity leave. I have value, even if my marriage is falling apart.

As I talk, he seems to look at me differently. A wide smile takes shape on his face. "You have to be pretty confident to be a journalist."

I shrug. "Not really."

"No. I think you do. You put your words out there. Have to stand by them. Don't sell yourself short."

I feel a smile forming. I grab the bottle to cover it and pour another few swallows into my glass. The bottle feels light. An hour and we've nearly finished the whole thing.

"Of course, you have every reason to be confident," he says.

"What do you mean?"

He looks squarely at my face and tilts his head.

My cheeks grow hot. I pick up the wine bottle and pour the last of it into his glass.

"Will you be covering that rock star's wife who hit all those people? The one who has the case coming up next month?"

"No. I'd have to recuse myself." I take a long sip, trying to act casual. "I know the prosecutor."

"Your husband."

Though his tone is matter-of-fact, the statement works like a shrill high note, breaking the glass that had blocked out reality. Again, I'm the depressed patient married to the cheating spouse.

He's the shrink. He drains the last of his drink. The waitress must see the deliberate way he polishes it off because a second later, she slides the check in the center of the table. He reaches for it.

I stand to place my hand on his. "Let me get this." I grab my wallet from my purse and slip a fifty into the leather folder, enough for the wine, tax, and tip. I slide from the interior seat. "You can pick it up the next time I save you from a bar brawl."

He towers over me. My eyes come to the level of his defined chest. I'd like nothing more than to walk home with my head leaning on his pectoral, his arm draped over my shoulder. But that's not going to happen. I'm married. And though that means nothing to my husband, it means something to the man in front of me.

The air outside is blanket heavy. It presses on my shoulders, adding to the weight of my embarrassment. I let myself forget that Tyler was only accompanying me because he felt sorry for me. I allowed myself to hope.

We walk in silence toward our apartment buildings, crossing busy Twelfth Avenue, where the lights are too bright and the noises too loud, heading toward the river. The park is dark save for a few streetlamps along the promenade. Laughter sounds from somewhere on the lawn. Music wafts from the party boats over yonder on the Hudson. A couple pushes a baby carriage. Everywhere, life is being lived. Shared. But I am headed to an empty bedroom. The idea is so disheartening that I suddenly can't stand being out in the open. I want to get home, crawl beneath the covers, hide from Tyler's well-intentioned pity. Sleep for days.

"My building is right up there." I extend my hand. "Thank you."

"It's late. I'm happy to walk you home."

The offer makes me even more pathetic. I'm a suicide risk who may not make it back to her apartment. Frustrated tears well in my eyes. I stare at the sky to keep them from falling. Clouds glow in the dark, reflecting the brightness of the New York skyline. They look lit by lightning.

"That's okay. I'm so close." My attempt at a smile forces a tear from my eye. I recall my outstretched hand to wipe it away. "Thank you again. It was really nice of you to keep me company."

Tyler rubs the back of his neck. "Hey, Beth, Listen. I know there might be a temptation, given what you're going through, to see tonight as a rejection. But please don't. You're a—"

"Postpartum wife whose husband sleeps around while she's at home with an infant." I laugh. "I get it. Don't worry. I'm a real catch."

His hand brushes my exposed arm. "You can't let your husband's actions determine your self-worth. I meant it when I said it's about him. Not you."

"Everyone always says that. If I'm so desirable, then what's stopping you?"

His eyes go wide. He gestures with an open palm, one of those shrink-wrapped nonthreatening motions. "My license, for number one. You're my patient."

"Not anymore." I extend my arm for a handshake. "You didn't have to take the time to build me up tonight, though it was nice of you."

He takes my hand, shaking his head. "I wish you believed me."

His grip is so firm. I want to feel this hand on my body. I want to see those brown eyes look at me with something other than sympathy. I want, more than anything, not to go back to my apartment, alone, feeling sorry for myself. "Make me believe."

He pulls me into him. Full lips land on my own. My mouth invites his tongue inside. He kisses better than Jake. He tastes better than Jake. Right now, I want him more than Jake.

Tyler grabs my hand and takes me into his building. As we pass the doorman and head into the elevator, he explains that he lives eight floors up from his office. "Easy commute."

That's the last thing he says. We make out as the car rises to the ninth floor, entering his apartment as a unit, tangled together, his arms encircling my waist, my hands wrapped around his neck. I catch glimpses of bookcases and a black leather couch. A king-sized bed is visible to the left of the living room.

He peels off my dress and then devours the exposed parts of my body. I can't undo the button on his jeans fast enough. We fall onto the bed. His mouth travels from my clavicle to my chest to my stomach and then to my thighs. Suddenly, he's on top of me and I'm moaning. Screaming. The bed frame is banging against the wall and he's telling me I'm beautiful. God, if I could only see. I'm beautiful.

# LIZA

Writing about sex is tricky. Readers want details to stoke their own erotic fantasies, but they don't want to be in the imagined room listening to each moan, witnessing every awkward position change. Intercourse, even for the most liberated observer, is embarrassing. Porn is rife with examples. People say uncalled-for, dirty things. They obviously fake orgasms. They scream words more suited to the hook in a Daft Punk song. *Harder. Better. Faster. Stronger.*

To pen a love scene without verging into comedy, I have to close my eyes and imagine not what my characters are doing in bed but what they want deep down. Are they using sex to achieve greater emotional intimacy? Is it an opportunity to dominate someone or to be dominated? A chance to procreate? Sex is never about getting off. It's a physical form of communication, stripped of the linguistic armor inside of which people cloak their true feelings. A person cannot have a sarcastic orgasm.

After I finish writing, I feel hot and bothered. Itchy. I fire off an e-mail to myself with the latest version of my story attached and then stare at the photo of David and me on my home screen. I'm looking up at him, adoringly. He's mugging for the cameraman. In my head, Beth says he's handsome, but he's no Tyler.

I can't be in the room alone with her and my thoughts.

\*

The hotel bar is the Moulin Rouge gone modern. Black velvet chairs surround tufted ottoman-style coffee tables topped with mirrored drink trays. A sanguine light shines on the seating areas, emphasizing the bordello decor and the fact that most of the patrons are too buttoned up for this kind of establishment. The space is noisy. Though there's no music, a myriad of half-sober conversations create a sound cloud. Bits of discussion splatter my ears as I head toward the far end of the room where a glowing amber wall illuminates shelves of liquor bottles. The left side of my head still feels held in a vice, but the bar isn't spinning.

I spot my editor. He sits on a barstool, elbows on an onyx counter, underlit to highlight the brown veins in the golden surface. Trevor's face shines in the glow. Pickney flanks him, along with Harrison Mance, whom I've met twice before. Harrison is a decorated detective turned best-selling author who publishes with my house's biggest competitor. He inked a movie deal for his latest book. Trevor is getting his woo on.

Pickney sees me hovering. He waves me over with a broad smile that I, and everyone else pretending not to watch his every move, can't help but notice. I approach, still feeling dazed from my marathon writing session. Imagined details seep into my present. Are the silk threads in Trevor's cobalt suit catching the light or is my subconscious supplying a halo? Is he really that handsome?

I glance at my reflection in an antique wall mirror beside the bar. My eyes are lined in kohl and painted with extra mascara. My lips are scarlet. I look ready for something. Anything.

Trevor stops midsentence to remind his famous friends of my much less well-known byline. "Brad, you remember Liza." He turns to Harrison. "This is one of our authors, Liza Cole."

I half-hug Pickney first. He leans forward to receive my back pat, too cool to rise yet sufficiently generous to allow some familiarity. "Brad, it's been awhile. Congratulations on your latest."

Since I wrote through the awards ceremony, I'm guessing that he won Master of Suspense. It's an educated assumption. He's accepted the award for three straight years. And even if he didn't get it, there's never a dearth of reasons to praise Pickney on his latest novel.

Pickney accepts my compliment with practiced humility. He congratulates me on my newest book without saying anything more about it. I'm sure he hasn't read it. Given the reviews, I'm almost thankful.

Trevor asks if I'd like a drink, saving me from sharing any details about my bland addition to the larger canon. Before I respond, he calls over the bartender and orders a gimlet, my go-to cocktail at every conference. I'm flattered that he remembers.

Harrison is grinning in that awkward way folks have when they don't remember somebody but think they should. I bestow a bro-hug—half embrace, half back pat—and tell him how nice it is to see him again. As I disengage, Trevor's forearm brushes my back. He's reaching for our drinks. Still, the hairs stand up on my neck. I become hyperaware of his presence, of how many inches there are between his body and mine.

"It's good to see you, too," Harrison says, regaining his footing. "These things aren't the same without your face brightening the room."

I thank him for the compliment and make small talk, throwing in ample flattery for both novelists as I carefully sip my drink. Imbibing to excess isn't exactly frowned upon in my profession. My own literary heroes would fill a church basement had they not been such unrepentant boozers in real life. Still, technically, I'm working. Plus, I can't be sure that the stiff drink combined with the hormones won't make me sick. I don't want to leave too soon.

Mutual praise meanders into a discussion of beloved new books and detested television dramas, the stuff of idle conversation that, for writers, amounts to shoptalk. Pickney groans about the latest adaptation of Superman heading to the small screen. Hollywood won't take a significant risk on a new show unless it's adding to a masked-man franchise. Shame, really, since he had high hopes for his current series.

"What are you working on now?" he asks me, possibly because he realizes that there's nothing less sympathy inducing than the complaints of the rich, famous, and ridiculously successful.

"An affair-slash-murder mystery."

Trevor smiles at me as though he knows a secret. His dark eyes threaten to reveal it. "She won't say any more," he says to Pickney. "No outline."

I attempt a hearty laugh. What comes out is an unappetizing low-cal version. "I like to discover my endings along with the reader."

Trevor winks. "She wants to keep me in suspense."

Pickney excuses himself two more drinks in. He's sorry for being an "old man," but he must surrender the all-nighters to us "young 'uns." The apology is nice, albeit unnecessary. We all know that Pickney's popularity, rather than his age, demands the early bedtime. He's been chatting up fans and midlist writers like me all day, each of us courting his friendship. Fame must be exhausting.

Once Pickney departs, Harrison becomes increasingly drunk and incredibly forward. He brags about his latest work during a conversation of far better-known authors and tells me that I'd be the perfect female foil for his oversexed trilogy hero. "You're . . . How do the British say it? A 'fit bird,' eh, Trevor?"

To his credit, Trevor pretends not to hear him and calls over the bartender. I parry the remark with some ridiculous segue about the best books having bird references in the titles: *To Kill a Mockingbird, One Flew Over the Cuckoo's Nest, The Goldfinch,*

*I Know Why the Caged Bird Sings.* Afterward, I feign a yawn and say, speaking of birds, I really need to return to the nest. I'm on an early panel.

Trevor confirms my "packed" schedule, though he must remember that he and Pickney are the only ones with breakfast speeches tomorrow. My sole appearance isn't until ten. Most likely, he is happy to have me gone so that he can resume convincing Harrison to switch houses.

My fellow writer bestows a tight good-bye hug, way too familiar for someone who needed to be reminded of my name ninety minutes before. I pull away, feeling like a field mouse wresting free from a python. As a result, Trevor gets nothing but a halting wave, which I regret while making my way to the elevators. As I wait for the next car to arrive, I think about penning an e-mail apologizing for my rudeness. *Sorry I had to run. Harrison was giving me the heebie-jeebies. Thanks for the drink.* What would he write back to that?

The imaginary exchange so engrosses that I almost miss the presence of the man behind me. Once I sense him, my body goes into a full alert. I can tell he's large, strong, and standing inches closer than he should. There's latent intent in the lack of space between us. For a moment, I wish I had my gun.

When the elevator arrives, I step to the side, allowing the person behind me to enter so that I may check him out. Trevor lords over me. His Adam's apple peeks above the unbuttoned collar of his white shirt. "Realized I should call it a night too." The spark in his eye says he doesn't typically do what he should.

I swallow the urge to flirt. In my head, Beth is comparing his neck to a cannon, his shoulders to kettlebells. She's no Shakespeare. She needs to shut up.

"Something wrong?"

"No. Nothing." Again, I pretend a yawn. "I had a marathon writing session before I came down to socialize. Everything is still hazy."

We file into the elevator along with a couple of badge-carrying conference attendees: a man and a woman, married according to the gold rings on their held hands—though, not necessarily to each other. Business trips are notorious for bad decisions. The couple exits on the fifth floor. I repress the number seven.

"How's the writing? Or are we still not discussing that?"

"I'll talk about it all you want—in a month."

He pouts. I tell myself that the full lips pulled beneath his neat mustache make him look like an unhappy Schnauzer. In no world, however, would such a derogatory description fit. If Trevor were a canine, he'd be something sleek and powerful. A Rottweiler or a Doberman.

The elevator dings. "Saved by the bell. This is my floor."

"Courtney booked us all on seven."

The door opens. We both exit, me first since I'm a lady and Trevor has British manners. "Why seven? Lucky number?" A twinge of horror follows my question. Did I really just ask him that?

"Maybe." He smiles with one side of his mouth and steps forward. The motion opens his jacket. I glimpse the outline of his torso in his thin shirt. Beth's voice continues chattering. His stomach is a mountain range designed by a symmetry-obsessed God. This man is so sexy, he's turning my inner prose purple.

I force myself to look down the hallway, increase the speed of my walk. Heavy footfalls echo behind the click of my stilettos on the worn carpet. I pull my keycard from my purse as I stride to the door.

"This is me." I push the keycard into the slot.

The footsteps stop. "Good night."

He's standing a foot from me, close enough for me to smell his cologne. There's musk and tobacco smoke. Cigarettes and sex. I say good night. Or at least my brain does. But my mouth, outfitted with Beth's sultry voice, says something else.

"It was nice chatting with you earlier on the plane."

"You too."

"I appreciate the time."

Each word brings him closer. Is he moving or am I? My heart is racing.

"We should definitely talk more," he says.

The door beeps. I pull it open and escape into the jamb. Beth is still yammering in my head about Trevor's body. "Let's make a date for early next month, after you've read the book." I allow myself one last glance over my shoulder. "Good night, Trevor."

He gives me a smile and sign-off wave. I shut the door and then flop onto the bed. Beth is screaming. I bury my head in the pillow. "My husband didn't cheat on me," I whisper. "I have no excuse."

# Part II

Everybody lies about sex.

—Robert Anson Heinlein, *Time Enough for Love*

# Chapter 9

AFTER SEX, I DON'T SLEEP. Instead, I lie on my back and stare at the smooth ceiling pockmarked by pot lights, daydreaming about revealing my revenge to Jake. I imagine returning home at 6:00 AM, just as he is showering for work. I picture him peering through the steam-clouded glass door, his puzzled expression when he realizes Vicky is not in my arms. "Is she asleep?" he'll ask.

"Oh, I don't know, I haven't picked her up yet." I'll smile. "I'm only now getting in."

He'll ask me whom I saw, cocky as ever, assuming I spent the night crying over a bottle of Cabernet with one of my girlfriends. Again, I'll don a Cheshire cat grin. "Since you went out with your lover, I decided to find one of my own." He'll step from the stream, uncertain whether he actually heard me above the waterfall. "Well, I mean, since you unilaterally decided that we should have an open marriage, I figured I better get with the program. And you know what? Best orgasm of my life last night! I didn't know sex could be that good."

My fantasy fails me after that. In an ideal world, Jake would shut off the faucet and stumble from the shower, soaking wet, blinking in shock. I'd repeat my words for him for maximum absorption and then watch him shrivel from arrogant jerk to penitent spouse. He'd beg my forgiveness, tell me how sorry he is for making me feel this wrenching pain that he suddenly understands so well. He'd call up Colleen and end things over the phone while professing his love for me and our family over and over.

But my husband is not so easily broken. More than likely, Jake would argue that his affair is somehow more virtuous than my actions. I can imagine his case: what he did was selfish and cruel, but he never meant for me to find out and get hurt. I, on the other hand, slept with someone deliberately to skewer him. Intent is nine-tenths of the law.

Tyler murmurs something. Here, with my head against his chest, listening to the familiar whoosh of the sprinklers beyond the window, I can almost convince myself that Jake's reaction won't matter. I loved my husband. Probably I still love him. But much of my adoration isn't unique to Jake. I thought I loved Jake's arms around me at night. What I love, in fact, is the presence of a strong man in my bed. I thought I loved dressing up for Jake and seeing that impressed spark in his eye. But Tyler had that look tonight, and I loved it then too. I thought I loved talking to my spouse. But when was the last time Jake and I really had a good conversation?

Tyler murmurs again, more distinctly this time. He's saying something. His eyes are half open, lit by the moon slipping through the cracked window.

"Hey, you." I prop myself on my elbow and slide my naked torso up his side a couple inches.

"The sprinklers," he moans.

I lift my head to peck his lips. My kiss lands on his neck.

"It must be midnight." He scoots back toward the fabric head-board. "What time do you need to get back?"

My lips travel down his neck to his shoulder, licking the salt from his collarbone. I don't want to go back. This room, this man—they exist outside of time and space. As long as I am within these walls, I am not a shamed wife with a waiting infant but a valued, vibrant, sexy woman. "Vicky is at my mom's all night."

"What about your husband?" He sits up straighter. My lips head for the triangle of his hip bones. "You're not going to tell him?"

I sit on my haunches and lean back, flaunting my nakedness. My breasts are engorged to a cartoonish size on my lanky frame. This is the closest I will ever come to resembling a lingerie model without plastic surgery. I grab his hand and place it on my full chest. "I don't want to talk about Jake."

"But won't he ask where you were if you don't get home before him?"

I lean forward for a real kiss. He rolls to the side. His legs swing onto the floor. "This is serious." He grabs his boxers off the hardwood and shoves a leg inside. "We have to talk about what you'll tell him."

I scoot back against the headboard and fold the sheet over my body. "I don't know."

"Are you thinking of confessing that you also cheated?"

I grimace. "If your marriage is over, is it cheating?"

"You're still married."

He pulls the boxers to his waist. The moon and the ambient light from the buildings outside highlight his muscular back as he bends down, searching for something. His clothes are in the closet. Is he looking for mine?

I rise from the mattress and stand in front of him, spotlighted by the window. "I'll tell him the truth. I know he's been cheating on me and I don't know if I can forgive him. And . . ."

I reach for Tyler. He grasps my hand before it can land on his bare side. "And?"

I take a brave breath. "I've met someone."

My hand falls as Tyler retreats from me, backtracking beyond the window's direct light. "He'll ask you who. He booked the appointment." A charcoal filter obscures everything. I see the outline of Tyler's body crouch to the ground and then rise as though he's said a quick prayer. "He knows I was treating you. If you say my name, he'll put two and two together. I could lose my license."

The darkness prevents me from reading Tyler's expression. Still, I can feel the intimacy in the room dissipate. On the bed, I was warm. Now I'm freezing in the air conditioning. Instinctually, my arms fold atop my chest. "I won't say you. I'll tell him it's none of his business."

"He won't let you get away with that."

"He'll have to."

"Beth. He's a prosecutor. He'll keep badgering you until you give him a name. He'll be jealous. Angry. It won't matter that he's done the same thing or that he pushed you to this. He'll make you the villain. He'll come after me and my practice."

In my mind's eye, I can see Jake do all these things. He won't take my revenge lying down, even if he wants me back. Tyler would be the perfect target for his anger. "What do you want me to do?"

He steps back into the light. A hand lands on my forearm, urging me to abandon my defensive stance. As my arms fall, Tyler pulls me into him and hugs me, rewarding me for my deference with the return of his physical affection. "You should go home, wait for him. Confront him about the affair. Don't tell him about tonight." He brushes my hair away from my face with his fingertips and tilts up my chin so that I can look into his eyes. "You have nothing to gain by telling him. He'll say you're as bad as him."

"I want to be as bad as him."

His look chides me. "No, you don't."

"But I want to see you again."

He releases me from his embrace. "Beth, I think you're great. You're beautiful. Smart."

"But?"

"I have my daughter to think about. If I lose my license, how will I support her?" He shakes his head. "I am so sorry. I saw you and . . ." A loud exhale fills the room. "I let other things get the best of me. I didn't act professionally. There are rules against—"

"I'm not your patient."

"Even former patients."

"I'm not pressing charges."

"Your husband could. He could argue that I influenced you to end your marriage for my personal gain, abusing my position as your psychiatrist."

His reaches out toward me. The light hits the shiny spandex blend fabric in his palm. It's my dress, balled up like used tissue. My underwear is hidden inside, no doubt. "I can't see you again." His voice is gentle yet firm. It's a shrink's tone, borrowed from years of books on positive discipline. "You should go home to your husband."

I accept my clothing and excuse myself to the bathroom. He calls through the door that I am welcome to shower. Of course I am. Better for him if all DNA evidence of our act is scrubbed from my body. Should I reveal his name and my lawyer husband decide to go after him, it will be my word against his. He can argue that I made the whole thing up. Delusions as an outgrowth of postpartum depression.

The bathroom light stays off as I dress. The sight of my ruffled hair and rumpled clothing against the backdrop of the unfamiliar wall tile will humiliate me more than any mug shot. It's bad enough that I'll have to pass the park on the way to my building, dodging the rotating sprinklers spraying the walkway in my party dress, looking like yesterday's newspaper. I rub my eyes hard, forestalling the frustrated tears building beneath my lower lids. Crying will only make me hate myself more. And I do hate myself. I was half of a power couple with a healthy baby girl. I'll never be that again, no matter what I do. If I stay with Jake, I will be the laughingstock wife of a philandering husband. If I leave him, I will be the poor single mother with the waiting newborn at home.

I cannot abide either role. The only option is to make Colleen go away.

# LIZA

A golden glow rouses me from sleep. The sun peeks above the horizon, long arms stretching across the landscape and reaching through my uncovered bedroom window. I think about showering and food but can't motivate myself to leave the body heat cocoon beneath the covers. Instead, I slide my laptop off of the bedside table and reread the scene penned the prior evening.

I edit for an hour. Around nine, I become offended by the human smell of the room and take a scalding, soapy shower. The hot water reddens my skin and purges my pores. I pack my bag and check out, thinking about David and his weekend of work (with Cameron), trying not to think about Trevor. I grab Starbucks across the street from the hotel. Given the free morning brew offered in all the breakfast panels, spending five dollars on a latte feels wasteful, but I don't want to run into my editor right now. It was hard enough saying good night. I'm not ready for good morning.

I can't concentrate during my panel, though no one appears to notice. My fellow authors are too busy squeezing mentions of their current books into responses to questions about their first novels. The moderator is a timid woman, ill-suited to the job of dividing speaking time between the five egos on this dais. She's being talked over by an author who has seized every opportunity to rebut critics of her panned second book. If I were in charge, I'd make sure to call on individual authors in order to keep the panel from becoming an infomercial for the loudmouth's latest. But I'm not, and to be honest, I'm too distracted to care. At the end of the day, maybe one person out of the few dozen gathered will buy a book. If that sale doesn't go to me, so be it. I didn't come here to fight with my compatriots.

I didn't come here to indulge in sexual fantasies, either. Yet it's difficult not to hear Beth's running description of Trevor's body, forged, she says, like Spartan armor.

"Liza?"

The moderator's smile is strained. I'm that kid caught daydreaming in math class. She's the teacher who has called me out. "I'm sorry. Got a little lost there thinking about the relation of my first book to my most recent, *Accused Woman*." When in doubt, sell.

"The question concerned how authors identify with dark subject matter. You had to not only imagine a victim of child abuse in *Drowned Secrets* but also believably write about the response to that abuse from the perspective of a twelve-year-old girl . . ."

She trails off, hoping I'll fill in the blanks. The crowd stares as though I'm the driver in a slow-motion accident. Pressure builds deep in my hippocampus. "Well, I don't exactly know."

The moderator blinks, waiting for me to continue.

My palms open in a guilty appeal to the crowd. "I think when the writing is going well, you are so immersed in the character that everything's automatic. It's a bit like having an Ouija board instead of a keyboard."

The audience is silent. A person in the front of the crowd flashes a nervous smile as though I've just confessed to actually communing with spirits or something similarly insane. It's an analogy, people. Get with it.

"Well, how did you come up with the idea?"

"Um . . ." The audience's eyes speckle my body with dozens of laser sights. Sweat buds on my hairline. "I think I had this character in my head, and I really wanted to tell her story."

An audience member raises her hand. She is a younger woman with a notebook in her lap—an MFA student, if I had to guess. The moderator acknowledges her with the enthusiasm of a teacher calling on a class pet. "But how do you get characters in your head in the first place?" she asks.

She might as well demand to know how images show up on a television screen. Clearly, there's rhyme and reason behind it. But damned if I understand. "They're just there."

The student gears up for a follow-up. Thankfully, loudmouth starts before she can get it out. "What Liza says about this automatic writing, if you will, really resonated with me. When you've been immersed in the character for so long, you really do feel what they feel and write what they are thinking. You don't have to imagine it anymore. It's a bit like acting in that way. In my latest book, the main character, Jolene, is, of course, in a situation I would never find myself in, God willing. She's living in a dystopia where the government can hear your thoughts. Yet I can imagine her pain of not having privacy. I don't need to be nineteen, either. You know, as a person, you can identify. You can picture yourself, and it really is . . ."

I nod as though I agree with everything my fellow author is saying. In my head, I only hear Beth.

# Chapter 10

I CAN'T GO HOME. NOTHING is there except an empty bed with cold sheets. A dark room. That's too much for my ruthless imagination. Instead of the back of my eyelids, I'll see Colleen with my husband, flaunting her prechild body. Laughing at me.

The sprinklers tick their countdown to daylight. I flee the spray as fast as I can in my heels. Though the moon is only a quarter full, the city is as bright and beckoning as ever. I walk toward the center of it, a bug to a black light, following the traffic signals and restaurant signs until I find myself at the Chambers Street subway entrance.

The underground is lit up like the inside of a refrigerator. I slide my metro card through the turnstile and follow signs to the J train, letting my subconscious lead the way. My waking mind doesn't know why I want to head east toward the outer boroughs. All I'm aware of is a need to get away—far, far away. Away from my lonely apartment. Away from Tyler. Away from myself.

I pass through the sliding door into an empty car. Midnight is an in-between hour in Manhattan. People are where they planned to be. Few are ready to go elsewhere, yet. The train screeches down the track, rumbling beneath me, lulling me into a half-conscious state. I am here, sitting on this hard plastic seat, listening to the doors rattle as they open and the PA system tell me to be wary of them as they close. I am also not here. My mind has escaped to a not-so-distant past.

Jake and I are at dinner, a restaurant near Gramercy Park that looks like a cross between a posh townhouse and a train station. The tables are intimate affairs beneath oversized crystal chandeliers. Our table is beside a demilune window. It's the best seat in the house, and Jake has requested it special. He wants to discuss something important.

I sit across from him, dressed in something yacht-worthy. Tight and white. The kind of unforgiving ensemble I wore before Vicky kicked out my lower abdomen and stretched apart my hips. I'm nervous beneath my meticulously applied makeup. My husband seems more serious than usual.

He places his hand on mine. The ball of his palm is calloused from hours lifting weights at the gym, another consequence of the hair loss. If he can't have a mane like a twentysomething, he's damn sure going to have a body like one. He strokes the diamond on my left hand.

"I'm ready."

I stare at him, waiting for elaboration. He smiles at me as though I'm dense or defective.

"A baby." Again, he grins. "I know you've wanted to try for a while and I've been back and forth. But I realize that it's not fair to make you wait any longer. You will be a great mom, and you deserve a child. And I really want to be a father. So what the hell? Let's make a baby."

In retrospect, the memory isn't as sweet as I'd once thought. At the time, I'd leapt from my chair and landed in his lap, covering his squinched face with kisses. His admission had seemed to validate our whole relationship. I'd told him to forget a full meal. We should eat oysters and get to the fun part. I didn't think, until now, about the notes of surrender in his speech. It was almost like Jake had felt I'd earned the right to a baby, whether or not he was prepared to have one.

The train slows to a stop. A mechanical voice informs me that I'm on Marcy Avenue and Broadway, which is disorienting since

Manhattan's Broadway lies three blocks east of my apartment, and I've traveled in that direction for the past twenty-five minutes. Brooklyn, then.

I exit the car and ascend the steps. There's a park to my right. Dark with plenty of trees to hide behind. I hurry past it, more jogging than walking. Ready to run. Tyler's not popping out from a bar to save me this time.

I hear the highway on my left. I cut right, traveling down Division Avenue into the Jewish section of Williamsburg. A kosher grocery and liquor store dominates the corner. The Star of David marks a synagogue up ahead. Half the signs are in Hebrew. Car horns cut through the quiet like a machete. I veer right, instinctively heading toward the noisier, non-family-friendly side of area. That's where she lives.

Eventually, I hit Ninth Street. I'm drawn toward the East River and the apartment that she told Jake in an e-mail "overlooks the water, for now." Instead of a park lining the river, a massive construction zone flanks the bank, cordoned off by a chain link fence and makeshift cardboard wall. Through the mesh wire I see flattened dirt and the line of excavators that will dig down to the bedrock beneath the river, ensuring that the skyscraper-to-be is bolted to a foundation stronger than sand. Man-made dirt hills, as tall as a person, are located at the edge of the property. They've already started digging.

I cross to the sidewalk beside the future luxury apartment complex and turn to face the building across the street. It's a squat warehouse, illegally converted, no doubt, into loft apartments and artist spaces. Multipane factory windows overlook midtown. Some are lit, revealing their open floor plans and brick interior walls, betraying that their owners are inside watching television or entertaining, not making matzo or chocolate or whatever the factory was originally slated to produce.

I count floors, trying to remember Officer Colleen's apartment number. It was one something. Usually, that would denote the first floor, but things are wonky in Brooklyn. Maybe the basement counts.

One of the dark apartments blooms to life. The light reveals a white L-shaped couch with a kitchenette steps behind it. A naked woman walks to the eating area and straddles a stool at the breakfast bar. She must know people from the street can see her. Perhaps she's gotten used to the construction site being vacant at this hour. More likely she enjoys voyeurs.

Her hair is piled atop her head in a messy bun. She looks like Officer Colleen, but every dark-haired petite woman would look like her at this distance. A man saunters from a back room. He buttons a shirt over his boxers. The way he does it, elbows high, hands down, screams my husband. I've seen him do this same act thousands of times. Shirt secure, he strides into the living room and grabs what must be his suit pants off the back of the couch. He jostles his legs inside, hopping to pull the tailored trousers over his firm backside. She turns in the chair to face him and the window. Her legs are spread like how a man would sit on a horse. She's trying to get him to stay. Sharon Stone style.

I watch him as though he's an actor in a movie and not my husband and the father of my child. The window is a television set. What I am seeing isn't real.

He walks back toward the breakfast bar and reaches past her naked torso to a neighboring stool. A jacket waves in the air. He flings it over his shoulder, as though posing for a magazine. She stands, hands on her hips. He kisses her on the forehead and heads to the door. She follows him, brushing his side. Her walk is half sexy, half angry. I'm reminded of a cat scratching against a leg. They disappear. A moment later, she returns to the kitchen. Alone.

He must be coming down the stairs. I walk away from the streetlight and the chain link fence, pressing my back against the temporary wall around the left side of the construction site. The ambient light from the building in front of me is still too bright. He'll see me. I hurry along the temporary wall, papered with fliers for street fairs and unknown bands, until I see a door. The wood has been kicked in near the knob.

I open it and slip inside. Immediately, I stumble on something. My knee lands in the dirt, saving my face. Beneath my foot lies a broken combination lock, pried loose, apparently, from the smashed door.

I pick myself up and walk, more carefully, back toward the chain link fence, pitching my weight forward to keep the heels from pinning me to the dirt in the construction site. As soon as I get there, the door opens across the street. Jake exits. He looks over his shoulder, as though he senses me watching, before jogging down the avenue. I can imagine the need for his hurry. He hopes to find me asleep so that he can claim to have come in around midnight. Working until 12:00 AM or even one can go unquestioned. Two AM demands an explanation. What excuse has he prepared if I'm awake? Will he claim to have nodded off on his office couch?

I watch him through the fine metal mesh, crouching, waiting until he rounds the corner before standing back up. Beating him home isn't possible. Moreover, I don't want to. Let him wait for me for once.

A shuffling noise sounds behind me. Too soft to be human. Maybe a rat. Maybe a robber trying to sound like a rat. Whoever broke the lock might be living here. Hiding here. Homelessness swells in the city during the summer. People leave wherever they managed to find shelter during the winter months and return to NYC, where the constant flow of tourists provides plenty of marks for beggars. There's probably a group of men here, all of questionable mental health, getting high. They won't appreciate my infringement on their party.

I scan the ground for something with which to defend myself should anyone come near. A board. A hammer. Metal catches the moonlight a few dozen feet to my right. I hurry toward it, hoping for something pointy. It's a beam of sorts, far too heavy to lift. Behind it, covered in what appears to be pulverized ceramic, is something skinnier. I wrap my hands around its gritty exterior and yank it from the construction debris. It's a pipe, curved like a scythe, the kind that might have once joined a sink drain to the indoor plumbing. Armed now, I retreat to the broken door, prepared to take a swing at whomever might come near.

No one does. I step back out onto the sidewalk and cross the street to Officer Colleen's building. A multitenant intercom is bolted to the brick beside the entrance. Only half of the ten slots have names on them. *C.L.* is scrawled across a label in what appears to be a sharpie next to a number sign, a *1*, a letter *D*, and a fat gray button. I assume the letters are her initials. None of the other names start with *C.*

My finger hovers over the buzzer. I want to talk to her, reason with her, appeal to her sense of justice. Surely she can understand how awful it is to be a new mom, home with an infant, while your husband spends half the night with his girlfriend. She can't really justify her actions. She'll have to admit that whatever feelings she has developed for my husband don't trump my claim to him as his wife and the mother of his child. She'll let him go.

What if she won't let me up?

Music penetrates the door. Someone is having a party inside. The music is live. Lots of drums. A garage band jamming in one of the semiconverted loft spaces, most likely. Brooklyn's underground music scene is literally underground. Again, I stare at the buzzer menu. "Flying Free" appears to own the entire basement level. Either someone had hippie celebrity parents or it's a private venue.

I hit Flying's buzzer, and the door unlocks. No one asks for a name, despite the fact that there aren't any visible cameras to check whether I'm an armed gunman. The fact that I know the location of the party is, apparently, good enough. I pull back half of the double steel door and walk up a narrow staircase.

Each landing opens to hallways with heavy, factory doors on one side. Tribal drums pound from the basement, louder than the house music at any club. Guitars screech. I ascend the first flight, my speed fueled by the rhythm reverberating up the stairwell. Normally, my thighs would burn from the effort of running up stairs. Yet I feel nothing except my determination to make my husband's lover see reason.

A door opens several yards ahead. Quickly, I pivot to face the wall, holding the pipe and my purse close to my chest so it appears that I am searching for my keys. Scaring some poor tenant is the last thing I want.

Officer Colleen fills my peripheral vision. She's dressed now, skinny jeans and a tight black tank with a looser button-down open on top of it. It's one of those outfits that flatters both genders as long as the wearer is on the skinny side. A black bag hangs from her shoulder. Her mouth is painted a deep red. I realize with horror that she is heading out after my husband. She intends to show up at our apartment and spill the truth. She thinks he'll leave me and our daughter for her.

What if she's right?

I whirl around as she passes. The pipe is in my hand. It connects with the back of her head with a sickening crack, the sound of a home run at a baseball game. I see my hands trembling on the metal cylinder. Red is splattered on the wall. Something sticky spills from her scalp, gluing her hair into a clump.

What have I done?

I reach for her as she drops to her knees, ready to apologize and promise to call an ambulance. Though my cell is back at my apartment, her purse lies half open beside her body. There must be a phone in there. It's three easy numbers—9-1-1. I couldn't have hit her that hard. EMTs will be able to fix this. She'll have a concussion. Stitches.

Her hand claws for the bag. I see a flash of something black and silver inside it.

Before she can grab her gun, I swing the pipe again. It strikes the curve of her shoulder, and she screams as bone snaps beneath the metal. Her voice doesn't sound human to me. The figure beneath me isn't a person. All I see is a hand, long fingers like strange arachnid legs, crawling toward a weapon.

If I want to live, I must stop the spider from reaching the gun.

The pipe comes down on her back. She's pressed flat against the floor now, still struggling to raise her broken shoulder, to bend her elbow so that her arm can snag her purse's shoulder strap. I drop the pipe, grab the gun. I turn it over in my hands; the metal is cool and smooth. It's so much lighter than the pipe. Like it's barely even real.

An animalistic, gurgling sound comes from beneath me. Her face is pressed to the concrete floor. There's blood on my dress. Blood on the pipe. Bits of skull in her hair. Jake will never stay with me now. I'll go to jail. She'll go to the hospital. She'll raise my Victoria.

I fall back from her. Suddenly, there's a bang, louder than any drum.

I see myself standing over a lifeless body. Both of my hands are wrapped around the gun's grip. My right index finger is on the trigger. A thin line of smoke curls from the barrel into the hallway. I must be imagining this. Maybe I am asleep in my apartment. Maybe I took Tyler's advice. Went home.

Blood pools onto the concrete. This is real. Oh, my God. I fall to the ground, head bowed, ready for the army of neighbors that will pour from the apartments and overwhelm me, pin me to the wall as they call the police. An agonizing minute passes. Nothing happens. I think of my little Victoria and look back up at the body. Maybe, just maybe, fate has other plans. Perhaps I can return home to my baby.

I kneel and wipe the weapon on the dead woman's shirt, trying to erase my unseen prints. All it does is smear blood across the gun. I slip the weapon back into the officer's bag. There's no leaving all this here. My prints are on the pipe beside the body and on the gun. My DNA must have shed all over her during the attack. I pick up the pipe and shove it into my handbag. Then I slip my purse over my shoulder and put her handbag on the other one. Balanced with a purse on each side, I grab her feet and drag her to the stairs.

A high heel breaks as I heave the dead weight toward me. I pull off my shoes and squeeze them into my handbag. Barefoot, I yank her the rest of the way to the landing. I sit for a moment and catch my breath. My limbs vibrate from exertion. I shake out my arms and then pull the body until the torso is draped over my own and the head rests on my chest. Another moment to prepare myself, and then I scoot my butt down each step, hoisting her along with me while unknown body fluids leak onto my chest and bare legs. I move quickly, back banging against the edges in the process, trying to reach the landing before anyone comes through the door. Somehow, no one enters. Everyone must be at the party or staying elsewhere to avoid the noise. Or maybe the industrial factory doors have made the apartments sound proof and no one realizes that a fatal shooting has taken place.

I prop the body against the wall while I open the front door, praying the whole time that the basement party continues blaring downstairs. God or the devil answers me. I press my back against the door, holding it open while I fit my arms beneath the dead woman's pits and drag her from the building.

Once outside, I head straight for the broken door and into the fenced-in construction zone. I drop the body beside a man-sized mountain of dirt. My idea is to shovel the earth on top of it, hopefully hiding her long enough that whatever physical evidence I've left becomes sufficiently contaminated to be unusable. But the bloody trail I've carved into the soil makes me realize that she'd be discovered by morning. Besides, I can't move enough dirt without a backhoe.

On the far side of the construction site is the East River. My arms ache from supporting the dead weight. I grab the hands and drag it across the dirt. At the riverbank, the ground gives way to an old concrete pier. Near the end is a pipe railing, erected, undoubtedly, for the safety of the construction vehicles rather than the workers. The railing is too high to hoist the form in my arms above it. Easier to push it beneath.

I lay what was Officer Colleen down at the edge, ready to roll her off the pier. As I do, her bag slides from my shoulder to the ground. I see the gun inside. If the police find this, they'll realize that her gun was fired. Would it be better to dump them separately and hope the current carries them miles apart? Should I take her purse with the gun so that, if she is found, police assume that someone intended to rob her and committed murder in the process?

I move Colleen's bag to the side and then sit next to her body. Both of my bare feet press into her sides. I bring my legs back toward my chest and then kick out with all my energy.

The body barely makes a splash before vanishing beneath the dark water. With luck, it will be gone for good. The East River was named "Hell Gate" by early Dutch explorers because the current is stirred to rapids by the different tidal flows converging in it. It's why so few bodies dumped here ever surface. Jake told me that after a gang case once.

I remove Colleen's phone from her purse and pitch it as hard as I can into the water. The splash is audible, though I can't verify that the device has sunk in the darkness. Either way, I'm sure the salt water will destroy it soon enough. I wonder whether or not the police will be able to tell that her cell was at the construction site when they begin investigating her disappearance and track the last known signal. Maybe the phone will register as outside her apartment.

My purse still hangs from my shoulder. I jostle the pipe from inside. Dark spots splatter the metal. In the moonlight, I can almost convince myself that the marks are rust. I hold it like a boomerang behind my head before hurling it over the railing. It makes a big splash, the kind that would be noticed by someone, if anyone was around. Watching me.

An icy fear possesses my body at the thought. The gun is still in Colleen's bag. I slip the shoulder strap over my left arm, feeling the weight of the weapon at my side. The loaded pistol makes me feel simultaneously more secure and panicky. I used it before to protect myself. I could do it again. But it connects me to this murder. Even if the cops never find Colleen's body, my hands on her gun would reveal my crime. I have to get rid of it.

Throwing it in after Colleen doesn't feel right. I am relying on the East River to destroy too much evidence. One more item will somehow clog the drain, sending all the sewage bubbling back to the surface.

Over my shoulder, I see the mountains of earth that had called to me before. I choose the mound farthest from the construction hole. Using my hands and the weapon itself, I tunnel into the side of the dirt hill. It has rained recently and the earth is moist. To keep the soil from spilling into my hiding place, I must keep patting the sides, like sculpting a sandcastle. When I have a space deep enough to fit my arm up to the joint, I shove the gun inside. Finally, I smash my fists into the pile until the mound crumbles in on itself, filling the cavity.

With luck, this dirt is destined for landfill somewhere else. It will be loaded on the back of a truck and dumped at a new construction site. Everyone wants a flat piece of property, particularly by the water. The gun could end up buried beneath the new backyard of a seaside home, topped by grass and flowering weigela bushes, an iron rock beneath manicured landscaping. Every year, the soil will settle, and the gun will sink deeper into the earth.

The idea comforts me as I head out to the street.

# LIZA

The flight attendant tells me to shut my laptop. I plead for another moment with a raised finger and a sheepish glance as she scowls at me from the aisle. Something is wrong in the scene I finished moments ago. The gun, I think. How Beth gets rid of it is too complicated. She's thrown everything else into the water, why not the weapon?

*Because, I need to bury it.*

I hear Beth's voice in my head, comingled with my own writerly justifications. A death cries out for a burial. Instinctually, people will want the images of digging and soil. Hiding the gun in a mound of construction dirt will resonate more with readers than having Beth throw yet another item into the East River.

But I can't force Beth to do something stupid because it fits with a death aesthetic. Discarding the murder weapon in a different location from the body only makes sense if the gun itself ties the perpetrator to the crime. In this case, it doesn't. The Glock wasn't Beth's; it belonged to Colleen. Even if Beth is concerned about her prints on it, submersion is far more likely to destroy them than dirt. I gave Beth a crime reporter background. She would know this.

*I murdered someone*, Beth protests. *I'm not thinking straight. I want to bury it.*

"Ma'am, we're landing." The stewardess looks as though she wants to slap the screen down on my device. "Your laptop could fly from your tray table when the wheels touch down. If you don't store it now, I'll have to confiscate it."

I have not e-mailed myself my last chapter. Apologizing, I hit the save button, close the computer, and then slide it into the purse that barely fits beneath the seat in front of me. The flight attendant watches me do all this, a mother checking up on a child's chores after she failed to do them the first time.

We touch down with barely a bump, which I mentally argue means I could have kept my computer out longer. I know I'm wrong, of course. Rules have reasons. A laptop probably went airborne during a particularly rough landing once and injured a litigious passenger. I don't care, though. All I want is to get back to my story and figure out how to fix the murder scene.

Images of earth and metal continue to plague me as I roll my suitcase across the airport to the short-term parking lot and retrieve my car. Burying the gun is too similar to how the mother hides the murder weapon in my bestseller. *Well, it worked then,* Beth quips. Throwing the weapon in the river makes the most sense, I argue.

*BUT I BURIED IT!*

*BUT YOU SHOULDN'T HAVE!*

I get onto the highway, still thinking about the gun. That gun! I can't leave it there, waiting in a mound of dirt like a body in a wall or a telltale heart beneath the floorboards. It will make me crazy. It is already driving me nuts. Rather than concentrating on the road, I am inventing excuses for Beth to bury the weapon. I've outsourced the car's operation to an automatic part of my brain, the section that controls breathing and bathroom urges.

There's little traffic heading back from Queens on a Monday evening. I pull into the garage in under an hour and run to the elevator, eager to get back to my manuscript. A woman rushes in before the door closes. I know her vaguely. She has two boys, middle school age, and lives in one of the penthouses above me.

She wears her power suit from work. In my peripheral vision, I see her smile at me as though we've spoken and not simply acknowledged one another's existence with the occasional nod. Fortunately, she must sense that I'm preoccupied and doesn't attempt small talk.

As soon as the elevator doors shut behind me, I hurry to my apartment and twist the key in the lock. "Hi, honey," I shout as I enter, letting David know an intruder hasn't broken in.

Silence responds. I don't sense my husband's presence. Instead, there's a strange energy. An odd smell. Stagnant odors have been released from hidden places, as though a bin of decaying paper was uncovered and left in the center of the room. The shelving unit in the foyer has been rearranged. A glass vase with crystal roses—a wedding present from one of David's tchotchke-loving aunts—has been put on the same shelf as a wood-framed picture of my mom. The two items do not belong together. The books, too, have been moved. My fiction stack is now squashed by one of David's law textbooks.

I drop my suitcase in the foyer and walk through to the living/dining area. Legal documents are scattered on the glass table. David's briefcase is on the floor. It's the first sign that he might be in the house, though I doubt it. If he were in the bedroom, he'd yell, "Welcome home," or, at least, "Hello." Our home is not big enough to hide in.

"David?" I yell. "Babe?"

I pile the papers up and place his briefcase on top of them. Loose leafs secured, I open the French doors out to the balcony to drive the stale scent from the house. Street noise rushes in: honking on the FDR drive, the din of voices below. I look out at the building across the street. If I dared to lean out over the railing, I'd see the East River.

I call for my husband again as I walk to our bedroom. The sheets are in a tangle. David is the type to make the bed. Did he have to rush out? He knew I was coming home this evening. I tell myself that an unmade bed is not cause for panic. He'll be home shortly. He probably headed out for food.

I return to my purse atop my suitcase and retrieve the laptop. My anxiety inexplicably builds as I carry the computer back into my bedroom and place it on my desk. Beth must toss the gun into the river. Why didn't I write it that way?

Repetitiveness, I decide. My reluctance to have her act rationally must be because I don't want a series of paragraphs ending with a splash. Details can fix this, though. Beth can contemplate her act while staring at the gun, tying her observations about its small size to the weight of her guilt. She will be so preoccupied with the image of the weapon that she won't even notice it sink into the water.

I open the laptop and call up the manuscript. The cursor blinks at the end of my last sentence. I see only it. Not the gun.

I need my Ruger.

I slide back my closet door and stand on my tiptoes to look at the shelf above. The black lockbox lies in its usual spot. As I reach for it, my brain starts throbbing. I rub my temple with one hand as I swat at the box with the other. When I push the case far enough to the lip of the shelf, I take it down with both hands and place it on the bed. There's a combination lock on the front, three wheels that must be turned to the right numbers. One thousand combinations for a thief to try. One right answer: my wedding anniversary, June 28. 628.

The numbers are already in the right place. The lid pops open with a simple press of a button revealing an empty, gun-shaped space surrounded by black padding.

The throbbing becomes a pounding. It doesn't make sense that my weapon wouldn't be here. I haven't used it since the writers' police academy workshop. Did David take it? Why would he need a gun?

I grab my cell from my shoulder bag. The glare from the windows intensifies the pulsing between my ears. I close my eyes and let my fingers navigate to the speed dial from memory.

David answers on the second ring. "Liza. Are you home?"

"Hey, yeah. Where are you?"

"Liza?" Static clouds the connection.

"I'm home. Question for you—did you take my gun?"

"Liza. Are you home?" The white noise increases. He hasn't heard me.

"Yes. Where are you? I need to talk to you. Did you take—"

"Wait. Wait. Listen." David is nearly shouting. He never yells. "I'm at the police station. You need to come here. They have questions. They—"

A sucking sound chokes his words, air slurping through a straw. "I need you to come." His voice breaks. "They found Nick's body."

# Chapter 11

I CAN'T GO HOME LIKE this. Gravediggers are cleaner. Blood and dirt cover my dress, my arms. Soil and sharp bits of construction debris are embedded in my heels. I can only imagine what my face looks like.

Colleen's keys are inside her bag. The grit on my feet makes putting my heels back on impossible. I hobble out of the construction site, still barefoot, and cross the street. There are two keys on Colleen's ring: one is bronze and one is silver. The lock on the outside door is bronze. I open it with the corresponding key, keeping my head down so passersby on the street can't get a good look at me. I'm sure my cheeks are freckled with blood. There was so much of it.

I hurry up the stairs to the first floor and exit onto the landing. A dark reddish-brown splotch stains the concrete floor near Colleen's neighbor's door, which, given the keypad lock on the outside, is likely a shared artist space, only at use during the day. For a moment, I consider cleaning up the blood but then decide that it'll only delay the inevitable. Someone will figure out she's missing soon enough. Maybe even my husband.

I enter her apartment with the key and shut the door behind me. Her lights are off. I don't dare turn them on. From her narrow foyer I can see straight to the window through which I had watched her so easily. She could have neighborhood friends who will realize that someone strange is in her apartment.

I open one of the doors to my right and am greeted with empty hangers and an NYPD windbreaker. Hanging beside it is a man's suit jacket and pants in dry cleaner plastic. Jake has left a change of clothes in her apartment. The sight saps the last of my adrenaline. I fall to my knees, feeling fully connected to my feelings for the first time since I swung that lead pipe. Tears stream down my face. How could he do this to me? To Vicky? To this woman, even?

I imagine how it must have gone down. Like most things, it probably started innocently enough. She was working with him, found him attractive. Smart. Funny, maybe. He would have figured out that she was a bit enamored and turned on his charm, enjoying the ego boost, not thinking that it would go much beyond some flirty conversations and friendly e-mails. Then one night, their chatter became more than that. Maybe she confessed her feelings and he was curious. More likely, she said something sexual and he pounced on it. I won't only blame her. Yes, she shouldn't have fallen for a married man. But he was worse for taking her up on whatever offer she put out there. He made promises to me. She didn't owe me anything.

Yet she paid the price.

I struggle to catch my breath. It's too late to feel sorry.

I walk through the second door. Her queen bed is an unmade mess. Silvery sheets hang off the mattress. A blue coverlet is balled on the floor. Feathers from a busted-open pillow are scattered across her rug. Did she and Jake have sex or a pillow fight? Did she tear apart the pillow after he walked out on her?

I don't touch anything and walk through to her bathroom. It's small, separated from the bedroom by one of those pressurized walls that the city's young professionals are forever installing to add illegal Craigslist renters. There's a sink with a flat mirror above it, which I avoid facing. The toilet is pressed against a small shower, separated only by a chevron curtain. I fling back the plastic and begin peeling off my dress. The fabric that had covered my chest is damp with Colleen's blood. It slaps and sticks against my face as I pull it over my head. Once it's off, I drop it in the bathroom sink. Then I slip from my underwear and step onto the four gray tiles that serve as the shower floor.

I turn the water to its hottest setting. It blasts out of the square showerhead above with all the force of a fire hose. Freezing cold. I tilt my face back into the stream. It flows red into the drain beneath my feet. Thinned by the water, the blood looks like dye. Part of me is able to pretend that I've colored my hair some intense shade of auburn. This is no different than what the water would look like after a trip to the beauty salon.

I stand stock still beneath the stream until it starts to warm. Then I reach forward to a shower caddy on the ground bearing Colleen's shampoo, conditioner, and body wash. I pour the soap into my hands and begin rubbing it on my face. The smell is instantly recognizable. This is the citrusy scent I've caught on Jake's clothes. I'd thought he'd been using a new aftershave.

I scrub my face, my hands, my feet. I press the suds beneath my nails and shampoo twice before using the conditioner. Lather, rinse, repeat. When the water is finally scalding, I step from behind the curtain and let it run, blasting away all my errant hair and skin particles. Finally, I walk to the mirror and turn on the light.

The top of the glass is fogged from the hot water. I dip lower to view my full face and am surprised that the woman staring back at me is the same person who got out of the shower this morning. The word "monster" is not written on her forehead. There aren't any defensive wounds on her arms or strange stigmata on her hands. This woman is me. She's a murderer. But she's still me.

I towel off with a dry washcloth by the sink, which I then add to my bloody clothes pile in the basin. This is the stuff I need to throw away somewhere no one will find it. I detangle my hair with a paddle brush on the lip of the sink and then add it to the stack. Afterward, I shut off the shower, certain that it has done its job by now, and walk into her bedroom.

Since it's an interior room, it lacks a window. I turn on the light and head to a freestanding wardrobe where Colleen must keep her clothing. The stuff inside isn't my style. It's all cutting edge and colorful, intended to call attention to the wearer, to assets I don't possess. I reach for the only items that we could possibly share: skinny black jeans and a black tank top.

I slip the outfit from the hangers, careful to only touch the garments that I intend to wear. The tank slips over my head easily and falls more or less where I'd expect. The pants hit my hips weird, but I can still wear them.

Using the hem of the shirt, I rub down the wardrobe handles. As I am about to close the door, I notice that shoes are stuffed beneath the hanging clothes. Her feet were surely smaller than mine. Next to a pair of seven-inch wedges are a flat pair of floral flip-flops, the kind of gaudy plastic thong sandals that nail salons dole out to pedicure clients. I slip them out and drop them on the ground beside my battered feet. They fit perfectly.

Dressed, I walk into her makeshift kitchen. Using the light from her open bedroom, I navigate to the cupboards. It takes opening three before I find everything I'm looking for: bleach, a plastic grocery bag, and paper towels. I unravel a wad from the roll and pour bleach on it. Then I go around the apartment, rubbing down every surface my fingers have grazed: cabinet handles, doorknobs, the shower controls, the light switches. The handle of the bleach bottle itself. It takes at least fifteen minutes for me to feel sure that my prints are not on any surfaces. When I'm done, I put the wet paper towel in the bag with the rest of the garbage: the bloody clothes, my shoes, the hairbrush, and Colleen's purse. This trash is destined for a series of dumpsters between here and Manhattan. The more separated, the better. Before I leave, I take one last paper towel and, wrapping my hand in it, open her apartment door.

"I'm sorry," I mumble as I shut it behind me. "It was either you or me."

# LIZA

The precinct is a windowless building on the East Side, a fortified strip club, only more sinister thanks to the assault rifle–carrying bouncers. As I approach, I feel small and timid, as though my name's not on the list. Though, apparently, it is. That's why I'm here.

I walk through a reinforced steel door, past the black-clad guard with the he-man torso, courtesy of his bulletproof vest. The officer's mouth remains in a straight line as he sizes me up like an usher at a wedding. Is she on the victim's side or the criminal's? My voice dries up in my throat, which is probably the point of all this. So much about the police is designed to intimidate. Take the military-cut uniform, all glinting badges and shields. Even if a cop doesn't have a visible handgun or bully stick or Taser (though he probably has all three), he has the blessing of the US government emblazoned on his clothes. How can anyone stand up to that?

A metal detector stands to the right of the guard. He shakes a plastic container at me and demands my keys and phone, both of which I immediately turn over. It is not until I walk through without incident and approach a small podium in front of another set of fire doors that an officer attempts politeness.

"May I help you?" The officer wears a belt weighed down with ways to immobilize people, though his voice is friendly enough. I explain that my husband asked that I help answer some questions about a missing friend.

"You want missing persons, then."

"No, I think he's been found." I repeat what David told me to say on the phone. "I want criminal investigations."

The officer directs me through the doors behind him to an elevator bank. I take it to the fifth floor, where I am met by a bulletproof glass window at chest level. A man with a boyish face looks at me like I might ruin his day.

"I'm here to see David Jacobson. My husband."

The officer continues interrogating me with his eyes.

"It's with regard to the Nick Landau case. My husband, he's a lawyer, asked that I come. He needs me to help him answer some questions. Mr. Landau was his law partner and friend. I understand that Mr. Landau's body was found."

He holds up a finger and disappears. I curse myself as he steps out of view. I'm talking too much, volunteering way more information than necessary, reverting to some deep-seated childhood desire to please. Pretty soon, I'll be explaining how Nick was dismissive of me and my friends and confessing that I never liked him.

I press my lips together and try not to sweat as I scan for someplace comfortable to wait. There's a line of plastic chairs against a wall that look about as hard as the poured-cement floor. When I look down, I can see up my nose in the shiny gray surface beneath the fluorescent overhead lights. At the end of the room is a metal door. There are black scuff marks near its base, probably from an officer's brand new boot.

Minutes of nervous fidgeting pass before the door opens with the bang of a weapon discharging. The hand holding it open is beefy, an appropriate stopper to the muscular arm attached. Tracing that extremity brings me to a young face with taut tan skin and dark hair worthy of a Just for Men ad.

The officer waves me toward the door. "Thanks for coming in." He extends his hand. "I'm Detective Bill Campos."

I shake and stop myself from saying something overly eager. *Anything I can do to help. Whatever you need.* Nick is dead. He was the best man at my wedding. I should seem appropriately bereaved.

"It's so awful." I touch the corner of my eye, as though I feel a tear there. "Is my husband okay?"

The officer gives me a weak smile. I've seen this look on my gynecologist's face, on my shrink's face, on the face of everyone whom I've ever told that I'm trying to have a baby and "exploring different options." It says things aren't looking good.

"He's in with someone at the moment. If you could follow me, we would appreciate asking you a few questions."

Though his tone is casual, it triggers my alarms. I've written enough romantic thrillers to know that the police wanting to question anyone alone is never no biggie. They're already talking to David. I'd assumed he was crying over the confirmed death of his friend. Maybe not.

"I'd like to see my husband first."

The officer holds the door open a bit wider. "I understand. He's helping out some of my colleagues at the moment. If you would follow me, we're trying to piece together what might have happened to your friend."

My back tenses. "You found his body, right?"

Officer Campos does his best impression of horrified sadness. Wide eyes. Shaking head. It's all a bit overacted. Surely this guy must see murder victims all the time. "We found him in the river."

"What happened?"

"Why don't you come with me? I can better answer these questions sitting."

We walk down a carpeted hallway. Seals of different police branches dot gray-painted walls. Another steel door is propped open at the end of the corridor. I pass through it into a bright room full of wooden desks and fluorescent lights. A few officers are hunched over computers. Most of the desks are empty at this hour, though. An American flag stands in one corner, several feet away from the New York State version. I flash back to grade school and the Pledge of Allegiance.

Officer Campos sits at what I presume is his desk and gestures to the visitor's chair opposite. He withdraws a notepad and pen from a drawer.

"I really don't wish to talk to anyone without seeing my husband. I'm sorry. It's not that I don't want to be helpful, but he was very upset."

Again, the detective gestures for me to sit. Some part of me that wants, desperately, to be agreeable, as any innocent person would be, pulls back the chair and perches on the edge of it. Fine, I'll sit. But I don't have to get comfortable.

"Mr. Jacobson, your husband, knew Nick well?"

"They were law partners."

"So it was mostly a work relationship?"

He looks at the paper, as though he's posing routine questions, checking boxes off a list. Nonchalance in a detective is not a good sign. This question is more pointed than he wants it to appear.

"No. He and David have been close since law school."

"What did you think of their friendship?" This time, he makes direct eye contact.

*I fucking hated it.* The words reverberate in my head in Beth's voice. I don't verbalize them. There's no reason for me to have felt *that* strongly about their friendship. Most wives don't love their husband's "bros." Most single guys don't relish the presence of the woman who tied down their wingman. "They worked well together."

"Did you see them together much?"

160

I shrug. "They saw each other at work."

"But you felt they worked well *together?*"

Why is he pressing this point? "They built a successful firm. Isn't that evidence?"

"Did they see each other socially?"

My left eye starts to twitch. Not another headache. Not now. "David, I'm sure, can tell you all about how often he saw his friend. I'd like to see him now."

"Did they—"

The overhead bulbs seem to glow brighter. Harsh yellow beams pour from each pot light. I shut my eyes and press my thumb and forefinger against the lids, trying to block out the spotlights. "No more questions. If you want to formally interview me, I'd be happy to come back with David present as my attorney."

Officer Campos leans forward in his chair. "I thought you wanted to help."

"I want to see my husband."

"He's answering—"

My stomach seems to drop into my bowels. I need to get out of here. "I'll wait outside then."

The detective rolls his chair back from his desk. He stands with a sorry expression on his face, as though he feels terribly for me for some inexplicable reason. "Word of advice? You might want a different attorney."

# Chapter 12

I PAY CASH FOR A cab to the Forty-Second Street ferry terminal and then drop a twenty for round trip tickets to Weehawken. The boat skims across the gray water at a speed that car commuters could never hope to achieve in the Lincoln Tunnel. Eight minutes later, I am walking over a metal gangplank to the terminal. Another minute and I'm facing the bedrock cliff that supports the majority of the town above sea level.

I cross the street and climb up a rickety metal staircase bolted to the rock face like a fire escape from suburbia. My mom lives on top of the hill, several blocks back from a pricey apartment complex overlooking the city, on a postage stamp lot reminiscent of how the area used to look before developers realized they could build condos overlooking Manhattan and charge three thousand dollars a month for the privilege of waking up to the midtown skyline.

My thighs tremble as I ascend the last step into a narrow park. The past five hours was more exercise than my body was equipped to handle. I am not in shape. The biggest pain, however, isn't in my wobbly legs. The night without nursing has swollen my breasts into two water balloons. One of my nipples has already sprung a leak. A circular stain darkens the fabric on the left side of the tank top. I'm lucky it's black.

It's 6:30 AM when I ring my mother's doorbell. She welcomes me in with a yawning smile. The circles beneath her eyes are darker than yesterday. Victoria still wakes up every two hours at night. Interrupted dreams are a form of torture.

"What are you doing here so early?" she asks, pulling me inside as though the summer air isn't a balmy seventy degrees already.

I gesture to my top. "I need to nurse. The pump doesn't work like the baby."

My mom pokes my hardened breasts. A vein that I didn't know existed bulges beneath the cleavage popping above the tank's scoop neck. "That looks painful, Beth!"

She steps back into the house and gestures to the stroller. "I fed her a bottle about an hour ago. She likes it better in there than the Pack 'n Play."

I lift Vicky from the bassinet. Her tongue protrudes from her petite mouth at my scent, though her eyes remain closed. I pull the right breast up over the tank top's neckline. She latches on in her half-asleep state and pulls the milk from my body. It's a release better than any I have ever known. I could fall asleep like this.

Milk dribbles down the tank from the leaking left breast. My mother asks if I need a towel.

"I hate this shirt anyway," I say.

"It looks nice on you." My mom tilts her head. "The pants aren't right though. Maybe the waist is a bit boxy."

Vicky starts coughing. I remove her from my chest and pat her back while the spray from the right nipple soaks whatever dry fabric remained on my top. "Sorry, baby," I say as I hold her upright against my shoulder.

"Let me get you a towel."

"It's all right, Mom. You know what you could get me though? Something from my old closet. A T-shirt. Maybe a pair of old jeans."

"Everything is from college."

"I'll squeeze."

I put Vicky back into nursing position. She fusses as she drinks from one milk fountain and then the other, annoyed by the speed at which the liquid rushes from my body. When I burp her, there is a deep gurgling sound. Moments later, my clothes are coated in sour milk vomit.

Vicky settles down right after. Possibly she'd already been full and had only nursed because she wanted to be near me. More likely, there was something wrong with my milk. All the adrenaline in my blood stream probably poisoned the supply. I fed my baby rotten milk. Tears threaten to fall from the thought. I'd rather be a murderer than a bad mother.

As I'm placing Victoria back in the bassinet, my mom comes down the stairs holding a blue Columbia tank top and drawstring sweat pants, one of those college gym outfits that everyone lives in for four years. I probably left it here because I was sick of wearing it.

She wrinkles her nose as she looks at me. "Give it here." She holds out one hand with my outfit and the other for the soiled clothing clinging to my chest. "I'll wash it."

I grab the hem of the tank and bring it up to my breasts, distributing the baby vomit. "It's done, Mom. I'll put it in the trash."

"But—"

"It didn't fit right, anyway."

I ball up the top and walk it, near naked, to the kitchen garbage. As my mom protests, I push it deep inside the plastic bag with the other refuse: uneaten pasta and red sauce from the smell of it. "Really, Mom, that outfit was ruined." I slip the shirt over my head and then go into the bathroom where I jostle into the oversized sweats. Colleen's pants follow her shirt into the trash.

"I could have washed those." My mom shakes her head at me as though I am the most wasteful woman in the world for throwing out perfectly good clothing saturated in human fluids.

"I need a favor."

She eyes me. When I said these words yesterday, she ended up not sleeping all night. She quickly covers the distrustful look with a tight smile and nods at me to continue. I am her daughter. She'd do anything for me—even if she doesn't like it.

"Jake cancelled on me last night and—"

"Oh, honey. I'm sorry. Was it work? Did you at least get to see him a—"

"I went out with a friend and spent the night. I'd rather Jake think I was here."

My mom folds her arms across her chest, a perfect replica of my own skeptical stance—or, rather, the original version. I'm the imitator. "What friend?"

I lower my head as though ashamed. A normal person would feel that way. Clearly, something is wrong with me. "A male coworker."

"Oh, Beth."

"I was lonely and wanted the attention. Nothing happened. I just drank a bit too much. I'm not used to it now that I'm nursing. I passed out on his couch."

My mother frowns. She hates cheaters. My father was a philanderer. She hates my father. Now I seem as though I took after him.

"I'm not proud of it, Mom. It was a mistake. It won't happen again. I was disappointed that Jake canceled, and I've been a bit depressed, honestly, being home with Vicky all the time." I'm playing the overwhelmed mom card. That always gets a bit of compassion. "Jake is always working late. I went out for a drink by myself and ran into this guy—"

"Who?"

"It doesn't matter! Please, just, if anyone asks, say I slept over here last night."

"Won't you see this man when you go back to work?"

"Nothing happened."

"Come on, Beth. You changed your clothes."

My mother is looking at me the same way she did when I was a little kid and she'd catch me picking my nose and wiping it on the side of the couch. *What is wrong with you? You think I didn't see that?* I could tell her that I changed when I realized Jake wouldn't take me out, opted for this black ensemble. I could reiterate that nothing happened. But she thinks she's seen me.

"Mom." I reach for her, but she recoils. "It was a mistake. I'm sorry. Do you want Jake to divorce me over one act of stupidity?"

My mother looks away. I've disgusted her. She's ashamed that she raised me. Feeling horrible for poor Jake. "Everyone says they'll never do it again," she says.

Pictures flash in my mind. The pipe. The blood. The smashed back of Colleen's head and her face, battered and broken beyond recognition from striking the floor each time I slammed the metal pipe into her back. Tears fill my eyes. I wipe them away with my forearm. More come, wetting my cheeks, filling my nose, falling from my chin. I shake my head vigorously. I will never, ever, ever do anything like this ever again. Never. "I'm so sorry." My voice comes out as a rasping, wail. "I'm so sorry. I'm so, so sorry. I will never . . . I'm so—"

My mom opens up her arms. "Oh, Beth." Her voice cracks, as though she, too, struggles with tears.

"I'm so sorry." I fall into her embrace. She feels warm and comforting. Thank God for mothers.

"It's okay. It was a mistake." She strokes the back of my head and shushes into my ear. "Don't worry. It'll be okay. You were here all night."

# LIZA

I wait for David in a stark gray room, sitting in a classroom chair that is as uncomfortable as the ones I remember from high school. The precinct lacks cell service, so I amuse myself by flipping through stored photos. Here's a picture of David and me at an anniversary dinner. Here's one of us posing with Chris and Emma last year. Here's one I took of Dave and Nick.

They stand side by side. David's arm is draped over Nick's narrow shoulders. My husband is tilted forward with his mouth slightly open, as though he were giving a camera direction. Nick, for his part, is smirking with his lips pursed. The expression is probably to show off his high cheekbones, but it could be that he's suppressing a laugh—possibly something to do with me.

After ten minutes, David emerges from behind a steel door. His pink complexion looks drained. The only time I remember him being this upset was a year ago. Nick had called. David had rushed out in the middle of dinner. Later, he'd said that there'd been a problem with the lawsuit against the school. He'd missed something important and needed to work it out. He'd had the same pallor.

"What's going on?"

David shakes off the question and gestures with his head to the officer behind him. Whatever transpired in the police department, he won't discuss it anywhere near the station. His secrecy makes me nervous. If he can't tell me in front of the cops, what the hell is he hiding? What did they do to him? What do they think he did?

A police officer says something about following up. I'm not listening to the detectives so much as looking at David's reaction to whatever they say. He blanches with each word. By the time the officers are done, my husband looks exsanguinated.

A protective instinct ignites inside me. "We are mourning our friend and you are pressuring him like this?" I yell. "That's unconscionable. We have rights. You can call our lawyer."

Instead of making similar threats, David walks in a daze to the exit. We pass through the metal detectors in silence and exit onto the guarded street. Once outside, I again ask what happened. He pleads that he is too tired. We will talk when we get home.

By the time we enter the apartment, the suspense has made me physically ill. My head throbs as I lead David to the living room love seat. City lights stream in from the French doors, spotlighting the white leather sofa onto which David slumps, shielding his eyes with his palm.

I turn the chandelier above the dining table to its dimmest setting and then draw the blackout curtains. David's hand drops from his face. I ask if he'd like water. When he shakes his head no, I assume my position: sitting beside him, looking squarely into his lowered eyes. "Tell me everything."

David coughs, as though the words are lodged in his throat. "They found Nick's body in the East River. They showed me photos." He rubs his lids with his fists. "He was beaten. Badly. Horribly. I mean, God, Liza. His head was bashed in with something. A tire iron, maybe. There were flecks of metal. And . . ."

David takes a choppy breath. "He'd been shot. The cops think that the killer put a .22 into his gut and then, once he was immobilized, beat him to death."

In my mind's eye, I see Beth with the lead pipe, reddened with blood, raised like a baseball bat. A knifelike pain stabs my frontal lobe. White spots speckle my vision. I drop my head into my hands and rock back and forth. I lack the constitution for true crime. Violence against my made-up characters is all the brutality I can withstand. Thinking about Nick's real warm blood coming out of his real bludgeoned body, the fear that he must have felt as a real, live human being facing his all-too-real death . . . it's too much for me. I can't let myself imagine.

David pats me on the back, happy, I think, that I am finally as broken up about his friend as he has been. "God, Liza, his face was barely recognizable, just this waterlogged . . ." I feel his body tremble beside me, as though an electric current has been applied. The cops tortured David with these details. Why would they get so graphic? What could they hope to gain?

"His skull was destroyed. He might have been alive when—"

I put up a hand, unable to swallow any more gory details.

My racing heartbeat resounds in my head. "I don't get why the police told you all this."

"I don't know." David stands. I look up long enough to see him walk from the couch to the curtains. He pulls back the heavy fabric. A long rectangle of light from the neighboring building breaks in, bathing my husband's button-down and suit pants in a white glow. I can't stand to see that halo.

"I don't understand who would do this. I mean, the savagery . . ." David gasps. "The hate they had to have . . ." A sob cuts off his words. I peer from beneath my lowered lids at him, trying to see his expression without taking in the light. His body shudders and shakes as though he dove into a cold ocean. I have never seen my husband cry this hard.

"Why would they show you the photos?" I mumble the question, unable to silence my inner monologue with the throbbing in my temples.

He rubs his hands back and forth over his bald head. "For all I know, I'm a suspect."

"What reason would you have to hurt Nick?"

"I don't know!" He whirls on me like an angry dog. "I don't have a fucking clue! I don't even own a gun. I had no reason to want Nick dead. He was my friend. The best man at our wedding."

I recall Detective Campos's line of questioning. "Do the police think you and Nick had disagreements about the firm?"

David shakes his head in disgust. "I don't know, Liza. I do know that without Nick, our biggest clients might leave. So you tell me. Why on Earth would the police think I'd hurt my friend?"

If I were writing a book, I could invent a variety of reasons. Nick was stealing money from the firm and David found out. David had messed up a case and Nick was blackmailing him. Nick planned to leave and take their best accounts. As I consider motives, needles stab into my forehead, forcing my eyes shut. In the blackness, I see the empty space in the lockbox. A horrifying thought flares in my brain. It consumes the oxygen in my lungs. Suddenly, I'm gasping. Choking.

David killed Nick with my gun.

Fear wrests open my eyes. I watch David step from the window and survey the room, scanning for evidence. His red, tear-stained face looks wracked with guilt. "The police always spend the first part of an investigation leaning on those closest to the deceased. That's probably all this is. They might come here at some point." His index finger shoots toward me, accusing me of wrongdoing. "If they do, demand a warrant and call me. They'll probably have one since they know I'd have any search overturned in court otherwise. Still, ask. If they don't give you anything, make sure you tell them, 'I do not consent to this search.' Okay? Those exact words."

My head swims with the migraine and the realization that I may be married to a murderer. Memorizing anything is too much. I drop my forehead onto my thighs. Bile sears my throat. I swallow it along with any idea of revealing that I know my gun is missing. I don't want David to think that I suspect him or, worse, to confess anything to me. Ignorance is bliss. Whatever he did, I don't want to find out for certain. I don't want to know anything at all.

"Say it, Liza!"

His volume startles the words from me. "I do not consent to this search."

"Good. Good." David is pacing. I hear his shoes against the hardwood. Three steps right, turn, three steps left. "By the way, I was looking for a note Nick sent. Um, for a case . . ."

His tone has changed from angry to distracted. He's trying to hide the importance of this note. Does it show a motive for him to kill Nick? *I don't want to know.* I mentally repeat the words like a silent prayer. *I don't want to know. God, I don't want to know.*

"I have to go the office. If they come, call me."

It must be after midnight. Maybe after one. What is so important in the office?

It's an effort to raise my head. I see that David's briefcase is in his hand. Despite the dim lighting, the room is far too colorful. My gut is clenching. I need the bathroom. "But—"

"Liza. Whatever you do, don't say anything to the police, okay? Spousal privilege. Tell them you're invoking spousal privilege."

I can't answer.

"Liza, say spousal privilege."

My stomach does a last somersault. I wretch and cover my mouth, running to the toilet before the next spasm spews the contents onto the floor. The front door slams as I hurl over the bowl.

# Chapter 13

JAKE ANSWERS THE DOOR BEFORE I can put my key into the lock. He's showered and dressed for work, though he's not wearing a tie, socks, or shoes. It's past noon. Dark circles swell beneath his lower lids. Last night, apparently, was not a restful one. Welcome to the club.

As I enter with Vicky, he tries to reach into the stroller. I push my baby past him into the apartment, knocking his arm away with the bassinet's sunshade. Victoria fell asleep ten minutes ago. He cannot play daddy now and wake her because it's convenient for him. Besides, she's played already. Vicky stayed awake the whole boat ride back to the city and during the lengthy stroll through the chain of parks and piers lining the Hudson River en route to our condo. Her navy eyes had observed everything. She'd been so engaged, I'd even taken her to play on the lawn outside Chelsea Piers. As I'd swept her bare feet over the blades of grass, she'd gurgled an openmouthed infant laugh. Neither of us had been in a hurry to return home.

"Where were you?" Jake grips his hips. A laugh bubbles in my throat. More than a month of sleeping around and he's angry that I didn't come home.

If he only knew what I'd done.

"I was at Mom's."

"Your mother's?" His arms fold across his chest. "Without your phone?"

"I forgot it." I push Vicky into our bedroom. It's bright in here, not that she cares once she's fallen asleep. Still, I walk to the window and lower the blackout curtain.

"I had no way to reach you." Jake stands in the doorway, indignant.

I put my finger to my lips and point at the stroller. Then I brush past him again, a Manhattan native navigating around a midtown tourist, and reenter the living area. "You could have called my mom," I hiss.

The bedroom door shuts. He follows me into the living room. "I didn't know you were there."

"Where else would I be, Jake?" My feet ache from hours of walking in cheap flip-flops. I am tempted to take off Colleen's shoes and massage my arches, but I can't draw attention to my footwear. Instead, I sit on our fabric couch and pull my legs up to the side, tucking my feet beneath me so Jake can't see the shoes. I'll need to dispose of these. Trash collection is tomorrow. Perhaps I'll take Vicky on a stroll through Battery Park later and toss them in a garbage can, somewhere far enough from my building that they could never be traced back to me. Maybe by the Staten Island Ferry terminal. Tens of thousands of people pass through there each day. If I go around rush hour, no one will notice me.

"I don't know where you'd be." He stands behind the coffee table. "There are hundreds of places: a friend's house, a hotel. In a ditch somewhere."

A yawn swallows my face. Now that I'm sitting, my body is acutely aware of my all-nighter. The adrenaline is gone. I could pass out this instant.

"I mean how could you be so irresponsib—"

"You cancelled on me." I rub my hands over my face, trying to wake up for this conversation. It's important that I sell Jake on my alibi. "Obviously, if I'm not here waiting for you, I'd be with my family."

He bends toward the glass table and picks something up. He brandishes the items like a trial exhibit. A stone glints in the sunlight flooding the living room window. "I found these."

My rings. I fight a smile. Knowing that I'd thrown them on the floor or fearing they'd been wrested from my fingers would have made last night that much worse for him. "I was upset." I shrug. "I told you that I wanted to talk and stressed that it was important. And you still canceled."

"A work thing came up."

I close my eyes so he can't see me roll them. The action spurs another yawn.

"I was worried."

*Not worried enough.* Jake's big blue eyes shine with little boy hurt. They remind me of Vicky's. A swirl of emotions suddenly overcome my fatigue. Anger, sadness, fear, regret. Love. They bang into one another like subatomic particles at high speed, fusing together, leaving empty vacuums in their wake. For a moment, I fear I might explode with screams and rage and tears. Then Jake's brow lowers, and a strange calm descends. It's as though I've been drained of all the muddled emotions that define the human experience. I feel detached. I am watching myself huddled on this couch, lorded over by my self-righteous spouse. The distance gives me clarity.

I don't love this man anymore. I'll also never love any man the way I loved him. Never again will I be a twenty-one-year-old ingenue so enamored of the idea of someone finding me special that I refuse to see this other person for who he really is. No one loves selflessly. I won't do it again.

A knock on the door stops my thoughts. Every muscle tightens. I glance at the window. Newer buildings don't have fire escapes.

"You expecting anyone?"

*A SWAT team?* "No." I cover my fear with annoyance. "I just got home. Are you?"

Jake's walk is stiff as he approaches the door. I realize with a twinge of schadenfreude that he thinks Colleen has come for a visit. His stomach is probably somewhere in his colon right now.

The door pulls back. A blue uniform peeks above Jake's shoulder. "Excuse me, ADA Jacobson. Sorry to bother you at home like this. May we come in?"

I tuck my feet farther beneath my bottom.

"I called out today. What is it that can't wait until tomorrow?"

"It's about Officer Landry. Officer Colleen Landry."

*Here it comes.* I feel as though I am in a car traveling eighty miles per hour toward a brick wall.

"What about her?"

"She's been reported missing."

"Oh?" Jake looks at me over his shoulder. "Maybe we should talk outside? My six-week-old is sleeping in the bedroom."

The officers step back into the hallway, giving Jake room to go outside and close the door behind him. If they were here to arrest me, they'd never leave me alone with a child in the apartment while they talked to my husband. They don't suspect me . . . yet. I have to know what they're thinking.

"Jake, you can invite them in. As long as we all keep our voices down, we won't wake Victoria." I approach the door and reach around Jake to extend my hand. "I'm Jake's wife, Beth."

The officer is a wall of a black man. Broad shoulders, broad torso. He gives me a guilty smile and steps into the room. His partner, a middle-aged blonde woman with wide shoulders and deep frown lines, follows behind him. "What's wrong?" I ask.

"An officer, Colleen Landry, is missing. A neighbor called this morning after seeing blood in the hallway outside her apartment. It's Colleen's. And there was a lot of it."

Jake blinks at the man as though he hasn't understood him. After a beat, he scratches the stubble on his cheek. "Have you checked with family? She has a sister in the Bronx."

"Her sister hasn't heard from her," the female officer says. "Neither have her pals. She was meeting up with a girlfriend last night for late drinks and never showed."

My gut twists. Colleen hadn't been headed to chase down Jake and confront me after all. I let my jaw drop. "Is that the police-woman who was in your office yesterday? The one you were working that case with?"

Jake's hand rakes down his mouth and drops to his side. "Yes." He clears his throat. "She was a witness on a prior case, and she was in my office." He glances at the male officer. I wonder what he might be trying to communicate with his eyes: *Please act as though our relationship was professional.*

"Helping with a current case," I offer. "The one about the socialite who backed her car into those people."

He gives a sheepish smile to the two detectives as though they know something by virtue of being here. Maybe the whole police department is aware that Jake and Colleen were lovers, that I was the stupid wife with an infant at home.

"Can I get you anything?" I ask while walking into the kitchen. "Water? Juice." If it weren't for Colleen's shoes on my feet, I might be enjoying Jake's distress. He's so close to being outed.

"No, thank you."

The female officer eyes my husband. "Officer Landry's friend said that Ms. Landry was meeting with you before she failed to show for drinks."

My husband glances at me. I try to keep my wide-eyed, curious expression intact. "We had dinner," he says. "I wanted to pick her brain on a case."

I stare at him, doing my best to feign what I would be feeling if this were my first hint that my husband had been cheating. The gut-wrenching emotions I felt when I first saw Jake's hand on Colleen's back are inaccessible to me. Still, I blink at him and let my lips part, pretending to be suspicious yet hopeful that maybe there's an innocent explanation.

"Where did you go?" The female officer looks at me as she asks. Is she trying to tip me off to my husband's affair? If she is, then she can't think I had anything to do with Officer Colleen's death. Then again, she could simply be gauging my reactions. I focus on Jake, pretending to be interested in the answer.

He clears his throat for the second time. All the moisture in it must have evaporated. "You know, I think I'd rather do this at the precinct. I have work to catch up on, and that way, I'll be near the office."

"Jake worked late last night." I pump earnestness into my voice as though all I want to do is be helpful to my husband. "We had dinner plans, but this case kept him."

The male detective nods as though he doesn't know my husband has been feeding me a crock of horseshit. "And what time did he get off work?"

"She wasn't here," Jake snaps.

"I just came in five minutes ago, actually. When Jake had to cancel on me because of the case, I went back to get our daughter from my mother's house and ended up spending the night."

"What time did you get in?" Again, the female officer asks Jake for a direct answer.

In response, he walks to the coat closet and grabs his suit jacket. "As I've said, I'd prefer to answer these questions downtown, detectives."

The detectives nod and follow Jake out the door. Before the female officer leaves, she passes me a business card. "If you think of anything," she says cryptically.

I nod at her, doe eyed, as though I haven't any idea what she means.

# LIZA

Someone is chasing me. I run from them all night, racing through unfamiliar alleyways, sweating in a black tank that I've never owned and ill-fitting jeans. I flee my pursuer into the subway, diving into empty cars. I speed away in a vehicle, right foot pressing the gas pedal to the carpet, yellowed knuckles gripping the steering wheel. Still, there is no escape.

I wake in a confused fever. Where am I? Who am I? What is real? Sunlight, too pale for the afternoon, pours through my bedroom window. Its visual alarm reflects off my laptop's metal shell into my tired eyes. The end of the month will be here before I know it. Trevor won't give me an extension.

The blanket is still pulled tight to the headboard on David's side of the bed. He didn't come home. Likely, he crashed on his office couch. *Or he went to Cameron's apartment*, Beth says.

"Right now, that's the least of my concerns." I answer her aloud, comforted by the familiar sound of my scratchy, gravely morning voice. David wasn't sleeping with anyone in his emotional state. He probably didn't sleep at all.

I roll from beneath the covers and head to the bathroom. Last night's vomiting has left me dehydrated. There's barely anything to evacuate. Still, I go through the motions: toilet, shower, brush teeth, dress. The acts feel superfluous. My husband might have killed a man. What does it matter if my breath smells?

Yet what else is there to do besides go about my day? I can't sit around waiting for officers to arrest my husband. And there's still a chance that David didn't do anything at all and this is all in my head.

In the light of day, my murder theory seems less plausible. David and Nick were getting hate mail after that big judgment. Perhaps David took my gun because he feared that whomever had hurt his law partner was coming for him next. Maybe he hadn't asked me for it because he hadn't wanted me to worry. For all I know, my gun is in his desk drawer.

The thought that David might be innocent barely comforts me. Alone in the apartment, with only my imagination for company, I can invent too many reasons for my husband to have wanted his business partner dead. I can devise too many ways for him to have done it.

*So go out*, Beth admonishes me. A woman of action, she would not stay here like a polite chess player, waiting for her opponent to make the next move. She would meet someone. Do something. But what?

*The bar.* Again, the suggestion comes in Beth's voice. When her husband stood her up, I sent her to a local pub. But I think the idea is about more than my story or drowning my sorrows. Given Sergeant Perez's brief description, Nick had likely gone to the bar where he'd taken Christine before his disappearance. An upset woman had asked about him. Maybe that woman was involved. Maybe, if I figure out who she is, I can give the cops— and myself—another suspect besides my husband.

I don't know the name of the place. Christine hadn't remembered it, and Sergeant Perez had probably withheld it deliberately. Still, it's possible to find out anything on the Internet with a few scant details. I open my laptop and search for a list of descriptive phrases that I remember from Christine's story: "Brooklyn." "Marie Antoinette." "Speakeasy." "French." Within seconds,

Google returns a customer review page for Le Bonhomme. There are photos. Red leather banquettes line one wall. Massive mirrors with ornate frames coated in gold leaf are posted above each table. This must be the place. The web page has a phone number and hours: 4:00 PM until 4:00 AM.

No one will answer if I call now. I resolve to head into Brooklyn for an early dinner and close my browser. My manuscript lies behind it. I see the cursor flashing beside the period of the last sentence. Obsessing over my husband's possible guilt isn't helping anyone. Time for me to write.

*

I work all day, stopping only to slurp up a bowl of watery instant oatmeal and refill my coffee mug. By three o'clock, I have been staring at the computer screen for so long that my vision is blurred. The objects in my apartment have a hazy quality, as though plopped onto a green screen. I save the latest version of my novel and e-mail myself a copy. If I want to get to the bar before it gets crowded, I need to leave soon.

I bump into my ottoman en route to my closet, forgetting that the layout of my bedroom is tighter than the one in Tyler's imaginary studio. Nothing that I own is trendy enough for any place that Nick would have frequented. I settle on a pair of last season's skinny jeans, sans this season's factory scuffing around the knees, and a white V-neck blouse. My go-to black heels would help dress up the outfit. Unfortunately, I haven't put them in their usual place and don't trust myself to recall where I left them. Instead, I grab a pair of black sneakers. The woman in my full-length mirror seems as though she doesn't care. Strangely enough, this makes me look hip.

I bring my laptop with me for the long subway ride. There are four stops between my apartment and Fifty-Ninth Street. There, I will switch trains to head into Greenpoint, Brooklyn.

The trip will give me another hour to work. Editing also has the added bonus of keeping anyone from talking to me. Tourists seeking someone to take their hundredth picture or strange men wanting to know if a clearly vacant seat is "taken" won't bother asking a woman with her head behind a computer screen. Too much is happening for me to navigate polite conversation.

*

I emerge above ground in an area that looks like the bastard child of Manhattan's Chelsea and the Bronx. Brownstone-lined streets intersect avenues of bodegas selling ethnic cuisines. In the distance, a glass skyscraper nears completion beside what I am pretty sure is a row of abandoned factories. Most strikingly, there's graffiti. As I approach the waterfront, brick facades are splashed with blue-and-white bubble letters. Illegible scripts shout garbled messages on shuttered doors. The scrawled writing is more sad than threatening—a last FU from the struggling artists being pushed out of any neighborhood within five miles of the city. The Nicks of the world have arrived. No doubt the spray paint will soon be sandblasted, perhaps replaced by the high-priced art of a Banksy rip-off, though only if the developer decides that "edginess" drives up prices.

I walk down the street listed on the website until I see a gilded door, curved like the entrance to a castle and slapped on the brick face of one of the abandoned-looking factories. There isn't any sign, and the door doesn't have a knob or a handle. This must be the place.

I rap my knuckles against the fancy entrance, more annoyed with the gimmick than thrilled by the faux secrecy. The door retreats with the screech of rusted metal, probably for effect. A shirtless man in a gold bowtie, like a male version of a Playboy bunny, peers around me. When he doesn't see anyone, he welcomes me to Le Bonhomme.

Christine has a knack for descriptions. The place does resemble a French queen's chambers, only with booths instead of beds. More accurately, it seems to be fashioned after the sitting room where courtesans entertained before heading to more private quarters. It smells like a heavy male cologne, something with absinthe and rosemary.

The hour is too early for the after-work crowd. Only one of the several booths hosts patrons. Two men. Perhaps a couple. Their presence alone, sitting across from one another, does not make this a gay bar. The bartender's work attire of a silken red scarf and tight black pants, however, strongly hints in that direction. The man could bench press me. Another clue.

I take a seat on a red velvet stool and request a tequila gimlet. It's the only mixed drink I can come up with while still struggling to digest the decor. The bartender looks at me like I am in the wrong place and hands me a menu. All the cocktails are special to the restaurant, he explains. He doesn't do plain old tequila and lime.

I point to the first one. It has an accent over the vowel and raspberry listed in the description. It doesn't matter. I'm not drinking so much as I am trying to create a financial transaction involving information. If I am tipping this guy, he might be more forthcoming.

As the mixologist starts taking bottles from the back bar, I slide my phone from my purse and scroll to the picture of Nick and David. "I am sorry to bother you, but I am hoping that you may have some information on a friend of mine." Surprisingly, my voice doesn't sound all squeaky. The stress of the past few days has forced me to get over some of my social anxiety.

The bartender squints as though I might be a crazed stalker or badly cast bounty hunter. He doesn't say anything.

I place the phone on the bar. "His name is Nick Landau. The man on the right."

The bartender pours raspberry vodka into a shaker with one hand and red raspberry juice in with the other. He glances at the screen.

"He's my husband's best friend and law partner. He disappeared about a month ago. His name has been in the paper. Apparently, he was last seen here."

The bartender keeps looking at the image. His lips remain shut. He adds another liquor to the shaker before vibrating it above his shoulder like an odd instrument.

"We don't want money or anything from him." I cough. "We just want to know what happened."

The bartender grabs a champagne flute and strains the lipstick-colored concoction into it. "We don't really talk about guests. Don't want to *out* anyone for coming. Understand?"

All doubts about the sexual orientation of the bar's primary clientele disappear. The man probably thinks that I am a girlfriend trying to figure out whether her boyfriend is using her as a beard.

I sip my drink. It's good, but too sweet for me. Still, I effuse over the man's efforts. He smiles in a thin way that shows he's all too aware that my compliments are because I want something and moves to straighten the glasses on the back bar. If another patron were here, he'd probably start chatting him up right now to avoid me.

"My husband and Nick were prominent in the LGBT community after their law firm sued the city on behalf of a bullied teen," I blurt out. "Please, look. He thinks Nick could have been the victim of a hate crime."

This gets the man's attention. His arms puff out as he walks over to me. He picks up my phone from the counter and taps the screen to zoom into the photo. "The guy on the right, smiling. Nick, is it?"

"Yes."

He hands me back the phone. "He's a regular. Takes dates here often. Great tipper."

I remember Christine. Did Nick have a thing about bringing women to gay bars? "Female or male dates?"

The bartender's mouth pinches on the side as though I'm particularly dense. "Honey, look around. Men bring men here."

Nick was gay! Things that never made sense to me before become clear. Why he was never particularly affectionate with any of his "girlfriends." Why he hadn't been interested in sleeping with a clearly willing Christine. Why he still wasn't married, while David and I had just celebrated twelve years.

My mouth must be hanging open because the bartender's hands are folded across his oiled pectorals as if to tell me to get on with it. I clear my throat and pose another question. "The night he disappeared, Saturday, July ninth, Nick came here with a man. A woman came in later. She was upset."

The bartender regards me skeptically and shakes his head. "I wasn't here. I spend most of July in Fire Island. But I can ask the rest of the staff if you text me a photo."

I type in his number as he rattles it off and then send him the picture of David and Nick. There's a beep under the counter that I assume is his cell acknowledging receipt.

"Do you have a photo?" he asks.

"I think you just got it."

He rolls his eyes. "Of you."

"Me?" I don't understand. Maybe bartenders for gay clubs aren't necessarily homosexual. Or he's bisexual? A flush rises to my cheeks. "I—"

He chuckles. "You're cute, hon. But I also want to ask around about you. How do I know you're not the girl who came in here all upset about her boyfriend and then had her homophobic brother or some other asshole murder him?"

I want to protest with a list: (a) I'm married. (b) My husband is straight. (c) We've been together twelve years and are trying to have a baby. (d) I've never been here in my life. But I hold my tongue. He wouldn't believe me, anyway. After all, I hadn't realized Nick was gay.

I pull my wallet from my purse and remove a business card. My last book cover is on the front. A flattering photo of me is printed on the back with a few lines of positive criticism for my first book, the *international bestseller*. "This is me."

He examines the image and then stares back at me, comparing features. Recognition sparkles in his eyes. He flicks the card with his finger. "I read *Drowned Secrets*. Good book."

# Chapter 14

Victoria sleeps in her bassinet, body positioned for a police pat down. Her arms are raised in a stick-'em-up position. Her legs are spread. Yet there's no tension in her expression. Her bow mouth is untied. Her lids are closed without fluttering. She does not have bad dreams.

Fatigue weighs on my eyelids. REM is not an option. I know Colleen waits for me in my subconscious, bloody and beaten. Banquo's ghost, prepared to accuse me of murder and usurp my position as Victoria's mother.

I need to think like the detectives. They are questioning Jake. They must suspect murder. They've seen the blood-soaked floor. And Jake must be a suspect. He was the last known person to see Colleen alive. I'm certain to land on the short list, too, if anyone figures out that I knew of his affair.

Although, how would they discover that? Jake thinks he's slipped everything past me. My mother believes she's lying about my whereabouts to cover up an indiscretion with a coworker. The only person who knows that I knew is Tyler. Surely he wouldn't say anything. He was my shrink, after all—though sleeping together probably voided any doctor-patient confidentiality agreement. If a policeman came to his door asking questions, would he say he treated me? Would he confess everything?

I need to find out. I grab my house line off the nightstand and call his office. He answers on the third ring.

"Hello. Dr. Tyler Williams."

"It's Beth."

"Oh, hi. Did everything go all right last night?"

"That's what I wanted to talk to you about. Are you free at all today?"

His voice drops. "Did you tell him anything?"

If I say no, he'll assume that he's safe and won't see me. "Can we meet?"

"I have one more appointment for the day coming up in twenty minutes."

"I'll see you in an hour and half then. I'll come to your office."

*

Tyler doesn't leave me loitering. He's waiting at the door. As soon as I get within fifty feet of his office, he waves me and the stroller through like a frantic traffic director and locks the door behind us. His facial expression does not befit a shrink. Visible worry lines crease his brow as he motions to his couch. I push the stroller around to the side of the room and then settle down on the sofa, hoping he'll sit beside me.

He takes his usual chair. "So what happened?"

No "nice to see you." He only cares about how close my husband is to filing malpractice charges. "I didn't tell Jake anything. I didn't even go home last night. I went to my mother's house. She has assured me that, if Jake asks, she'll claim I was there all night."

He scratches his neat goatee. "But she knows something occurred."

"She believes I went out for drinks with a male coworker after Jake stood me up. I've made sure, the best I can, that this won't come back to you."

His expression relaxes. "Thank you." He starts to rise from his chair, hand extended, as though we've made a business deal to bury our rendezvous and all that remains is to shake on it. Me, bare-skinned beneath his body, can be deleted from his memory.

"I apologize for all this," he says.

"The police came to my apartment this morning."

Tyler slumps back into his chair. His Adam's apple bobs.

"Jake's girlfriend is missing. Apparently, she was supposed to meet a friend late last night for drinks and didn't show. A neighbor found blood outside her apartment and called the cops."

Images of the stained floor overpower me like an unseen wave. I am caught without enough air. I start gasping. Hyperventilating. Suddenly, Tyler is beside me, brandishing a paper bag from the ether. He places it over my mouth, a parent securing a child's oxygen mask on a plane going down.

"Just breathe." His palm, warm and wide, rubs my back. A few long inhalations and I'm ready to speak again. I focus on the feel of his body next to mine. I can get through this. I have to concentrate on Tyler.

"The cops came to the house to question Jake," I continue. "I'm sure he was with her last night. That's why he cancelled our date last minute."

A real sob escapes, even as I lie by implication. The weight of my actions threatens to crush me. If only Colleen weren't dead. If only I could go back to when I discovered the affair and confront them both in that restaurant, tell her that she could have my cheating spouse. I'd gladly give him up now.

Tyler takes my hand in his larger palm. He strokes my fingers. For a moment, I close my eyes, remembering his touch from the night before. He'd made me feel beautiful. Worthy.

"Do you feel safe?"

"No." I take a halting breath.

"You think he did something?"

Of course he did something! His betrayal made me a murderer! I clear my throat, making way for the lies to slip out. "Jake was always kind of violent and controlling. I never said anything because I was embarrassed. If his girlfriend threatened to leave him or to tell me what was going on, I could see him flipping out. He didn't know I knew." I gasp, my best imitation of a horror movie victim. "If he finds out where I really was last night . . ."

Tears escape my eyes. They are real, fueled by despair over my future. I will never again have a sound sleep. The fear that someday someone will figure out my crime will hang over me like a suspended boulder.

Tyler cradles my cheek with his palm. "Don't worry. I certainly won't say anything to him. It will be all right."

His assurances annoy me. Obviously he won't talk to Jake. He doesn't want my husband to go after his license for sleeping with me. Plus, nobody in his right mind would tell a likely murderer that he fucked his wife the prior night.

"I'm so afraid." I sound meek. I can't tell whether I'm acting or if the stress of the past twenty-four hours has sapped all the confidence from my voice. "If he thought I knew what he did . . . If the police found out and it somehow got back to him . . ."

Tyler pulls me into his chest. Here, with his arm around my back and my head against his strong shoulder, I feel protected. I want to stay. Hero types are my downfall.

"Please," I whisper. "You can't tell *anyone* that I knew about the affair. Even the police. It could get back to Jake."

He makes a shushing sound as though I'm an infant. "They can't ask me about our sessions."

"What if they gave you a subpoena?"

"I can't be compelled to talk about anything you said. I'm bound by confidentiality. I'm your doctor."

I lift my chin to gaze into his empathetic brown eyes. He's not scared. He thinks his doctor-patient privilege protects him and, to a lesser extent, me. In fact, he feels more secure now that I have my own reasons to keep our one-night stand secret. But he should be afraid. I covered up a crime. I know that once the police start investigating Nick, they'll want to verify my comings and goings. They'll check the security cameras around our building. I wasn't thinking about avoiding them when I went to Tyler's apartment. My face is undoubtedly on a CCTV tape somewhere. Tyler's doorman saw us too. And although Tyler's practice is in the same building as his first-floor apartment, the timing of our rendezvous is wrong for a session. Once the cops see us walking to the elevator, hand in hand, late at night, they'll know it wasn't for a standard psychiatric visit. Confidentiality will crumble.

"But what if they find out that I was with you that night? If they see me on a camera somewhere or your doorman recognizes me? What will you do?"

"I'll tell them . . ." His eyes widen. "I'll tell them . . ."

I cup my right hand over the one stroking my left and look him straight in the eye. "You'll tell them that I developed feelings for you. My husband was ignoring me, and I mistook your attention for affection. You were trying to calm me down."

"But what if they have footage in the lift?"

I close my eyes, considering the possibility without seeing the worry lines across his brow. We definitely kissed in the elevator— though that probably works to my advantage. It would be better for the police to think that I was having sex with a lover than out killing Colleen. Faced with any footage, my best bet is to tell the cops that I'd been seeing Tyler, maybe even to hint that I'd intended to leave my husband for him. But I can't ask Tyler to come clean. Once he admits to sleeping with a patient, his career is over. He'll have nothing to lose by telling the whole story, making clear just how angry I was at Jake and his girlfriend.

I squeeze Tyler's hand. "If they have elevator footage, you can say that I was kissing you. You didn't push me off because of my fragile state. But you talked to me until midnight and got me through my crisis. Then I went to my mother's."

He nods slowly, taking in everything I've said. Evaluating me. He thought I was a desperate housewife. Deferential to her husband. Nonconfrontational. Unaware. Weak. It is occurring to him that his assessment was off. "Thank you, Beth."

I grab the stroller. I should leave before he realizes all that I am capable of. "Thank you, Tyler, for helping me."

"Be careful."

I press my lips together as if holding back tears. Really, I'm stopping the retort on the tip of my tongue. *I always am.*

# LIZA

The apartment is in disarray when I return. Papers are strewn over the dining room table. Books have been tossed from shelves onto the floor. Clothing—David's from the look of it—is thrown over the living room couch. A thousand pins pierce my lungs. Is he packing? Is he fleeing the country? Is he leaving me?

My voice trembles as I call out my husband's name. He emerges from the master bedroom, face flushed from exertion. The sunlight penetrating the French doors tinges his blue eyes an animalistic yellow.

"What's going on?" I ask.

His nostrils flare. "I'm looking for that note. I have to find it."

The fear that had gripped my body moments before releases. "Are you sure it's even here?"

He flips on the overhead lights and then scans the room with his hands on his hips. The artificial brightness highlights areas of mess. David's expression changes from panic to disgust. He looks at me sheepishly.

"Is it from the court?" I ask. "Can't you get a new one?"

"No. I . . ." His eyes water. He shuts them and presses the heel of his palms into the lids. "I don't know what I'm doing."

My husband is going grief (or guilt) crazy. I love this man. I don't want to know which one. "Hey, I'll help you look, okay? Just tell me what it is we're searching for."

My offer only makes things worse. "No. I got this." He sniffs. "Um, what have you been up to?"

I consider whether or not to tell him. Will learning that his best friend was gay make things worse? Or will he be relieved to know that police are exploring a theory about Nick's death that doesn't involve him?

I choose my words carefully. "My contact at the police academy spoke to the detectives on the case. They're looking into a woman who was following Nick. Apparently, he'd gone to a bar by his apartment before he went missing and some upset lady was asking after him."

David's chin retracts toward his neck, a turtle retreating into his shell. He may not be ready for this revelation.

I take a deep breath. "The bar was a gay bar, babe. I know you probably won't believe this, but the bartender said that Nick went there often on dates—with men. He was homosexual."

David's expression relaxes. He should be shocked. Protesting.

"Wait, did you know already?"

He clears his throat. "He came out last year."

I notice a new tension between my temples, as though a rubbery sinew is being pulled to its breaking point. "And you didn't tell me?"

"Why would I? Nick's sexuality was his private business."

"I tried to set him up with friends." I rub my temples, trying to stop the tugging. "You could have at least mentioned that I was wasting my time and my friends' ti—"

"I always told you not to bother with Christine, but you wouldn't listen."

"But he couldn't have only been gay. Nick had girlfriends. That one with the pixie cut. That mod-looking girl."

David shrugs. "They were friends. Just friends. Coming out was hard for him. He didn't want to be labeled."

"It's not taboo to gay." The rubber band snaps. A jackhammer starts trying to break open my skull from the inside. I stride to the couch, my eyes in slits, and slump down on top of one of David's suit jackets.

"The world isn't New York City, Liza." I can't see David's expression, but I imagine that he looks annoyed from his tone. "You think everyone is accepting because you're a progressive elitist who grew up in the Hamptons, went to an Ivy League university, and then settled in Manhattan. For you, sexual orientation is like hair color, right? Change it every week if you want. No one gives a shit." David releases some of his normally well-covered Texas accent. He's spent so long trying to sound like an Upper Midwest news anchor that I know he must be upset. "Nick was from fucking Mississippi, a pray-the-gay-away state. His parents raised him to think something was fundamentally wrong with homosexuals."

I peek between my fingers to see David scowling at me. "He was thirty-eight and he lived here, though. A stone's throw away from Stonewall. I mean, gay marriage is legal now."

I cradle my aching forehead in my palm and force my head back to look at my husband. He is staring at me like the bartender from earlier. The expression says, *Are you really this stupid?* "The ink on the marriage law is still wet, and there are plenty of people out there who want to erase it. They think being gay is like a psychological dise—"

A knock interrupts. David's head snaps toward the foyer. He is not expecting anyone.

The sound comes again, three short raps and a word that I can't hear over the heartbeat in my head. David walks toward the exit, arms hanging stiff by his thighs. I brace myself for whoever is on the other side of the door.

"Mr. Jacobson, Detective Campos."

I force my knees to straighten and hoist myself from the couch. The detective from yesterday stands in the doorway with a piece of paper in his hands, which he passes to my husband. I squint to see it through my headache haze. There's a government seal on the top.

"I don't consent to this search," I shout.

David shoots a scowling glance over his shoulder. Wasn't that what he wanted me to say? I'm disoriented from the events of the past thirty-six hours and my pounding brain. I'm not sure that I can trust the images in front of me.

Behind Detective Campos are two uniformed cops. They stand in the hallway, thumbs in the pockets of their suit pants, leaning back on their heels as though they have all the time in the world for David to scrutinize the document—as though, no matter what my husband does, they will be coming into our home.

I hover behind David in the doorway, reading the warrant over his shoulder. It doesn't say much. It includes our names and address. A superior court judge whose signature I'd never be able to transcribe has signed the lower half of the document. The officers have permission to search the premises for evidence as well as seize any firearms and locked gun boxes.

The hairs stand up on my limbs like a sudden burst of static. They want my Ruger! But it's not here. I don't know where David put it.

"Everything checks out," Detective Campos says.

David hands back the warrant. He rubs beneath his nose like the men in the hallway have activated an allergy. "May I see the affidavit?"

Campos pats his pockets for show. "It's with the court clerk."

Cops usually don't mock the innocent-until-proven-guilty. I expect David to put Campos in his place with some obscure legal argument. Instead, he motions with his head for me to step back.

I retreat into the living/dining area. The officers follow me inside, their strides wide from the weight of the gear on their hips. Before I can apologize for the mess, Detective Campos is commenting on it from the center of my living room. "What happened here? A bomb went off?"

I look to David, hoping he has an excuse ready. His head hangs like a chastised puppy. This is not the right time for him to fall apart. I can barely see at the moment. "Excuse the mess." I pull my hand away from my temples and feign an embarrassed smile. "We are in the midst our annual preautumn purge. Time to put the summer suits in storage to make way for fall and winter gear. You know small New York apartments. It's impossible to fit everything."

Under the circumstances, I'm amazed by the ease with which the falsehoods roll off my tongue. Though I guess I shouldn't be. Creating believable fiction is my craft. I'm dedicated to it.

"The gun lockbox is in the bedroom closet." David points down the hallway. Either he is pretending that he didn't take the Ruger to hide his involvement in Nick's murder, or he's forgotten bringing it to his office amid the stress of the past twenty-four hours.

One of the uniforms follows my husband back into our bedroom. I slump against the living room wall feeling as powerless as a chained dog. In moments, they will all realize the gun is missing. What will I say?

*I buried it.* Beth's voice shouts over the pounding in my skull, like a rock singer screaming over drums. I press my fingers into my temples to silence her. My character hid her gun in a hole. My Ruger must be in David's desk drawer (providing he didn't toss it in the East River along with Nick's body).

I cannot cast aspersions on my husband. When they ask, I'll tell the officers that I must have misplaced it. Sergeant Perez thinks he saw me at the police academy range recently. I can say that I took it there to practice and may have left it in a locker.

196

Detective Campos circles the living room, taking mental inventory of our furnishings and the items scattered on the hardwood floor. He walks into the kitchen. I hear a cabinet open. The thought of this stranger rifling through my belongings makes me panicky. Quickly, I return to the foyer, where I have a direct view into our galley kitchen. What could he possibly be looking for?

*He wants to see if you have champagne tastes on a beer budget.* Beth answers in the matter-of-fact way that I imagine her using when talking to other reporters. *Financial problems could give David a reason to, say, get rid of a law partner who'd discovered that he was spending clients' investigation budgets on his housewares.* I push her suggested motive from my head. David was not a spendthrift.

*Show the detective he isn't bothering you*, Beth counsels. *You have nothing to hide, right?* I've created a character that would be far more adept in this situation than I am. I need to think like her.

"Would you like a glass of water?"

"No. Thank you." Detective Campos peers around the half wall separating the kitchen from the living/dining area. He looks toward the hallway leading to the bedroom. Not seeing anyone coming, he crouches and opens the double doors beneath the kitchen sink. His lackadaisical search must be meant to make me squirm. Surely he doesn't think I store jewelry behind the dishwashing detergent.

The detective opens the cupboard to the right of the sink. It contains a fancy dining set gifted at our wedding. The pressure in my head builds.

Beth suggests that I make him laugh. An innocent person would want the police to rule out her and her husband as soon as possible so that they could get to the real investigation. She wouldn't be on the defensive.

"We should have never put those fancy plates in there on the wedding registry." I force a chuckle. "I guess everyone does that when they get married right out of college. They ask for all these things they think grown-ups should have: champagne flutes, pretty cheese boards, serving bowls. Then they realize that stuff only comes out at Thanksgiving and Christmas, and it's taking up half the kitchen."

Detective Campos snorts. It's not a guffaw, but it's better than nothing. He closes the open cabinets and goes for one above the range. "You give any more thought to my recommendation of getting your own lawyer?"

My back stiffens. The detective would like nothing better than for me to get an attorney and relinquish spousal privilege, to spill my marital secrets. But I won't. David is *my husband*. He proposed by a driftwood fire in the freezing cold because my best friend told him that I'd always wanted to see the Montauk lighthouse at night. He told my mother over and over how beautiful she was when the chemo had made her bald and bloated and she couldn't stomach her own reflection. He held me when she'd died. He supported my failing writing career, paying all the bills while I penned novel after novel that barely moved the financial needle. Someday, I pray, he'll be the father of my child. Whatever David did to Nick, I will not turn on him.

"David would never hurt Nick." I say it with as much conviction as I've ever said anything in my life. "He loved him like a brother. So while I appreciate you trying to figure out who did this, being here is a waste of time."

"You write crime novels?" Campos's head is behind a cabinet door. His voice rises at the end, though, so I can tell he's asking a question.

"Romantic suspense."

He's rummaging through my cheese boards and serving platters. Wood is knocking against ceramic. He'd better not chip any of my good bowls. "But you went to the police academy writer's workshop, right? So you know how warrants work."

Clearly, my sergeant friend has shared details about me with the detective. But why? To explain how he knew me? Idle conversation?

My stomach twists. Maybe there'd never been a woman asking about Nick at that bar. Perhaps the sergeant fed me that information to see how I would react.

But that would mean I was the suspect. Not David.

*Run.* The command comes in Beth's voice. *Get what you need and get out of here.* It was what I was going to have her do in the next chapter.

"I'll spell it out." The detective speaks while slowly removing and examining each knife from the wooden cutlery block on the adjacent counter. "To get a warrant for your gun, I have to prove to a judge that there's probable cause that the firearm was used in the commission of a crime. So the fact that we're here means that both I and a judge believe this search is *probably not* a waste of time."

The detective's sarcasm leaves little doubt that I am on the potential perpetrator list. Beth is repeating that I must leave. *Run.* But walking out the front door in the midst of a police investigation would only lend credence to Officer Campos's ridiculous suspicions. I didn't have any reason to hurt Nick. He resented me for taking away his best friend, and I disliked being resented. So what? That's something to complain to my girlfriends about. It's not a motive for murder.

Though I can't flee the apartment, I don't have to stay in front of the detective as he tries to push my buttons either. I leave the room for the living area. The air suddenly feels jungled. The headache is giving me a hot flash—or maybe it's the hormones. I fling open the French doors and step onto the Juliet balcony. The sun has nearly set, leaving an eggplant sky in its wake and a string of brake lights below. It's cooler out here. I can smell water. I place my hands on the railing and look east, toward the river.

My head swims. I jump back toward the safety of the open patio door, afraid that I could tumble to the street below. Once in the doorway, I put my hands on my knees and take in air in short gasps.

The scare works like electrodes, shocking away the rest of my migraine. My breathing normalizes and the pressure in my head begins to drain. Before it's fully gone, I hear one of the officers call me. "Ma'am, would you come back inside?"

"I have a headache. Fresh air helps me feel better."

"We'd appreciate if you were inside while we search." I look over my shoulder to see a younger officer with a pale-blond buzz cut, a grimace twisting his small mouth. He steps toward me, arms out, hands open in an imploring fashion. "Please."

Reluctantly, I retreat into the living area. Heavy footsteps sound in the hallway. David enters the room, followed by one of the uniformed officers. The glow from the balcony doors makes his skin look jaundiced. His eyes appear glazed with confusion.

"Liza, the lockbox is empty. The officers tore apart the closet and couldn't find your gun."

Years of criminal defense keep David from stating anything more than the facts. He doesn't ask me whether I know the location of the weapon because he knows that my suggestions will provide grounds for another search warrant. Still, his eyes seem to beg me for an answer. Does he really not remember taking it?

"Do you know where your gun is, Ms. Cole?" Detective Campos emerges from the kitchen. He is no longer hiding his distrust.

I snap my fingers as though a thought has only now occurred to me. "I used it recently at the police academy range. Sergeant Perez has let me in a few times to practice when I'm working on scenes with guns. I'm sorry for not saying so earlier. I forgot.

I'm on fertility hormones, and they mimic the first trimester of pregnancy. I've got mommy brain without the baby."

The detective gives me a wan smile.

"There are lockers at the academy where I could have left it."

"Anyplace else?" Though the detective asks, I can see from David's face that he fears what I might say.

I look at my husband, signaling with my sustained eye contact that I won't help the cops get to him. "That's all I can think of now. Again, I'm sorry for misplacing it. These hormones would make me lose my head if it weren't attached to my body. But I'll look around for it, definitely."

"And we'll continue to look here." I swear I catch the detective scrunch his nose so that he nearly winks at me. David seems to notice too. Something changes in his eyes.

*Get out. Get your things and go.* It might be that the migraine is over, but Beth's voice sounds stronger. My purse is in the foyer with my laptop inside. I walk over to it and slip my arm into the handles.

"I have an editorial meeting that I really need to get to," I say. It's a lie, but a plausible one. Better than saying that I need to get back to writing. A chapter can always be put off for a few hours. Editorial meetings, on the other hand, are on Trevor's schedule and involve multiple people. I can't change them as I see fit. David knows this.

I grab the door handle and tell David that I will call him later. Detective Campos asks me to wait a minute and approaches the exit. He removes a pencil from a belt pouch and uses it to press back the lining of my shoulder bag so that he can peer inside. Satisfied that all I have is my computer, he tells me that I am "free to leave."

I am sure that this last act was to antagonize me for David's benefit. My spouse stares at me, jaw open, dumbfounded that the police could think I had something to do with Nick's death.

"You're really not going to find anything," I say, directing my words at David. "No one here had any reason to hurt Nick."

The detective smiles, a cat-got-the-canary grin. "You might be surprised."

The streetlamps are coming on as I exit the building. It's doubtful that many people will be in my publishing house at 7:00 PM on a Monday, but I decide to head there anyway. The police could be following me. If I'm pulled into an interrogation room in the next week, I want to be able to claim that I had mixed up a meeting time and was surprised to find my editor gone for the evening.

I take a cab downtown to the Park Avenue building. There are officers on nearly every street corner, but no one seems to take an interest in me. A good detective wouldn't be obvious, though.

I pull back the building's heavy front door and walk through a shiny lobby to a security guard manning three turnstiles. I hand over my driver's license, providing a record of my appearance, and then head to the elevator bank. As I approach my publisher's offices, I hear the distinct whirr of a vacuum cleaner. If the cleaning staff is already here, there's no way people are still working. I debate whether or not to hang around for an hour until my tail—if one exists—tires of me. Then I see Trevor.

He notices me as soon as he exits the glass office doors. "Liza?" He tilts his head as though I may be an apparition. Maybe editors, like writers, also suffer from thin realities.

"Hey, Trev. I am sorry to show up like this. Um . . ." Tears suddenly fill my eyes. I look at the tiled ceiling and blink rapid fire, shooing them with my lashes. "The police found Nick's body. They are searching our home. I think, maybe . . ." My throat closes up. I can't say that the officers suspect me. How would I even begin to explain that?

I feel the weight of Trevor's hand on my shoulder. He gives it a squeeze and shakes his head, as though disappointed. "They suspect David?"

The fact that he has zeroed in on David calms me. Maybe I am imagining Detective Campos's attitude. Any suspicion of me is insane, after all. I didn't want Nick dead. I expel the tears with a long exhale. "Thriller editors." I sniff. "Always trying to guess the plot."

He doesn't smile. "Come with me to dinner."

I'd like nothing more than to go out with a friend at the moment. But dinner might give anyone following me the wrong impression. "I'm not that hungry. The idea of strange men going through my drawers has kind of sapped my appetite at the moment."

"Drinks?"

Heading to a bar with Trevor will look worse than going out to dinner. "Coffee?" I suggest. The hour is wrong for it, but editors and writers can always use more caffeine.

"I know a quiet local place."

I follow him an avenue over to a ritzy espresso bar. It's the kind of shop with decorative bookshelves stocked with European literature and unabridged Shakespeare collections, a place where people hang out to seem well-read and artsy whether or not they actually are. The inside is nearly vacant despite half a dozen leather booths and a long zinc bar set with stools on each side. I'm shocked more people aren't hunched over laptops. Writers love to "work on their novels" in places like this. Makes us seem legit.

When I see the menu on the chalkboard above the bar, I understand the emptiness. A fifteen-dollar latte is too expensive for anyone without a slew of bestsellers. I gesture to the chalkboard with the artisanal bean selections and outlandish prices. "Let me guess: all organic beans picked by Buddhist monk–trained monkeys." The joke isn't great, but it's all I have. Humor is the only lid against the well of tears in my chest. I don't want to cry in front of my colleague any more than I already have.

Trevor cracks a smile. "My treat."

I order a black coffee on the principle of not paying triple the Starbucks price for something with milk in it. Trevor orders an Earl Grey tea because he's unafraid of being a walking British stereotype. We slide into a booth and comment on what Manhattan eateries charge while waiting for the waitress to bring us our bland beverages. I, for one, don't want to be in the middle of saying "murder" when the barista shows up.

My drink arrives too hot. Though I'd like an excuse for silence, I can't sip this without burning off my lips. Instead, I hold the bowl-sized mug at chin level and blow onto the steam. It smells bitter.

Trevor pushes his tea to the side and leans his elbows on the table. "Are you concerned about this investigation?"

"I'm sure it's all routine." I try to steady my voice as I say this. I am positive it is anything but routine.

"What are they looking for?"

"My gun."

Trevor blanches.

"I'm not sure where I left it last," I say, pretending that my absentmindedness, not David's forgetfulness (or willful deceit), is the reason it is missing. "It wasn't in the lockbox in the house. I might have left it at a gun range that has lockers . . ." I put down my mug and gesture to my head. "These fertility hormones I've been on—I might have mentioned that I'm taking new ones— they've made the past month a bit hazy."

"Did David have access to your gun?"

"He has access to everything. We've been together twelve years. He knows all my combinations. He has my e-mail password."

Trevor raises his eyebrows as though I've just confessed to posting my social security number on an unsecured web page.

"If I didn't tell him them, I'd probably forget."

Trevor nods, shaking the instant camera film in his brain. I don't like the picture he's forming. I want him thinking that David is innocent—as he very well might be.

I set my nearly full coffee on the table. Hot liquid splashes over the side and onto the back of my hand. Instinctively, I jam the scalded skin in my mouth. Trevor watches, eyes crinkling with concern as though the accident is evidence of a fragile emotional state.

I drop my hand on the table. "David had no reason to want to hurt Nick. He was his best friend and law partner." My voice is a pleading whine. I am imploring Trevor to agree with my argument and help convince me of it. "With him gone, David is drowning under the weight of all the work. He's afraid the firm could go under."

A splotch spreads between my thumb and pinky. It throbs with my heartbeat. Ice would be great. I wonder how much a place like this charges for it. I shake my hand, trying to cool it in the air conditioning while I attempt a casual tone. "The cops hassling us makes no sense. I talked to a sergeant from that writers' academy I went to last year, and he thinks a woman spurned by Nick might have killed him. Apparently, Nick was gay. Can you believe it?"

Trevor reaches across the table and lifts my injured hand. He stares at the red spot, his thumb resting on my knuckles. Though he's probably evaluating the severity of my burn, the gesture feels intimate. Longing empties out my insides. I miss affection. Since Nick's disappearance, David has been so prickly. Since before Nick's disappearance, if I'm honest with myself.

"I need to tell you something." Trevor keeps his head down as he looks up at me. The result is a sad puppy stare that makes me nervous. "I probably should have said something before."

My breathing quickens. Trevor has never before "needed" to tell me something. Snapshots of our friendship scroll through my mind. Has it meant more than that to Trevor? To me?

"Remember the launch party for *Accused Woman*? The one at the Thrill and Chills Book Store a few months ago?"

This is not what I thought he was going to say. I flash back to an image of me in a plastic chair with an unnecessarily tall stack of books on the table, trying to put on a brave face for the disappointingly small crowd. I nod my answer. The more time I spend with Trevor, the more I communicate like him.

"David and Nick showed up right as you were doing the reading."

Again, I nod for him to continue. I don't remember this. Though I do recall David saying he had to work late and barely showing. He'd been a few months into the teen suicide case.

"On my way over to the bookstore, I saw them walking down the street."

My neck tenses. I feel the familiar twisting in my temples. "Yes?"

"I'm pretty sure . . . I think . . ." He looks at me, a defense attorney about to tell a wrongfully convicted client that her appeal has been rejected. "I saw them kissing."

A bomb goes off between my ears. An immense pressure fills my head, like my brain is being squeezed in a vice. It's followed by a high-pitched ring, as though I've developed sudden tinnitus. Trevor is still talking, but I only know because his mouth is moving. I read his full lips.

"I'm sorry."

"What?" I know what he's said, but can think of no other response.

"I'm sorry." His voice returns full blast, as though he'd turned the volume dial to the max, unaware that the sound had been on mute. I fight the desire to put my hands over my ears. "I should have told you sooner. Sometimes people have arrangements, and I didn't want to embarrass you in case you had an agreement." He clears his throat. "But if you only just found out about Nick . . ."

"David's not gay." My voice is too loud. The lights in the coffee shop are blinding. Where's the exit?

"Well, I suppose it's a sliding-scale kind of a thing for some people."

"You must be mistaken." I realize that Trevor is still holding my hand. I yank it to my chest. "Maybe they were talking close."

"Liza, I'm pretty certain of what I saw."

"No." I stand. "We're trying for a baby."

Trevor rises. "I know. That's why I thought you should be aware of it. If Nick was planning to reveal their relationship and ruin your marriage, maybe David did something to keep him quiet?"

My breaths have become short and raspy. I could be sick, right here on the shiny, stained cement floor of this chichi coffee shop. The bitter smell wafting from my cup is suddenly retch-inducing. I have to go. Now. "Thanks for the drink."

"Liza. I'm worried for—"

"You've read too many suspense novels, Trev," I say while backing up to the exit. "David's my husband. He's not gay. And he's not a killer."

# Chapter 15

I DO NOT EXPECT TO see Jake in the living room. Yet when I walk through our apartment door, there he is, sitting on the couch with his head bowed against his folded hands. Is he saying a prayer for Colleen? Pleading for himself? Asking God to spare me from discovering his actions?

When I enter, he jumps from the couch. His eyes are rimmed with red. "Beth." He says my name in a breathless fashion. "Can we talk?"

A vindictive voice in my head is dying to repeat, verbatim, his argument to me the prior night: *I can't rearrange my schedule on such short notice. I'll make it up to you soon. We'll go out someplace nice. In the meantime, you should get some rest. I mean, Vicky doesn't let you really sleep. Think of it: without her and me bothering you, you can get a good eight hours for once.* Saying any of this, though, would tip my hand. Such snark wouldn't be warranted for what I'm supposed to believe: Jake cancelled on me last night because of a difficult case. His dinner with a female colleague was a working meeting.

I push Vicky into the room. She stirs in her bassinet as we enter, disturbed by the tense energy in the apartment. I pick her up and hold her to my chest.

"Can you sit down?"

I feign concern as I sink into the couch. Inside, I am dancing a hula to a female empowerment song. Jake is going to admit to the affair! His confession will be a permission slip to do what I please. I'll be able to kick him out without raising any suspicion about my prior knowledge of his indiscretions. He's giving me a get-out-of-jail-free card.

I chew my bottom lip as I carefully pull aside the V neck of my dress and place Victoria on my exposed breast. Biting the dead skin from my lips is one of those unconscious acts that I perform when really worked up. Jake should see my telltale signs of stress.

"I need to tell you something."

*Get on with it.* I swallow the words. "Honey, you're scaring me. What's wrong?"

"The woman the police came about wasn't just a coworker." His face reddens as though he's constipated, straining over the toilet. "I slept with her."

I admire his tense choice. *I slept with her.* Not *I was sleeping with her,* which would indicate that he'd been screwing her up until the time of her apparent death. His phrasing could mean once a long time ago or a thousand times up until the moment she moaned her last. He's leaving me to guess.

"Are you saying you had an . . ." I trail off as though it's too difficult for me to verbalize the word "affair." A couple of weeks ago, it had been.

"I'm sorry, baby." A tear snakes down his cheek. He leaves it there for me to see, a glistening reminder that he is broken up about his betrayal—now that he has been forced to admit it. "I made a mistake. I was working with her. She came on to me."

It is not enough for Jake to confess wrongdoing. A true lawyer, he has to outline the mitigating factors. Sure, he's to blame. But there's plenty of fault to go around. His affair is the result of the butterfly effect. If pretty women didn't exist . . . If his mother had not been so permissive during his childhood . . . If he hadn't been living in New York City, with its nonstop nightlife . . .

"And you'd been spending so much time with the baby."

Oh, it's my fault too. Of course. And let's not forget to blame our infant.

"I was feeling vulnerable and neglected. We hadn't been together since your last trimester, and then there were the rules about no sex the first month and a half after delivery."

He looks at me for sympathy, or at least to see whether I am buying any of his excuses. I continue nursing Vicky, relishing the visual of me as the consummate caretaker. The better parent. The better person, for all Jake knows.

"I was weak and I'm so sorry." He reaches for the hand not holding our baby. I tuck it around Victoria, blocking his view of her little head. His arms retreat to his side. "I want you to know that it wasn't serious. I didn't love her or anything like that. I'd planned on ending it before she disappeared. And I had nothing, *nothing*, to do with whatever happened to her. I saw her the night she went missing, but I came home to you. Something must have happened afterward. I swear. I have no idea what went on. I came home to see you."

I open my mouth as though crying on mute.

Another stage tear announces itself. "I am so sorry," he sobs.

*Not as sorry as you're going to be.* I look away so he can't see me *not* cry. After a minute or two, I sniff and return my attention to his guilty face. "Do the police think you were involved?"

There's a change in his body language. His posture straightens. Chin lifts. I've witnessed this shift before. Exit Jake, the husband. Enter ADA Jacobson, the prosecutor. He clears his throat. "The police are necessarily looking into the timeline of her disappearance, and I'm the last one known to have seen her. But they'll discover that I didn't do anything once they figure out when the blood was spilled outside her apartment. People must have seen me come home. Our building has security cameras that would pick me up. I bought a metro card on the way back with my Visa, so there will be evidence of that transaction. They won't be able to suspect me for long."

I don't know how to feel about his CCTV alibi. Part of me wants him to continue sweating it out. Another part of me wants the police looking as far away from Jake and me as possible. "Could you have said something that might have made her hurt herself? Maybe she was distraught. Maybe you said you were going to break things off . . . ?"

Jake's jaw drops. "Um . . . I was . . . she . . ." How to explain that he never said anything about leaving his lover. "Colleen wasn't the type," he says finally. "My guess is that she stumbled upon a crime of some sort. She lived in an old factory, illegally converted to condos. They don't run background checks in places like that. Maybe one of her neighbors was dealing drugs or was high. She pulled her badge, and he went ballistic." His eyes start to water. "Whatever happened to her, she didn't deserve it." The prosecutor's voice crumbles. He snorts, sucking up mucus into his septum. "She was a good person."

Rage at his defense of the woman who lured him away from his pregnant wife runs through me like an electric current. Robotically, I separate Vicky from my breast and place her back in the bassinet. She starts fussing at being separated from me. I crouch down and pull out a baby mobile from the stroller basket, clipping it to her sunshade. Animals, outfitted in circus gear, dangle above her head. I flick a switch on a side of the plastic and fabric contraption.

"Pop! Goes the Weasel" plays through a hidden speaker. In addition to piano, this version has a string interlude followed by little kids singing nonsense lyrics. The sounds entertain our child. She stares at the animals, content with the music and visual stimulation.

I turn to face Jake's hunched form. His head is lowered like a chastised child. Seeing him this way makes me want to punch a wall. He doesn't get to be the sad and sympathetic one right now, not after what he drove me to do. I can't look at him. I can't stay with him.

*All around the mulberry bush . . .*

"I need you to go to a hotel."

*The monkey chased the weasel . . .*

"Baby." Jake starts to rise from the couch.

*The monkey thought 'twas all in good sport.*

211

"Vicky and I will leave for a bit, give you time to get your things."
*Pop! goes the weasel.*
"Where are you going? To your mother's?"

I don't want to see my mom. She will tell me to forgive my husband because I also had an affair. I won't be able to explain that I only betrayed Jake after discovering him with another woman without risking her telling police. What I need to do is take a walk with my baby and dispose of the plastic thongs cutting into my feet.

"It doesn't matter where I go. You lost your right to that information when you started lying to me. We will be back in a few hours. I expect you not to be here."

"But—"

"You don't get to negotiate right now. This is what needs to happen."

The kids on the recording laugh and giggle while the piano plays. Vicky starts to coo. She loves this part. I push the stroller toward the exit and open the hall closet. My sneakers sit at the bottom beside Jake's loafers. I pull off the flip-flops and shove them into the stroller basket. The tops of my feet are chafed and blistered from the rough straps. Slipping on sneakers is painful.

As I'm tying my laces, I hear Jake rise from the couch. I shut the closet door and see my husband, his shoulders rounded like a man headed for the stocks. The kids' recorded squeals morph back into music.

*I've no time to plead and pine . . .*
I bristle as he draws near but then move aside for him to kiss Vicky.
*I've no time to wheedle . . .*
He casts me a longing look as I take the stroller handle.
*Kiss me quick and then I'm gone.*
I push the carriage out the door. The lock clicks behind me.
*Pop! goes the weasel.*

# Part III

Elizabeth, Elspeth, Betsy, and Bess,
They all went together to seek a bird's nest.
They found a bird's nest with five eggs in,
They all took one and left four in.

—English Nursery Rhyme

# LIZA

I burst through my apartment door, not caring if I surprise the officers tearing apart my house. Migraine medication is no longer an option. The pain is so intense that I could go raving mad. My mind is trying to escape the pressure by separating me from my physical being. I feel as though I am having an out-of-body experience. I'm watching myself fumble with the keys and wince beneath the blaring hallway lights. This is happening to somebody else.

The foyer is empty. I rush through to the bathroom, yank open my pill drawer, and find my emergency sumatriptan syringe. This will stop it: the blinding, heart-wrenching, screaming pain.

I barely have the strength to shake the pen from the box and insert the cartridge. I yank my pants to my knees and jam the needle against my exposed thigh. There's a pinch and the promise of relief. I remove the pen and then fall onto the closed toilet seat. I concentrate on my breathing. Nothing else. In. Out. In . . . Out . . . When I'm no longer nearly hyperventilating, I turn on the faucet, cup my hands beneath the stream, and drink fistful after fistful. Finally, I strip down and stumble into my bedroom.

It's in shambles. The bedding has been pulled to the floor. Clothing, mostly David's, but some of my things too, has been tossed onto the mattress. Drawers are open. I can't handle this sight right now.

With my eyes half closed, I feel my way to the bare Tempur-Pedic. I fall on top of it and curl into fetal position. One by one, my systems shut down like an overheating computer force quitting processes. I can't walk. I can't move. I need sleep.

\*

I wake to a yellow orb outside the window. Somehow, I've slept ten hours. Maybe more. I roll over and look to the digital clock on the nightstand: 7:00 AM. Slowly, I pull myself upright. Where is David? Did he come home last night?

I roll my legs off the mattress and survey the damage. Clothes are scattered on the floor. The closet doors are half open. From the bed, I can see that the lockbox has been taken from the top shelf. The removal of something I own from my house is as violating as someone pulling down my underwear in public and slapping my bare behind. What have I done to deserve this? A ransacked apartment. Broken uterus. Gay husband.

I look at my hand. My diamond engagement ring shines beside my wedding band. David proposed on my favorite beach. He married me. He suggested that I start fertility hormones. Why would he have a child with me if he was homosexual?

*Because he felt bad for you.* The answer comes in Beth's voice. For once, she's not being hypersexual, overly emotional, or cursing like a drunken soccer fan. Her tone is almost sad, as though I've learned a secret that she already knew. David understood that I wanted a baby more than anything in this world. At first, he'd hemmed and hawed about getting me pregnant because he'd known that he was attracted to men and, deep down, must have realized our relationship wouldn't last. But he also knew that to leave me, at my age, with my history of fertility issues, would guarantee my childless future. So he stuck it out—even after starting an affair with the man he really loved—in hopes of giving us a parting gift. But then, none of the standard fertility treatments worked, and David realized that having a child with me could take years, if it happened at all. He couldn't ask Nick to wait forever.

The suicide case would have brought Nick and David together romantically for the first time. Probably, it pushed both men to face their feelings, prompting long conversations about their childhoods in Mississippi and Texas, being bullied and belittled for what they felt. They would have opened up to one another. Admitted their mutual attraction. Fallen in love.

A tear tumbles down my face, a mosquito bite at dusk. Many more are to come. Trevor saw David and Nick kissing not because he needs glasses and stumbled upon two similar looking men, but because *kissing* was what my husband had been doing with his male law partner before my big book launch. David intended to leave me for Nick. His choice explains the year of detachment and dismissiveness, which I mistakenly attributed to his frustration with my fertility issues. He was pushing me away, hoping that I'd end things myself and spare him the apologies.

I sit on David's side of the stripped bed, too weak to rise. Why would David kill Nick, though? He wouldn't have murdered the man that he loved simply to prevent me from finding out about their affair. He was willing to leave me. I would have learned of his relationship with Nick eventually.

The realization sneaks up on me, a robber with a knife to my throat. All of a sudden I can't move. Can't swallow. Can't breathe.

Nick was stealing my husband. I had the motive.

Oddities for which I've invented excuses flash in my mind. I see David's confusion after the police couldn't find my gun followed by Sergeant Perez's satisfaction as he insisted that I'd become a good shot. David really hadn't appeared to know the location of my Ruger, and he isn't an actor. Perez had been so sure that he'd seen me at the academy, and he's trained to differentiate between similar people. What if I *had* taken my gun? What if I *did* go to the range? What if I suspected the affair and took protection into Nick's rough neighborhood to stake out his apartment and catch David in the act?

But why wouldn't I remember?

I writhe on the mattress as the answer rips through my brain. The hormones! Dr. Frankel warned me that they could cause memory loss. And they're still in the experimental stage. What other side effects might they have that she doesn't even know about?

I bring my forearm to my face. My throbbing vision makes the white lines sink deeper into my epidermis. I'd been willing to sacrifice anything—even my sanity—for a baby. But I'd never imagined the drugs could make me a murderer.

*

I call the fertility clinic from the cab. The secretary tries to push me off until my next appointment. "I need them out now," I yell. "You don't understand. I have to be seen now. I've got to remember. I have to know."

Panic prevents me from controlling my volume in the vehicle's small interior. The driver checks the rearview mirror to monitor me, as though he fears I could start ripping apart the plastic seats or throw open the door and run before paying the fare. I hear the child locks click.

"Okay, Ms. Cole. Please calm down. We will fit you in right away."

A nurse is waiting for me at the clinic door. She rushes me through reception into a private room as though my hysteria is contagious, capable of infecting the developing fetuses swelling in all the successful trial subjects waiting for Dr. Frankel's glowing smile. The needles burn beneath the skin. I claw at my bicep, turning those faint raised lines into raw red tracks. The nurse keeps her distance as she tells me to sit on the examination chair and wait for the doctor. She sounds like a dog trainer.

I'm not to disrobe. I keep on the denim shirt dress that I threw on before racing out of my apartment. I take off my purse and place it beside me.

Clothed, I can appreciate the room in a way that I never could while shivering in a paper gown atop wax paper, bracing for a probe. I smell urine masked with lemon-scented disinfectant. The sonogram cart appears ancient. Its monitor is scuffed black around the edges. The urine collection cups have a gray film of dust outside. A hair clip lies on the counter, dark strands clinging to a knot inside it. Did the staff not have time to get the room ready for me, or has it always been this way? Did my hope for the treatment make me view this place as a state-of-the-art medical center when it was really a dirty lab with human rats?

Dr. Frankel's smile is even more strained than usual when she enters. My chart is already under her arm, and a laptop is balanced on her left palm. Instead of inquiring how I am doing, she asks, "What seems to be the problem?"

"It's the forgetting," I say, still scratching at the injection site like a cocaine addict. "I am doing things that I can't remember. I need these needles out. I need you to take them out today."

She rolls her stool from beneath a desk and sits down, placing the laptop on her thighs. "What, specifically, have you forgotten?"

Frustrated tears fill my eyes. How can I explain this? Saying that I killed my husband's gay lover and forgot doing it sounds insane. She might have me committed rather than remove the implants.

She stares at me from above her monitor. Waiting.

"The other day, a friend said he saw me at a gun range. I can't remember going in the past year."

Computer keys clatter. "Maybe he was mistaken? Did he talk to you at the range?"

My throat tightens. I shake my head.

"Did you check if you had signed in there, or did anyone else see you there?"

I have to come up with something that has proof. My gun is not in the apartment. That's a demonstrable fact. "I can't find my handgun either. I'm always very careful with it. I keep it in a lockbox on a high shelf in my closet. But it's not there."

"So you think that you misplaced it?" Dr. Frankel's mouth rests in the same sympathetic pose as always, but I detect a spark of amusement in her eyes. She thinks I am freaking out over a general distractedness—the kind that anyone might experience when also battling headaches and low-grade nausea, working on a tight deadline, and juggling fertility clinic visits.

"You don't understand. I have no idea where it is. None at all."

"Hormones do impact memory, and I can understand it being disconcerting. When I was pregnant, I'd have my keys in my hand one minute and wouldn't remember for the life of me where I put them the next. I thought I was going nuts. My husband thought I was bonkers."

She smiles. I want to slap that practiced empathy off her face. I want to shake her until she understands that I am not talking about keys or leaving out a carton of milk or misremembering where I left the car in the mall parking lot.

"I'm not talking about little things." My voice rises in pitch and trembles, an opera singer sustaining a shrill high note. "I'd *never* leave a gun lying around."

"Maybe you hid it in a new spot that you thought was safer, and then it slipped your mind."

I want to scream. "It's not only the gun. I've learned things— important facts about people that I care about—that I can't remember knowing at all. I may have done things—life-changing things—that I can't remember doing. I'm not forgetting details; I'm forgetting days."

Dr. Frankel's curls shake as her head turns from side to side. She shuts her laptop with a decisive clap. "Hormones impact short-term memory, Liza. Small things. Forgetting major events or a day's worth of activities are not side effects that could be caused by any hormonal imbalance from this medication. What you're talking about would be evidence of a psychotic break or brain trauma from an accident." Her eyes narrow. "Or excessive alcohol consumption."

Dr. Frankel's arched eyebrows raise. "Have you been drinking on this medication?"

"Not really."

She looks disbelieving. In her mind, my rushing here in a frantic state is probably a classic symptom of substance abuse. I run a mental tally of the alcoholic beverages that I've consumed in the past week: a few glasses of wine with Christine, a half bottle on the plane with Trevor, a cocktail the Sunday evening of the conference. Health questionnaires put five or more drinks per week as the highest answer on the multiple choice asking how often you imbibe. Circling it is a sign of a problem.

"I had a writers' conference recently that involved a bit more wine than is usual for me. But the forgetting was happening before."

My doctor's brow furrows. "You never mentioned memory loss as a problem before."

"I didn't realize that I was losing time until recently." The words fight their way from my closing throat. "But some of the things that I've forgotten happened more than a month ago. I'm only now realizing that I might have done them, that I could have done them."

Tears spill from my lower lid. "Please." My voice breaks. "I need the hormones out."

Dr. Frankel frowns at me for the first time ever—that I can remember. She stands and walks over to me. "Lay back."

I do as I'm told. A small penlight shines in her palm. She instructs me to open my eyes wide. Her face hovers above mine as she flashes the beam in my pupils. "You're retinas are responsive," she says, waving her fingers for me to sit back up.

"What does that mean?"

"Nothing seems wrong with your brain." She resumes her seat on the rolling stool. "I can schedule a CAT scan if you'd feel better about it."

"Please just remove the needles. The hormones have to be causing this." Tears overwhelm my words. "I just . . . I need to know what I've done. I can't function. I—"

"Liza." Dr. Frankel says my name like a slap. "You need this study to help you get pregnant, and it needs your results. What we learn from this drug—how it shrinks uterine scar tissue and aids implantation—promises not only to help you carry a healthy baby to term but also to help other women suffering like you to conceive in the future. Dropping out now would compromise the study results. It might keep the drug from getting to market."

Shame increases my tears. "I'm sorry. But you don't understand what . . . I may have . . ." My confession burns in my throat. I swallow it.

Her expression softens. She squeezes my hand. "I promise you, Liza. This medication is *not* making you forget major actions. If you did something momentous, you'd remember it. What it may be doing is causing you to jump to some irrational conclusions, particularly if you've been drinking on it and under a lot of stress."

I want to believe her. "Are you sure?"

"Yes. These drugs could never cause the kind of memory lapses that you're describing. I know we call them experimental, but they're really a combination of the same hormones in many other fertility drugs. The experimental part is more the delivery system than anything else." She fixes me with her round brown eyes. I see my desperate reflection in her pupils. "I know how much you want to have a baby, but I would never put you or any of my other patients on drugs that could cause psychological damage, even to bring a new life into the world. At the end of the day, you're my patient. I'm here to take care of you."

My clenched muscles start to relax. Maybe this is all a misunderstanding based on my hormone-hyped emotional state and a single shred of forgotten behavior. Maybe, knowing that I would be in the Hamptons alone, I took along my gun. Then, after drinking myself sick with Christine, I forgot doing it. Maybe, as David said, we are being investigated simply because he was Nick's business partner and the police know conflicts can arise from such close relationships. Maybe David is only a touch bisexual and he was experimenting with Nick but not planning to leave me.

*Maybe you already know the truth*, Beth says.

The emotion in my doctor's face seems sincere. She wants what is best for me, and what is best for me is to forget all about a Nick and have a baby. I nod and tell her that she's right. I am acting nutty. Paranoid. I will stay on the drugs. I want a child. These implants are my best chance.

"Okay." She releases my hand. "So I'll see you next week. We will stay on top of how the hormones are impacting you emotionally, and you'll call me if you start getting overwhelmed or feel out of control or—"

My purse buzzes. I offer an apologetic smile as I grab the phone inside. I don't recognize the number on the screen, but I answer anyway. For all I know, it's the police.

"Elizabeth, I've been . . ." It's David. He sounds as though he's been bawling. My stomach twists into a knot. I know what's coming. "I've been arrested and arraigned. I need you to bring bail."

# Chapter 16

THE PARK IS OVERCROWDED. GYM towels and picnic blankets cover the grass, transforming the fenced lawn outside my building into a patchwork quilt held together with green stitching. Atop every fabric surface is a sunbather in some stage of undress. I spy a group of co-eds, no doubt escaping from Greenwich Village's paved common spaces. They wear triangle bikini tops and flaunt their prebirth bellies in the direction of a nearby volleyball court. These are the kind of girls that men like my husband salivate over. The Jakes of the world stalk such women with their wolfish grins. They separate them from their female herds with strategic flattery. *You're the prettiest. You're the smartest. You're so much more desirable than your friends.* They scatter promises of adoration and fidelity at their feet, breadcrumbs leading back to their lairs. Then, when the young women are lost, permanently disoriented from seeing themselves and their surroundings through a male gaze, the Jakes return to hunting.

I wish to warn them not to be the lamb I was, a twentysomething transplant to the city starving for affection, thinking a husband and a baby would fill the spaces inside me. *Do not* court the hungry stares of the volleyball players across the way and instead toast your youth with your plastic cups of blush wine. Discover yourself before you find a man. Otherwise, when he leaves, you won't know where to go.

But I can't give them any advice. I've killed one of their kind, and I still don't know where I am going. I only know where I don't want to end up.

I push the stroller past a gaggle of moms hovering over a baby playground. Before, I might have joined them, introducing myself with a question about their respective children's ages. But I am not one of them anymore. I can't imagine making small talk about spit up and whether organic onesies are worth the price. I'm surprised that I ever managed it.

Vicky is cooing at me. She's happy from her marathon of "Pop! Goes the Weasel" and the fact that the stroller's motion shakes the animals appended to the bassinet's sun shade. I talk to her as I walk, supplying the advice that I wish I'd had in my twenties in hopes that she picks up on my speech, if not its content.

Every now and again, I feel the prickle of a focused stare on my back. When I look over my shoulder, however, I see the same nondescript crowd of city dwellers: people of all colors dressed in too much black, navy, and gray for the season. I don't really look too hard for the source of my unease. There's no reason for the police to track me, and I've been careful enough that there shouldn't ever be one. My guilt is creating goose bumps.

I walk down the esplanade, scanning for dumpsters. Manhattan authorities eliminated most public trash cans after the Boston Marathon bombings showed they could be exploited by terrorists. Dumpsters were spared due to the ability of their reinforced walls to contain blasts.

It's not until I reach the Staten Island ferry terminal that I see one: a massive container with corroding blue paint and white bubble letters spray-painted on its sides. The receptacle begs to be emptied. Black garbage bags are piled so high inside that they force open the rubber lid.

I stroll past the bin, glancing around to see whether there are cameras or particularly interested patrolmen. No blue uniforms stand out in the throngs of commuters. Again, I stroll to the container, this time parking my baby right beside it. I crouch to the basket beneath Vicky's bassinet and grab the flip-flops along with an unused diaper, with which I hastily wrap the shoes. When they're covered, sort of, I stand on my tiptoes and drop them atop a closed trash bag. There's no need to push the thongs farther into the garbage. No one is looking for Colleen's shoes. By the time they do, these will be in a landfill.

With the last of the evidence gone, I feel a lightness that I haven't since before learning of my husband's affair. Nothing in my possession connects me to Colleen anymore. I've discarded everything, even Jake.

I push the stroller away from the trash and breathe in my freedom. I'm single in Manhattan for the first time since turning twenty-four. And at least for the next four weeks until my maternity leave ends, I don't have a job to worry about. What should Vicky and I do? How should we amuse ourselves?

I look down into the bassinet. My daughter's mouth moves back and forth, sucking on an imaginary nipple. Her eyes are closed. The sunshine and fresh air has worked its magic.

New question. How should I amuse myself?

Tyler's handsome face comes to mind. What better way to kill time?

# LIZA

Bail bondsmen do not have offices on the Upper East Side. The types of establishments that grant loans to the wives of suspected killers know there's little money to be made operating out of the ground floor of a ritzy condominium. They set up shop in commercial buildings across from jails and courthouses—the kind of locales that don't frown upon neon lights in the window advertising "Get Out Fast."

The closest bondsman is south of Houston. A taxi driver ferries me thirty minutes through traffic from my fertility doctor's office to a grimy street in the financial district lined with electronics repair shops. I spot the place a hundred yards before we pass it. Who could mistake a yellow awning with spray-painted black handcuffs? I ask the driver to let me out on the corner even though he could easily stop in front of the store.

My legs wobble as I exit the cab and head to a neon sign boasting "Affordable Bail." It's an oxymoronic phrase if there ever was one. Securing David's release will cost a million dollars. Seventy percent of the cost of our majority-bank-owned apartment. His entire post-tax salary for the past five years. More than the sum of my life's earnings.

When David had revealed the price, my head had hammered so hard that I'd feared a stroke. He'd explained that we only needed to post 10 percent of the coupon, as though that was supposed to make me feel better. I'd responded that a hundred thousand would liquidate our savings, effectively bankrupting us. Any more would have had the virtue of being impossible.

David had not taken kindly to my preference that he await trial in jail. He'd assured me, voice filled with righteous indignation, that when the state ultimately drops the charges, he will sue for every penny of his bail, plus personal damages. He'd also threatened to have Cameron secure his release with a loan from the business, if I "couldn't be bothered." The idea of David's secretary showered with his gratitude made me ill. After all, she wouldn't be on the hook for the money if he skipped town.

I reach the store and loiter outside, reluctant to hand over the bank check in my wallet. In all likelihood, we'll never get this money back. I've written too many stories about "wrongfully" accused characters to think that the state files charges willy-nilly against upper-middle-class people. Either the defendant is being framed, or he's guilty of something.

The exterior of the bail bondsman's reminds me of a dive bar: brick outside, neon signs in the picture window. Inside, however, it is set up like a miniature version of my local Chase bank. There's a bar-height wooden desk topped by a likely bulletproof glass wall. On the other side, a heavyset man eats lunch at a blond Ikea-type desk, biting into a foot-long sub with the paper peeled back to reveal bread as thick as my bicep. He wears a pinstriped shirt and tie, no jacket. His neck has been tanned to the color of marmalade.

I wait for him to finish chewing before announcing my presence. He looks up from the sandwich, takes another bite, and points to a door in the corner. I hear it unlock as I reach it. The man welcomes me into his office. Lettuce is wedged between his incisors as he smiles and asks how he may help.

I start bawling. Adrenaline and my doctor's wary stare kept me from crying over the phone, but I can't maintain composure in the face of a simple pleasantry. I know that's all his offer is.

This man doesn't want to "help" me. He wants to charge me the down payment on a mansion for a short-term loan that he'll get back the moment David shows for his court date. Yet the offer of help, said without condescension, sounds so good.

I follow him, sobbing, to a desk stacked with file folders. As I sit in a rolling chair, he offers a tissue from a drawer, which only makes me cry harder. He walks me through the documentation I need in the manner of an oncologist delivering a bad diagnosis. Yes, he's getting rich off of me, but he feels my pain. Everything is accessible through my smartphone or his computer. Bank statements. Property records. Twenty minutes later, my bail bondsman—I never thought I'd say those words—makes a call. I'm told that that my husband is out. I can go home.

*

I emerge from the underground into a painfully bright summer day. The afternoon sky is a neon blue, even though it's nearly 5:00 PM. I shield my eyes with my palm and keep my gaze trained on the sidewalk until I hit my block. My apartment building is unmistakable, even at a glance. A New York riff on Italian architecture, the midrise is unique with its white stone and micro-balconies cupped by ornate lattice work. When David and I had bought the condo, I'd imagined throwing the French doors wide and leaning over the railing to see the sun rise over the East River. The apartment had seemed so romantic. I hadn't considered the reality of the busy street beneath my feet, the obnoxious honking that would drown out my own thoughts, let alone conversation.

I wave to my doorman as I enter and then take the elevators to the eighth floor. Bail posted an hour ago. David may be inside by now. One last chance to figure out how to confront my husband about the charges that he murdered his best friend.

*David, I know you were seeing Nick. Trevor told me yesterday that he saw you two kiss on the street. Did you kill him?*

Do I really want to know?

The pounding in my head picks up as I ride to my floor. I close my eyes against the glaring elevator lights and wait for the car to stop. When it does, I exit into the hallway and head to my apartment. Rather than use my key, I knock. David should be prepared for me. You shouldn't surprise a murderer.

He opens the door looking like a well-dressed homeless man. Lines that I have never noticed wave across his forehead, reminding me of a beach after the tide has receded, leaving behind its sunken garbage.

He steps back from the doorway. I brace myself for our confrontation, to tell him that he needs to, finally, be honest with me and with himself. Suddenly, his arms surround me. His head falls into the crook of my neck. Tears wet my dress strap and soak my shoulder. Sounds sputter from his throat that I've never heard before. Wailing, moaning.

I lead him to the couch. Getting him to sit takes all the skill of a wild horse trainer. I hold his hands and guide him to the cushion, whispering things I don't believe about everything turning out okay. When he's finally on the couch, I grasp his hand and ask about Nick in the least pointed way possible. "David. Please tell me what is going on."

He runs his palm under his nose and over his eyes. The skin glitters in the light pouring from the window. Not a single square inch of his face is dry. "The police found a note that Nick had sent me in the pocket of one of my jackets." He gasps. "There was blood on it."

"They arrested you over a note?"

"Yes." He sounds as though he's gargling. "A note. They think . . . Oh, God. It was his blood. They think I . . ." He bolts from the couch and stands, shivering, in front of me. "I don't know how his blood got on it. It doesn't make any sense."

"What did the note say?"

I ask, though I can guess. This is the document that David had been tearing apart the house to find, the piece of evidence tying him to Nick's murder. I imagine a Dear John letter written with Nick's scathing wit and a threat to out David if he didn't walk away from the firm. The man was trying to take away my husband while I was undergoing extensive fertility treatments to have our child. He was ruthless when it came to getting his way.

David's mouth opens as though he can no longer breathe through his nose. He stares at me, panting. I imagine his thoughts are racing. How to tell your wife of more than a decade that you had an affair with the best man at your wedding?

"Why do you ask?" His face, pinked from crying, darkens to a plum shade.

"It seems pertinent. A spot of Nick's blood on a piece of paper shouldn't be enough to call out the cavalry."

"Who said it was a spot?"

"You did. Didn't you?"

His eyes narrow. "What do you think it said?"

His questions are squeezing my brain. I stand up, finally angry. "How the hell would I know, David? You're ranting about a note that has made the police think you murdered your best friend. Naturally, I want to know what the note said."

The fight that had flashed across David's face vanishes. He moves back to the couch and slumps onto the cushion. He rubs his eyes with the heel of his hands, pressing them into his eye sockets to a point that seems painful. "Nick wrote that he was in love with me. He said he'd been in love with me for years."

David confesses like a lawyer. He's not admitting any guilt. Nick wanted him. He's not volunteering whether or not he reciprocated those feelings. But I know already. David at least explored a romantic relationship. He'd kissed Nick. And my heart says that if David kissed another man, the experimentation didn't stop there.

"Did you love him too?"

David has to say it. Otherwise, I might stay. I'll invent a melodramatic fiction in which a lovesick Nick kissed David and then, rejected, shot himself before diving into the East River with his last breath. I'll keep pretending that the man whom I fell for so many years ago wants a life with me.

Lying to myself is in my nature. When my father left, I convinced myself that he was coming back even though everyone kept telling me that he was gone for good. Chris. My mother. My grandparents. When he didn't return after a year, I became depressed. I don't remember all the details. I do remember talking to doctors.

David looks at me miserably. "He was my best friend."

"I mean, did you love him like he loved you? Did you want to be with him?"

David's mouth contorts like a stroke victim. I fear a blood vessel in his head will burst or that his heart will give out right here. "Yes." The word slips out, so quiet that it could be the hiss of wind beyond the window.

I close my eyes, prepared to be battered by waves of pain. Instead, a strange warmth radiates from my belly to my extremities. As it tingles to the edges of my fingertips, an extreme calm washes over me. It's as though my soul has left my body and is watching me, unfeeling, from a distance. I see myself rise from the couch, hear myself speak. "I need to be alone for a while. I'm going to the house."

I watch as I pick through my disheveled closet, selecting jean shorts off the floor and tank tops from a shelf, choosing bras and underwear from disturbed drawers. I grab sunscreen. My laptop. Everything is stuffed into a canvas shoulder bag unearthed by the police search.

As I walk through the living room, David calls my name. He attempts a smile, but the look is so pained, it resembles a grimace.

"I want you to know that this—our life—hasn't been playacting. I wanted, so much, to give you a baby. I love you too." His voice breaks. "Just, differently."

The acknowledgement that my husband has never felt for me like I have for him should be a corkscrew twisted in my heart. Yet I don't feel anything. It's as though the man sharing this admission is a stranger. I nod at him and walk through the foyer. My only vague discomfort is the slap of the bag against my butt.

It's not until the door slams behind me that I slide back into my body with a long slow breath. It's safe to come back now, I suppose. Hope is gone. My marriage is over. There will not be kids. School pickups. Family vacations. David will go to prison for Nick's murder, or he won't. It doesn't matter. Either way, he won't be with me.

As I walk down the hallway, a beep sounds inside my purse. I fish inside for the handset and see that I have a new message from an unknown number. Probably it's the police wanting to know about my role in this: How long has David had access to my gun? Did I realize it was missing?

I click the icon and listen to the voice mail. "Hi, Ms. Cole." The voice is young. Male. Uncertain. He doesn't sound like a cop. "My coworker Frank at Le Bonhomme said I should give you a call. I was there the night that Nick came in with his new friend. The one in the photo."

The bartender leaves a number. I wait until I am in the garage, in the seclusion of the driver's seat, to call him back. Though I'm resigned to hearing about Nick and David on a date, I can't promise that the details won't set off the waterworks again.

The kid answers on the third ring. From the clinking glasses and background chatter, I can tell that he's probably in the bar right now.

"Hi, this is Liza. I'm returning your call about my missing—" I choke on the word "friend." "About Nick."

"Right. Yeah. Hold on." His voice is muffled as he shouts something to another patron. When he returns to the line, the background noise is more of a murmur. "Well, like I told police, Nick was a regular. He lived in the area. He had started coming with the new guy in July, a few weeks before the papers said Nick disappeared. Usually they came during the week, right around when we'd open. That Saturday was the first time I'd seen them together on a weekend."

The revelation doesn't have any impact. I am dead inside. "Okay, thanks."

"And you wanted to know about the woman, yeah?"

I'd forgotten. "Yes. Right." My muscles tighten even though I know that she can't have been me. Dr. Frankel assured me that I wouldn't forget anything life-changing. Learning that my husband had a gay lover would certainly register on the earth-shattering meter.

"I'd never seen her before," the bartender says. "I remember her being really striking though. She was tall, maybe in her thirties."

I stare at the concrete wall beyond the windshield and flip through my mental database of Nick's dates. They were all striking and tall, at least compared to him. Most of the women were probably in their twenties rather than in their thirties. But Botox and alcohol can blur the difference.

"Anything else you can tell me about her?"

"Yeah. She had red hair. Not that brick color like everyone is dyeing it now, more like reddish orange. Ginger, I guess. Natural like."

I exhale, a long drawn-out whoosh like the breathing exercise at the end of a tough gym class. Though I didn't believe I was the woman in the bar, it feels good to have confirmation. In no world would I ever be described as a natural redhead.

"And freckles. Lots of them. Cheeks. Forehead. Everywhere."

My relief vanishes. Natural redheaded women with freckles are rarities, like white peacocks or black swans. I'm sure that I know the only one in the world who would be furious at seeing Nick and David together, who would want to break up their relationship at any cost.

I turn the key in the ignition. Chris is my best friend. She's always taken care of me. She's always said that she'd do anything for me.

I never thought that meant murder.

# Chapter 17

TYLER IS NOT HAPPY TO see me. He opens his apartment door with a tight-lipped smile appropriate for a funeral and doesn't welcome me in, despite the baby carriage at my side. "Beth, you're here. Is everything okay?"

I dab at my dry eyes. "Jake was home when I got there. He's in a rage about the police coming to the house this morning. I'm sorry. I needed to get out. I told him I was taking Vicky for a walk, but it's too hot to stay outside for long, and I'm afraid to go back to our apartment . . ."

I trail off and stare up at him. His lips are parted. The invitation is right there on the tip of his tongue. I only need to coax it out.

"I am trying to come up with an excuse to go to my mother's, but she's still at work, and she's not answering her phone." Again, I pretend to fight tears.

Tyler steps back from the doorway. "You can stay here while you wait to hear from her."

In the light of day, his apartment appears different: a plain bachelor pad rather than a sumptuous studio. It has an open layout, similar to my own apartment sans the separate bedroom and eat-in kitchen. The living room has a large couch worthy of a dorm's common room and an obscenely large flat-screen television on the wall. There's no dining room. Instead, a breakfast bar with four high-backed stools separates the kitchen from the main entertaining space. The bedroom is in a nook at the back.

I push Vicky's stroller to the side of the couch, away from the light pouring in from the windows. "She's sleeping," I say. "I really can't thank you enough."

His tight smile widens a bit. "I'm just sorry that you are going through all this. Can I get you some water or tea?"

I am a coffee drinker, and I certainly didn't come here for Earl Grey. Still, I accept the tea. It's a gateway to other things.

He removes two mugs from a cupboard along with a fancy glass contraption with a well and a filter. From another cupboard, he withdraws a tin of tea leaves. While his back is turned, I pull down the Columbia tank to show maximum cleavage and tilt my torso in his direction.

Tyler keeps his back to me as he takes the teapot, now with leaves added, to a standing water cooler in a corner of the room. He presses a red lever, and boiling liquid begins filling the well. Steam rises in the climate-controlled air. "We have to let it steep a minute," he says, returning the clear pot to the kitchen counter.

As he sets it down, I see his eyes dart to my chest. The memory of his lips on my breasts can't be that far gone. I round the breakfast bar, grasp his hand, and tilt my head to look into his eyes. He stares back, waiting for me to say something. Studies show that sustaining eye contact with a stranger for two minutes results in passionate feelings—even love. I figure I need twenty seconds for lust.

Tyler blinks. "This tea—"

I stand on my toes, grab his face, and plant my lips on his full mouth. For a moment, his eyes remain open. They don't stay that way. His lids close. His lips part. When he kisses me, I know he understands why I came here.

We move to the bed. I inhale the musk of his skin. It works like incense, chasing away my mental demons. Here, with Tyler's hands on my body, I can forget all about Jake and Colleen and what I did. It was a bad dream. This man, this bed, the pants falling past chiseled thighs, the fingers pulling at the drawstring of my sweats: this is reality.

As he slips off my underwear, he suddenly freezes. "What about Vicky?"

"We'll be quiet."

Recalling that my infant daughter is in the room changes his demeanor. Instead of the wild romp that it seemed we would have moments before, he kisses me as though my lips are chapped. His fingertips trace my neck and move to my breasts, the feathering stroke after a massage has ended. He slips on a condom and positions himself on top of me, bearing his weight on his elbows and knees so that I am not pinned to the mattress. When he enters, he doesn't make a sound.

Such tenderness feels like love, not sex. I am not ready for this.

Images of Colleen's crushed skull flood my vision. I pant from the force of them. Tyler slows his already lethargic rhythm as though he might be giving me more than I can handle. The images come faster. I see the pipe. The gun. The blood.

I start coughing, a violent hacking fit that doubles me over and waters my eyes. Tyler withdraws from my body like he's spotted signs of a venereal disease. He tells me I need tea.

No amount of liquid will wash Colleen from my mind. I was stupid to think that I could rid myself of her and start my life anew. She'll never leave me. I'll never be able to forgive myself.

I start bawling, silent sobs that shudder through my whole body and blind me with tears. Tyler returns without a mug. He helps me sit up and then positions himself to my right, far enough away that there's no chance of our naked bodies touching. Any desire he'd felt is long gone.

"Beth." He speaks softly, subduing his accent. This is his shrink voice. "You shouldn't feel obligated to sleep with me because I am letting you stay here for a few hours. In fact, we shouldn't do anything besides talk. You need to process everything that has happened."

"No." The word barely makes it out between sobs. "There's nothing to make sense of. It's all over. My marriage is over."

"Even if that's true—"

I gasp. "I don't want Jake anymore."

Tyler reaches toward me. For a moment, I think he is going to pull me into his side and kiss the top of my head. Make me feel better. When I look at his outstretched hand, I realize he's holding a box of tissues.

"Even if you intend to divorce your husband, you need time to feel good about not wanting him anymore. To mourn your marriage."

The word "mourn" recalls Colleen's dead body. I grab a handful of tissues and press them to my face. Tears swell my nose. My mouth can't close from crying. As I try to wipe my face, tissue sticks to my wet lips and tongue, bits of wafer that won't dissolve. I cannot be saved.

"It's all my fault." I repeat the phrase, sobbing. "It's my fault. Something is wrong with me. I don't deserve to—"

"No, Beth. No. Don't say that." Tyler gives my shoulder a supportive squeeze, reminding me that we can be friends even though it's clear we will not be lovers again. "The disintegration of your marriage is not your fault. And whatever your husband did or didn't do to his girlfriend is not your fault either."

I wipe the tissue beneath my snotty nose and take shaky breaths, trying to compose myself.

"You need to be there for Victoria," Tyler says. "You *don't* need to be punished."

I nod, though I know he's wrong. A woman is dead. Punishment is coming.

# LIZA

It's dark by the time I reach the Hamptons house. Stars—millions of them, as opposed to the handful visible in Manhattan on a clear night—paint the sky. I see Antares, the heart of the scorpion, glowing red in November's zodiac constellation. David taught me about that one.

I'm exhausted from the revelations of the past twelve hours. My legs shake as I exit the car, as though I'd been running a marathon rather than occasionally pressing a gas pedal. Fatigue flows through my blood like too many glasses of red wine. Everything has slowed. I can't confront Christine like this.

After entering through the side door, I flop down on the first available reclined surface: the living room couch. I shut my eyes with a foggy intent to rest for a moment and then call my best friend.

Once my lids lower, the plan dissolves into ether.

*

A black screen fills with the sound of the ocean. Waves rush to an unseen shore in a furious crescendo, only to fizzle on the sand. Gazing at the sea are the watery eyes of a young girl. Ten, maybe older. She has the height of a preteen but lacks the telltale signs of puberty. I feel as though I know her or I did once, long ago. She sits, half naked, on a lounge chair. Her flat chest is covered in a poorly tied Hawaiian-print tankini. The bottom is missing. Her trembling fingers clutch a bloody tissue.

Grunting draws the child's attention to a pool. The water is tinted like a bruise, blue fading into a purple spot tinged with red. A woman stands waist-deep beside the discoloration, her hands around a handle. Metal slams against concrete.

I know this person too, though my mind can't piece together where from. She's the kind of woman about whom people whisper, "She was a beauty in her day." Now frown lines frame her mouth. Her eyes are pulled down by dark circles. She wears a sopping button-down shirt. Her hair has been yanked haphazardly from a chignon so that half is still pinned while other sections hang to her shoulders.

"Mom." The girl whispers the call. She hugs her arms over her askew bikini top and shivers. "Mommy." She starts rubbing her forearms. The bloody tissue in her hand shreds from the friction. Bits of paper fall to the floor. "Mom." Still, she whispers. "Mom."

The child drops the tattered tissue and stars clawing her arms. Tracks of blood follow the lines of her jagged nails. Terror fills her dark eyes. "Mom!" She screams. "Mom! Mom!"

The woman splashes to the steps, running beneath the water. Blue slacks cling to her legs as she emerges onto the deck. The spearhead of a garden shovel hangs beside her knees. It clatters to the ground.

The mother kneels beside the girl and grasps her hands, stopping the fingers from tearing into any more flesh. "Shh," she hushes. "I didn't know. I'm so sorry. I never thought . . ." Though tears fill the woman's eyes, she doesn't let them fall. "We found him in there. Okay? He'd been drinking. None of this happened. Okay? Nothing happened. We just found him."

The girl considers the woman with a glazed expression and then turns her attention back to the sea. A blank calm erases the terror that had twisted her features.

The mother slowly releases her daughter's hands. She watches them, waiting for another attack, but they hang limp at the child's sides. She runs back to the shovel, picks it up over her shoulder like a musket, and rounds the house to the side yard. The girl stands and follows. Her face still, like the ocean just before dawn.

Again, there is grunting. The shovel sticks from the earth beside a line of flowering weigela bushes. The woman steps on its head, burying the metal deep in the ground before heaving it upward to dislodge a mound of dirt. She continues digging until a hole, the depth of a forearm, appears beside her feet.

The shovel goes in. She stands on the blade and then tugs at the handle until it pops out. The stick is tossed to the side. She motions for her daughter. The child crouches beside her. Together, they push back the earth with their hands until there is nothing except a sprawling bush. Wine-colored petals cover the site so that not even the earth looks disturbed.

*

I wake, unable to breathe. Panting. Gasping. Drowning. Tears have soaked my pillow. My neck is wet. Instinctively, I reach to where David would lie next to me and claw air. Everything that has happened in the past twenty-four hours returns with dizzying clarity. I have left my husband. I am in my house in Montauk. The woman in my dream was my mom.

A pale-yellow glow looms outside the patio doors. I stumble from the couch and walk through the dining room to the half bath. My reflection stares at me. Her eyelids look sunburned. I turn on the faucet, splash water on my face.

"Stupid nightmare," I tell my mirror image. The woman had been my mother, but I'd cast her in a distorted version of my bestseller, *Drowned Secrets*. "It was just a bad dream." My reflection sobs in response. She doesn't believe me.

I am still wearing yesterday's denim shirtdress, now speckled with wet splashes and stinking of hormones. Christine has seen me looking worse. I've seen her on day six of the same pajamas. How I look or smell doesn't matter.

I reenter the living room and grab my phone from my bag. Chris's voice mail answers my first call. I dial again. I have to know what role she played in all this. Did she know that Nick and David were seeing each other? Why didn't she tell me? What did she do when she found out?

She answers on my third try. "Hey, Lizzie." She yawns. "What's up? What time is it?"

"I'm in Montauk. Please come over." My voice is raspy. I can barely get the words out.

"God, Liza, what's wrong? Are you okay? Is David there?"

"David's home. I need to talk to someone. He's been charged with Nick's murder."

There's a gasp on the other end. "Okay. It's all right. Everything will be fine." She's awake now. Her voice is sharp. Adrenaline filled. "Are you in the house?"

"The living room."

"Okay. I need you to go to the beach behind the house, where people can see you. Don't stay in the house. Go where people can see you, okay? I'll be right there. The beach. Wait for me on the beach."

I don't understand why I can't be in the privacy of my home. "Okay, but—"

"Liza, where's your gun?"

*

Chris stays on the phone as she rushes out of her house and drives the ten blocks to mine. Every few seconds, she asks me to reassure her that I don't have my Ruger and that I am sitting on the beach. She demands to know what the sand feels like, what the waves look like, anything to keep me focused on the present. I tell her that my sandals are going to leave awful tan lines on my feet and that I am concerned about grains getting caught in the stitching of my purse. This makes her feel better.

Whenever I attempt to discuss David, she tells me that we will talk about him all I want as soon as she gets there and then inquires about the weather. My foul-mouthed friend speaks in the soothing tones of a suicide hotline operator. I have the sense that this isn't her first time talking someone off a ledge.

I hear a car stop in front of the house simultaneously through the phone speaker and from somewhere behind me. Chris's foot-steps crunch on the gravel driveway and then slap against the deck boards. I turn as she is clearing the tall grasses at the edge of the house. She slides down the beach, still in her blue-and-white-striped pajamas, ginger hair shining in the morning sun.

Before she sits beside me, she looks at my hands, scanning for my Ruger. I open my purse in front of her as though she were an airline security agent and then drop the bag back onto the sand and raise my hands in surrender. She smiles weakly at me and settles down on my same dune. Her arms open. I fall inside her embrace and lean my head on her shoulder.

"What happened?"

The waterworks are no longer on full blast, but the dial could turn at any moment. I try to share my story in one breath—before I'm sobbing too hard to speak. She gets the facts of the case against David without my opinions. The cops arrested him for Nick's murder after finding a note with Nick's blood on it in his suit pocket. Nick had written that he was in love with my hus-band. They'd been having an affair for months, maybe the better part of a year. On the night Nick disappeared, he'd been seen at a bar with David.

When I finish, she hugs me tighter and repeats how sorry she is. She says nothing about the bar.

I peel away from her. "How long did you know?"

Her chin retreats to her chest. "What?"

The motion seems too theatrical to be genuine. I can't watch anyone else that I love lie to my face. Instead, I look at my fingers pressing a print into the sand, the kind hospitals give new mothers of their babies' palms. "A bartender at the gay bar where Nick and David were seen said a woman came in asking about them." I grab a handful of sand and watch it slip through my fist like a timer. "She had red hair and freckles."

Chris's tense energy changes beside me. I sense her shoulders lower. Her back curves. She inhales and exhales, preparing for a story.

"I saw them together. Nick called and said that I should meet up with him at the place we went before." She scoffs. "I should have known he'd have a motive other than sleeping with me. But the power of wishful thinking, right? I convinced myself that he'd gotten distracted on our first date and wanted to try again."

I turn to face my friend. She twists her hair into a coil. In the white sun, it looks like a rose-gold rope. "When I arrived, he was with David. I didn't assume a date, though. I thought maybe that it was an intervention of sorts for you through me. Nick had said that David wasn't working hard enough because he was taking care of you. I thought maybe now David was here to tell me that the fertility drugs were making you . . ."

She trails off, but the word she wants is "insane." Her political correctness takes me aback. Christine doesn't have to fear calling me nuts. The only people who can't be called crazy are crazies. Am I acting loopy? Do sane people even ask that question?

"I wasn't about to listen to two men complain about a woman's hormones," Chris continues. "So I didn't go over to them. Though I did have a drink. I'd gone all the way out there, right? It was crowded, and I deliberately stayed in the corner behind some big dude so they didn't see me." She releases her hair. It stays wound on her shoulder like a stretched copper spring. "I didn't suspect that Nick and David were on a date until they left together. They weren't kissing, but maybe they were walking a bit close. Anyway, I asked the bartender about them and he said that Nick had been bringing David by a lot recently. The way he said it, kind of smirking, made me think something could have been going on."

I examine Christine's guilty posture. "Why didn't you tell me?"

"I didn't know for a fact and I didn't want to upset you. I mean, you were already under so much stress trying to get pregnant." She looks out at the water and blinks. "I didn't want it to push you over the edge and have anything happen again."

She swallows this last word as though she regrets it.

"What do you mean, 'again'?"

She digs her feet into the sand and tightens the coil of hair on her shoulders. I recognize these behaviors from our childhood. This is Chris at her most nervous and defiant. "'Again' like when you got depressed after your dad left."

She isn't looking at me. Reminding me of my brief bout of depression should not be this difficult for her. It's not as though she's a stranger to psychiatrists. She saw one after her divorce. I wonder what she's hiding. Is it that she followed Nick back to his house to talk sense into him and ended up shooting him? Chris has access to her father's gun. She might have taken it if she'd been heading into a bad area in Brooklyn.

Unspent tears make Chris's hazel eyes glow green. My best friend has always looked out for me. If she killed Nick because she believed me too fragile to handle the affair, then I'm responsible. It's my fault he is dead.

I grasp her arms. "Please, Chris. What are you not saying? I won't tell anyone, but I have to know. I just can't take more lies. I am going crazy from all the secrets. I don't know what's true anymore. What's real. I can't take it. I can't live like this."

I am on my knees, begging and shaking my best friend. To my right, I can hear the water. I fight the urge to run into it, to bury my head beneath the waves until I can't breathe anymore.

Chris looks at me as though she heard my thought. "You tried to kill yourself, Lizzie. In high school, after you found out that you couldn't have kids because of the abuse."

I release my friend and fall back onto my haunches. "No. Why would you say that? I talked to some doctors because I was depressed that my dad left and I'd realized he wasn't coming back." An image assails me as I speak. A white bottle with a red label. Over the counter. Generic brand.

"Your mother killed your father in front of you." Chris wipes away the tears on her cheeks with sandy fingers. Crystals sparkle like glitter on her spotted skin. For a moment, I don't think she's real. She's a figment of my imagination. I'm inventing what she's saying.

She shudders. "He'd been molesting you for years. Since you were eight, I think. You didn't say anything until the touching became more . . ." She coughs, driving fresh tears from her eyes. "Invasive. He had you convinced that everything was a normal expression of affection until then. You opened up to me about it. I told my mom. She told yours. Your mom came home to confront him. You'd been here alone a lot that summer while your mom was in the office and your dad was, supposedly, selling houses. She caught him in the act and—"

A sob cuts off her words. I look out over the ocean, trying to make sense of her story. My story. The childhood she describes is a nightmare out of one of my books. It's not mine. I had an alcoholic father who skipped out on the family and a loving, devoted single mom who died young of cancer. It wasn't an ideal childhood. But it wasn't that horror show.

Tears slick the skin beneath Chris's nose. She looks at the ground as she wipes them away. "Your mom hit him with something. Knocked him into the pool unconscious. He drowned. She never went to jail for it, but everyone kind of knew she did it. Even the police. No one really wanted her to pay for it, though. Ultimately, the cops bought the line that he must have been drunk and dove into the shallow end. It was plausible enough. There'd been a dent on the bottom of the pool. The police psychologist who talked to you kind of put two and two together, but the cops couldn't prove it. They couldn't find any weapon that—"

"Wait, I know this story." Anger pulls my legs upright as I realize the source of Chris's tale. This is the plot of my first book. My best friend is recounting my own fiction rather than admitting to killing Nick.

I dust the sand from the back of my bare legs, not caring that the wind is carrying it into Chris's eyes. "This is what happened in *Drowned Secrets*. You don't think I'd know a story that I wrote?"

She stands and reaches for me. I step back from her, leaving her hands hovering in the air. "You based that on your life, Liza! On suppressed memories."

I take another step back. "No. I made it up. I make things up. That's what I do. I make up—"

"That story was real." Chris's voice has lost its practiced calm. "The doctors said that the trauma of what your father did and then guilt over your mom's actions made you disassociate from the experiences." Her hands fall to her thighs. "You probably remember bits and pieces, but you've convinced yourself that they're dreams or things you've seen on the television or . . . your fiction."

Christine walks forward and grasps my hand. The pressure of her fingers pleads with me to be strong, to remember.

"Your mom and I didn't know, at first. When you wouldn't talk about what happened, we thought it was too painful to discuss. Then when you started to demand that everyone call you Liza rather than Bitsy or Beth, we thought it was because your dad had used those nicknames and you didn't want to be reminded..."

She trails off, tears tumbling down her cheeks. I can't look at her. She can't be telling me the truth. I don't remember my father touching me.

But why would she lie?

I slip my hand from her palm and turn toward the water. The morning mist has burnt off. Sunlight dances across the ocean. It's surreal that the day is bright and beautiful. I've stumbled onto the wrong movie set.

Chris sniffs loudly. "It wasn't until high school, when you didn't get your period and went to see the gynecologist, that we realized you didn't remember. The doctor told you that you couldn't have kids from scarring related to the abuse, and your mom had to explain. You tried to overdose on aspirin. If you hadn't already had such bad headaches and the bottle had been fuller..."

I close my eyes and see the pills in my palm, two dozen perfect little circles, promising to make the pain go away. If I'd been shorter. Smaller. My legs give out. I fall to my knees on the sand and then drop back onto my butt. Hot grains scald my thighs. The pain reminds me that I am here. I am here and I am real even though I have invented my entire history.

Chris sits beside me and drapes an arm over my shoulders. She pulls me to her side, offering her chest to cry on. Shame burns my cheeks. Chris loves me enough that I thought she might kill for me. How could I fail to trust my best friend?

"The suicide attempt made you forget the abuse again. Your mom told you that the hospital stay was for depression." Chris sniffs. "My mom said that the doctors told your mom to tell you the truth. There's medication to help you reintegrate your memories. But your mom thought it better for you not to know. She said that the only reason you had been able to finish high school, get into a good college, and have a semi-normal life was because you didn't remember. She was afraid that if everything came back up, you wouldn't want to keep on going."

Puzzle pieces fit together. Suddenly, I understand why I fear my childhood home when it gets dark. That would have been when he'd have come for me, in the between hours after school ended and before my mom returned from work.

Chris wipes her face on the shoulder of her pajama shirt. "I was so worried that the doctors would reveal the abuse when you first went for fertility treatments. But I guess the scarring mimics severe endometriosis, and with the gynecologists not knowing your history, they must have assumed. And then I really did hope that one of these treatments would work, that the drugs would dissolve the scar tissue and it wouldn't matter why it existed in the first place. I mean, medicine makes new things possible all the time." Tears carve tracks into her cheeks. "I really wanted you to be able to have a baby and never again have to face what had happened."

Seeing Chris in pain for me over something I don't even feel is real is too much. I focus on the water in front of me. It undulates like a curtain in the wind, pulling back, billowing forward. A breathing metaphor. The past is always hiding behind the present, threatening to peek out and drag everything down.

Chris hugs me to her side. "I'm so sorry. I should have told you before. Your mom and I were wrong to keep this from you. You are strong and you are going to survive this. In a year's time, David won't matter. None of this will matter. You are going to be okay."

I know Chris wants to believe this, but I can't agree with her. Instead, I grab fistfuls of sand and open my fingers just enough to allow a stream of grains to slip through. Over and over I do this, watching the seconds pass. I tried to end my life and I don't remember it. My father sexually abused me for years and I don't remember it. My mother killed him and I don't remember it. What kind of person forgets the most formative events of her life?

Not a strong one. Maybe a murderer.

"I think I did something horrible and suppressed it," I whisper. "I need to get something."

I grab my purse and head back toward the house, as if in a dream. Chris calls after me, begging me to explain where I am going, what I intend to do. But I can't answer her. I'm not sure myself. I only know that I must find my Ruger. For the first time since discovering it missing, I have a sense of where it might be.

When I hit the deck, I turn left toward the side yard. Chris steps sound behind me. She's following, close enough to stop me from doing anything crazy while allowing some space. I approach the line of weigela. Clusters of flowers sprout from the plants like red-dyed dreadlocks. The bushes have sprawled over the years so that the side yard doesn't have a garden bed as much as an unkempt hedge.

A wine-colored shrub calls out to me from my subconscious. I kneel beside it and brush back its tangles of blooms until I see the dirt beneath. I scratch at the ground with my short fingernails. The earth is soft, like fresh mulch. It gives way easily. Clumps of soil fill my palms.

I keep digging, trying to get a hole up to my elbow as my mother did in my dream. In my memory. Again, Chris asks what I'm doing. She tells me to stop. I can't, though. Somewhere deep inside of me is a need to be here, sitting on my haunches, fists beneath the ground.

My fingers hit something. Hard. Metal. I pull back the overgrown bush and carefully remove the object. It's too small for the head of a broken spade, though it has a handle. My entire body starts vibrating as though the ground is shaking beneath my feet. I rub my eyes with the back of a soiled hand and stare into the smudged palm of the other one. There's a fat rubber grip connected to a long barrel. A silver slide catches the sunlight.

"What do you have there, Liza?" Fear fills Chris's voice.

I don't answer. But this is my gun.

My hand trembles so badly that I am afraid to put my fingers anywhere near the trigger. I pull out the magazine. The weight of it alone tells me bullets are inside. It lands on the ground with a dull thud and sinks into the loose soil. I pull back the slide. A round pops out into my waiting palm. I examine the copper bullet with its red tip as though it is a strange wasp that I fear might sting me. Slowly, I tilt my hand and watch it fall from my palm into the mound of dirt beside the hole.

*It needed to be done.* Beth speaks in an assuring voice.

I face Chris with the weapon in my hand. "Don't worry. I unloaded it. But I knew it was here, which means . . ."

My voice breaks. Chris kneels beside me. She rubs my back slowly, urging me to continue. I don't have to tell her to keep what I say secret. Her set jaw assures me that whatever I tell her she'll take to the grave.

"I must have used it. I probably found out about the affair somehow and then went to confront David and Nick. I must have killed—" I cut myself off with a deep breath. The air burns in my lungs like smoke.

Chris places both hands on my shoulders. "Liza, you did not murder Nick. You didn't even know that he was sleeping with David until this week."

I gnaw at my bottom lip as I shake my head. "With my history of suppression, I could have found out before and then forgot. But while I knew, I might have—"

Chris hushes me. "You are my best friend, Lizzie. I've known you for how many years? You're the most loving, caring, honest, good human being that I know. You didn't kill Nick."

I want to believe her, to trust that murder is not in my character. But I didn't know who I was until moments ago. I have the backstory of a bad person.

"Nick was shot, Chris. He was shot and I buried a gun."

"There must be another explanation." Her eyes widen. "Maybe David buried the gun."

"At my house? Where I knew to look?"

Again, she shushes me, patting the air this time for me to control the hysterical wavering in my voice. "It was buried beneath the hedge like where the woman disposed of the murder weapon in *Drowned Secrets*. Maybe that's where David got the idea."

"Come on, Chris. Why would he do that?"

Chris digs her hands into her hair, picking up the twisted section into a ponytail. She holds it atop her head, thinking. After thirty seconds, she lets her hair drop with a long exhale. "In case the police suspected him . . ."

She doesn't need to finish. Her eyes say the rest. She thinks David wanted the gun to point to me. My husband was setting me up for Nick's murder.

# Chapter 18

ENDINGS DON'T STOP TIME. MY marriage and a woman's life are finished, but Vicky is howling in her bassinet, begging for my breast. Her life goes on and so must mine. I am a single mother. I don't have the luxury of wallowing in guilt.

I tell Tyler that I'm heading to my mom's house across the river. With all the lies I've told about Jake, he'd feel honor bound to keep me from my apartment as long as my husband might be there. He doesn't know that I've kicked Jake out already. It didn't fit the damsel-in-distress narrative that I'd used to convince Tyler to let me back in his bed.

He knows that we'll never see each other again. I can tell by the way Tyler lets his fingers linger in my palm as I step into the hallway and cautions me to "take care of myself." In another life, I'd be with a man like him. We would share our stories over bottles of wine, take our kids to picnics in the park, laugh at one another's jokes. Make love until morning. We'd build a happy blended family based on kindness and mutual respect.

But I'm a murderer. I don't get that happy ending.

Fortunately, Jake is gone when I reenter the apartment. Vicky is near hysterics from a full diaper. I lift my baby from the carriage and hold her against me with both hands, too weak from all the emotions and activity in the past twenty-four hours to trust myself with a dangling football carry. The changing table is in the bedroom. As I enter, I can't help but notice that the covers on Jake's side of the mattress are tossed back onto my spot by the window. His refusal to make the bed seems vengeful. In my head, I can imagine him excusing his sloppiness: *You can't kick me out and think I'm going to straighten up before I leave.*

Vicky stops crying the second I place her on the padded changing surface and release the tabs on her diaper. The blue line on the outside of her nappy that lets me know when it's wet extends all the way to the waist, a mercury thermometer about to burst in the heat. The diaper is so heavy and warm with urine that I can't properly fold it into the neat pentagon that fits in the hole of the fancy bin purchased at Babies"R"Us. Pee ruptures from the sides as I shove it inside while holding Vicky down on the changing mat with my other palm.

"I can do this all by myself." I say the words aloud to comfort me. "Jake wasn't helping anyway. I can do this alone."

I put on a fresh diaper with my clean hand. Now dry, she wants to nurse. All the liquids that have leaked out of my eyes and chest during the past twenty-four hours have left me dehydrated. I pull Jake's cover flat and place Vicky in the center of the bed on her back, feeling like a bad mom for leaving her unattended as I wash my hand in the kitchen sink and simultaneously grab a water glass from the cabinet.

My thirst makes me overfill it. It spills as I rush back into the room, creating a wet spot on the hardwood that I will have to wipe up later. I scoop Vicky back onto my torso and sit with my back against our headboard, drinking water with my right hand while she drains my left breast.

After she finishes, I put her on my shoulder to burp her. She spits up on the strap of my shirt, catching the ends of my hair. I tell myself that I could use a shower anyway as I put her to nurse on the other breast. When she's done, I hear a loud squirt followed by the distinctive sour-milk smell of baby poop. Again, I remove her diaper, this time wiping the mustardy grains from her backside.

I put on a fresh one, dress her in a side-snap onesie that says "Sleep, Eat, Poop, Repeat" and put her down for a short digestion nap in her crib.

I strip out of my college gear and get into the bathtub, not even bothering to check the reflection in the mirror. I can imagine what I look like after bawling over Colleen. I don't need confirmation.

While rubbing shampoo into my scalp, I realize that Jake didn't take any of his toiletries in the shower caddy. He probably only packed an overnight bag and intends to talk things out with me in the morning. I'll have to box his stuff up and have it ready to go by the time he gets here. I add packing my husband's things to my mental to-do list: feed Vicky, change her, entertain her, buy packing boxes from the UPS store—and tape. I can't forget tape.

The water rinses sudsy and clear. Not red. Not now. I tilt my face into the stream, as though the steady drops on my forehead might penetrate into my brain and flush the image of Colleen's blood flowing off my body. It doesn't work. Instead it adds the phantom sound of her falling into the water, like a log dropping into a stream. The sound intensifies as I head into the kitchen for another glass of water to help me replenish my milk supply.

I sit on the sofa as I drink my eight ounces. The couch is a holdover from Jake's bachelor pad days. He can have it. In fact, he can take the television too. I prefer reading to watching movies. I scan the room for anything I want to keep and realize that I can't find one item. I only want Vicky. I don't deserve anything else.

Instead of packing Jake up, I should box my clothing and Vicky's things. We can move to a cheaper apartment, maybe somewhere by my mother. Of course, then my commute would get longer. But my mother could help watch her when I needed to work late.

A buzzing sound stops me from listing the pros and cons of relocating to New Jersey. I track it to my purse, hanging off of Vicky's stroller in the foyer. Jake's number is on my cell screen.

He shouldn't be calling me so soon. Goose bumps, like those I'd felt walking to the dumpster, break out on my arms. Something is wrong.

I pick up without saying hello.

"Beth, we need to talk," he says. "I followed you in the park. I know what you did."

# LIZA

"You have to call the police." Chris says this as though she's stating the obvious, like we are talking about reporting a break-in or a suspicious stranger and not turning in murder evidence against my husband of twelve years. The best defense, she tells me, is a good offense. If I bring the gun to the cops and explain that David must have buried it, they'll be more likely to take my side than if the weapon comes up in court as evidence unearthed by David's investigator.

She might be right. Still, I can't do it. Though my husband didn't love me like he loved Nick, I have to believe that our marriage meant something.

"I need to talk to David first."

Chris looks at me as though I've forgotten our conversation or the fact that my husband lied to me for the better part of a year. "You can't warn him. That's idiotic, Liza. He'll go to the police and say you told him that you buried it."

Arguing with Chris is difficult enough without reeling from the revelations of the past hour. My head is a Newton's cradle where the horrors of my childhood hit against my present problems in perpetuity. My marriage began failing when I couldn't get pregnant. My father is the reason I can't have children. I married a man who could never really love me. I had a father who never loved me at all.

258

"I have a splitting headache." I press my fingers to my temples for emphasis. "I need aspirin."

Chris makes me promise to wait in the side yard for her to return with my pills. The house, with its kitchen knives in the drawers and its possibly full bottle of aspirin in the medicine cabinet, is far too dangerous for a person with a suicide attempt in her past and a plethora of reasons.

I pretend to agree with her logic as I direct her to the downstairs bathroom. As she enters through the side door, I slip the gun into my bag and run to my car.

I hear the screen door slide open again as I'm shutting the driver's side door. "Liza?" Chris sounds incredulous. "Where are you going?"

"I'm sorry," I shout through the window. "But I have to talk to my husband."

Chris runs out to the driveway, waving the bottle of aspirin, shouting for me to come out and talk this through. I jam my keys into the ignition and put the car into reverse. The sound of gravel rattling beneath the chassis drowns out Chris's cries as I back out onto the road and gun the engine.

The man who proposed to me by the lighthouse as purple flames lapped at the cold night air is not a monster. He loves me, in his way. How could he have stayed with me for twelve years otherwise? There must be a less sinister explanation for him burying my gun at my house than trying to frame me for murder. Perhaps, panicked after shooting his boyfriend, he hid it in the one place he considered safe, somewhere he thought no one would ever look. If I confront him, he will explain that. He'll tell me the truth.

Now that I've had a healthy dose of reality, I need to know everything that happened. Ignorance is never bliss. It is to walk around with a cancer in your colon, one that could be cut out safely within seven years but is instead allowed to grow, undisturbed, while you focus on other matters, unaware that it is spreading to your gut, infiltrating your bone marrow, your blood, all your vital organs until it has twisted your body into something grotesque and unsustainable. Until you're too sick to survive.

I need to know.

\*

The headache subsides during the drive home. When I hand the keys to the garage attendant, my thoughts have stopped throbbing. For the second time in two days, I feel an unnatural calm, as though somebody else—not I—will imminently accuse my husband of killing his homosexual lover.

The peace comes with heightened senses. As I enter my apartment, I feel David's presence in the house. I drop my purse on the glass dining table and remove the gun from the zippered interior pocket. I place the weapon beside my bag. Sunlight seeps through the French doors and saturates the metal. David will see it as soon as he exits the bedroom. He won't be able to deny that he had anything to do with Nick's death with the evidence staring him in the face.

"Dave?" I head to the master, listening for sounds of his activity. Is he sleeping? Working? Waiting for me?

The door is open, revealing him at my desk, back to the exit. He's hunched over his laptop, head close to the screen. I hear crying. Whatever he's reading is engrossing and upsetting. Another letter from Nick?

He doesn't seem to know I'm here. I slip into the room and round the bed, trying not to startle him. When I get close enough to touch his shoulder, I clear my throat. "David. Come with me into the living room. We need to talk."

He bolts upright as though he's heard a ghost. For a moment, I don't recognize the man standing in front of me. Fault lines carve his cheeks from his gaping mouth. His brow bulges above narrowed eyes. This man is capable of violence.

He raises a hand as if to hit me. I backtrack without thinking, stopping only when I feel the wall behind my shoulders. The bed blocks my escape to the living room. I'm penned in the corner, a trapped rat. David's hands wrap around my biceps.

"Did you think I wouldn't find out?" Spittle hits my face as he screams the question. My bare heels leave the hardwood. He's lifting me to his level so that there's no escape, no choice but to witness the pain twisting his features. "Did you think I wouldn't read it?"

I feel my lips part, my jaw drop, but his sheer volume silences me. My tongue fails to swell into any discernible syllable. The thick muscle hides behind my teeth, a snail cowering in its shell. His grip loosens enough for my feet to again feel the floor. "Answer me." He whispers this time, the hiss of a kettle before the boil.

His question doesn't make sense. What is he accusing me of? Has his guilt-riddled brain erased his memory of the murder? Has he convinced himself that I'm somehow to blame?

"I didn't do anything." Tears drown my words.

His blue eyes burn with an insane intensity, like the hottest part of a flame. His crime has driven him mad. In his warped mind, I'm the villain. My denial is expected. Criminals don't confess to the executioner. They invent alibis. Plead for mercy. I should be begging. I made a grave mistake coming here.

"Why, Liza? Tell me why he had to die." His speech is measured. I wish he would swear, call me names. This focused fury is worse than a fit of anger. If he were out of control, I could calm him down, negotiate, maybe even convince him that everything has been a misunderstanding. He is the murderer, not me. But he's resolved. His questions are rhetorical. The gun is on the dining table.

"Please." Sobs fold me in half. I press my hand to the wall, seeking leverage to stand.

He yanks my arm, forcing me from the corner. My knee slams against the jutting edge of the bed as he pulls me toward the oak writing desk and open laptop. The offending document lies on the screen. I'm pushed down into the desk chair and rolled forward.

"You expect me to believe this is a coincidence?" His index finger jabs at the monitor.

I recognize the structure of the paragraphs. Sentence-filled scenes followed by short bits of spaced dialogue. This is my book. David must have searched through my e-mail and found my story. He has my passwords. He knows I send myself copies. But why would he care about my novel?

The realization hits me like a gut punch. He's read my story and convinced himself that it's a retelling of my crime.

"It's a story," I plead. "It's only a story."

Though I catch the hand in my peripheral vision, I can't calculate the trajectory fast enough. It lands on his laptop, flinging it across the desk and onto the floor. Metal parts rattle. The bottom panel breaks off and skitters across the hardwood with the screech of an oncoming subway car.

"Liar." He turns my chair, wresting my attention from the ruined computer. A fist rises toward my face. He's been building up to this. I shut my eyes. "You're a fucking liar."

I don't protest. He's right. Blurring fact and fantasy is my trade. I am a con artist. A prevaricator. I make up stories. So why does he think this one is real?

The chair careens backward, smashing into the side of the bed. "You're going to pay for what you did to him." Tears tracks stain his cheeks. He wipes them away with the back of his arm. "I'm going straight to the cops."

He storms from the room. My gun is out there. He will tell police that I brought him the murder weapon, intending to admit to my crime. He may even believe it.

"I didn't do anything," I shout as I follow him. "Please, just wait a minute. Let's talk about this. Why would I kill Nick?"

He stops in the hall, right before it opens up into the main space. Dining area on the left, kitchen on the right. He can get to the front door through either the kitchen or the living room. He can only get to my gun if he chooses left.

"Why?" He whirls to face me. "To keep me! You thought I'd stay closeted if he was gone."

"That's not true. I didn't know you were gay. I didn't even know Nick was gay." I approach him and touch his arm. "Please. Think for a moment."

He recoils from my hand as though it's coated in Nick's blood. "Why are you still lying? I read the book. You saw us at the restaurant. I know—"

"It was just dinner, David. Just a made-up dinner at a made-up restaurant. I never saw you and Nick." I slip past him, stride into the dining room, and stand in front of the glass table, positioning my body to block the gun. I wasn't expecting David to be in denial. I can't show him the murder weapon until he is ready to accept responsibility.

He is watching my face, scowling at me rather than looking at the table.

"It was Italian."

"Half of the restaurants in the city are Italian."

"No!" David screams the word. "The river? The fact that he was shot? Bludgeoned? You . . . you did it. You . . . It can't all be coincidence."

A warm breeze brushes my back. The French doors are cracked to circulate the air in the stuffy apartment. I debate throwing them open, screaming for help. I can't trust David to listen to reason in this state, to not hurt me.

"I knew that you were looking for Nick and that the police were searching the river," I explain. "That was in my head while I was writing. That's why the body ended up in there in my story."

"No." David shakes his head as he advances toward me. I see the doubt in his eyes, though. He wants me to convince him of my innocence as much as I'd wanted him to tell me he hadn't meant to frame me.

"What about your gun?" he asks.

I step to the side, revealing the weapon on the table. "I found it buried at the house." I speak slowly, watching David's eyes open wider with every word. "You hid it in the same place that I got rid of the weapon in *Drowned Secrets*."

"What are you talking about?"

"David, I didn't kill Nick. Don't you see? You must have done it."

"No. You're crazy."

"I guess you took my gun because you were concerned going into Nick's bad neighborhood and—"

"No." His voice is louder now.

"You and Nick got into a fight and you were already conflicted about coming out. Maybe he threatened to tell me or he said he'd leave if you didn't choose him. I don't know. Maybe he broke up with you for not asking for a divorce fast enough."

His lips pull in and press together. He shakes his head.

"You must have shot him, David. It's the only explanation."

"No." He lunges at me and grasps my arms. "Stop it." A vein pops from between his eyebrows. His face is red with blood and fury. "I am not crazy. I did not kill Nick. I loved him. I loved him! I did not kill Nick."

Every word feels like a punch to the back of my head. He keeps holding my arms, screaming into my face. "I loved Nick. I loved him!" Suddenly, he releases me and grabs the gun off the table. He aims it, point blank, at my chest. "You lying bitch. You did it. You!"

The sight of the gun barrel between my breasts spurs an animalistic flight response. Before I realize it, I am running. Blood rushes to my extremities as I round the table and backtrack from David toward the balcony doors. My hand flails as I reach for the knob and throw it open.

I step onto the one-foot balcony. Wind takes my hair and twirls it around my neck, whips it in my face. For a moment, I consider letting it take me, falling backward and floating on air, far away from this mess of a life.

"You could have left us," David shouts over the rush of the wind and traffic below. "We would have been happy."

He flings open the other French door so it crashes against the apartment wall with a bang. The gun is in his right hand, braced by his left. He raises it at my head.

"Please, David. I didn't know anything about you and Nick," I scream. "You buried the gun. But I won't tell anyone. I didn't come here to urge you to turn yourself in. I came for the tru—"

A click interrupts my pleading. David stands in front of me in the doorway, finger on the trigger. He takes another step out onto the balcony and raises the gun to my eye level. Again, he aims and presses. Blood rushes to my head, sharp and painful as a brain freeze. I wince and hear another click, like snapped fingers only softer.

In my mind's eye, I see myself throwing the magazine into the hole. I remember clearing the chamber and tossing the round into the dirt. I had brought an empty gun to confront David. Not a loaded weapon.

"You tried to shoot me." A hot rage rushes through my veins, burning through my muscles and shaking my limbs. "You tried to kill me."

David's blinks at me, shocked that I am still breathing, that the gun in his hands is as deadly as a toy. "You're a murderer," he says.

Fight replaces my flight instinct. I fling myself at him, determined to rip the gun from his fingers, to tear the flesh off his body. After everything that I was willing to forgive, he tried to kill me.

There is no control. No rational voice cautioning me to go back inside, to call the police. There are only fists and flailing. Fury, as powerful as a mother's hormonal instincts, ignites inside me, incinerating all the feelings I have or ever had for my husband. I am blind with it. I barely see David's forearms rise to his face to block my blows or his back press against the railing as I slam my weight into his chest. I see his mouth make shapes of yelling, but I can't make out the words. It is as though a bomb went off beside me. I hear a high-pitched whine and my own internal monologue: He cannot pin Nick's murder on me. He will not do this to me. I would rather die. *I would rather them both die*, Beth says.

I shove both my fists into David's neck. His head snaps back, then his torso. I step back and watch his upper body disappear over the side of the railing as though he were a gymnast executing a back bend. His legs rise. His feet kick out toward me, threatening my stomach. I jump back to protect my belly.

There is a scream, too high to be David's voice, followed by a crunching sound. A car alarm. Shouts to call 9-1-1.

I lean forward from the doorway to peer down to the street below. David lies atop a parked car, below our balcony. His legs and arms are spread away from his body. His face looks up at me, forehead sunken from his skull exploding against the SUV below.

I stumble from the doorway and fall to my knees. I did that to my husband. David was right. I am a murderer.

Within minutes, the doorman is outside, announcing that the police will be coming in. I am ready for them, sitting on the couch, twisting a tissue between my hands. The tears I expect haven't come. A cool detachment has descended over me.

The police demand that I stand up, raise my hands. I tell them that my missing gun is on the balcony. My husband, I explain, murdered his boyfriend and hid the weapon at my mother's house. When I stumbled upon it and confronted him, he tried to shoot me and then throw me off the balcony. We fought. He fell.

They take me to the police station, where I sit on a gray metal stool beside a gray table in a windowless gray room and repeat my story a dozen times. Detective Campos and his buddies want every detail. When did David tell me about the affair? (After his arrest.) How long had he and Nick been seeing each other? (At least since Nick sent that note that the police found, maybe longer.) What was their relationship like? (Best friends turned lovers, apparently.) Did David want to be with Nick? (Yes.) Did Nick want to be with David? (I don't know.) Was I upset about the affair? (Of course. Wouldn't you be?)

On and on for hours, I provide monotonous responses to their questions. They take impressions of my fingerprints and pictures of my bruised arms where David had grabbed me in the bedroom. Everything is done "to rule me out." I'm no fool. I know David's death has made me even more of a suspect in Nick's murder. I don't care. My head hurts. I want to go home.

"When can I leave?" I ask.

Detective Campos brushes a hand over his thick dark hair. It's so black that it's nearly reflective under the bright fluorescent bulbs in the airless interrogation room. I've had so long to take in the details of the detective that I've committed his face to memory. He could be a character in my next book.

His lips press into a condescending smile. I'm frustrating him. All this questioning and my story hasn't changed. It's almost as if I'm telling the truth.

"Just a few more facts to nail down," he says. "What was Nick's note to David written on again?"

He is trying to trick me by implying that I told him already. "I don't know. I never saw it."

"Care to venture a guess?" He shrugs, as though the prize for the right answer isn't a life sentence. "Legal stationary. Parchment paper."

"I have no idea."

"A receipt?" he asks.

The memory floods my mind as though I've been plunged under water. Suddenly, it's all around me, all I can see: a small piece of paper in my palm, dog eared and crumpled like it has been read, folded, and reread many times. On the front is a bill for $150 from an Italian restaurant where David took me on an anniversary. On the back is Nick's tight cursive: "David, I love you. I always have. I admit that now. —Yours always, Nicholas."

I hear the detective call my name, but he sounds far away as though he's shouting for me on the surface and I am a diver, observing the depths. There is no going back for me now.

I am on a dark street in Brooklyn, gazing up at a lit multipaned window. Nick stands naked in front of it, flaunting his petite frame to the empty street. My senses are heightened. I smell the fetid river behind me. The disturbed earth of the construction site. I feel the hard metal of my gun through the leather bag pressed against my sternum. One thought races through my head: David is my husband and the future father of my child. I will not let Nicholas take him from me.

"Liza? Liza!"

The detective stands over me. I am no longer in the chair but on the cold tile floor. My brain feels as though I've been in

a head-on collision. The world around me is painted in chiar-
oscuro, highlighted by shadows.

The detective helps me sit up and scoot back against the wall.
"Are you all right?"

"The hormones." My voice sounds robotic.

"What?"

The needles pulse beneath my skin, pumping their poison
into my blood stream, into my brain. Suppressing my impulse
control. Sublimating my frustrated desire to procreate into violent action. Stripping me of empathy, of love.

I dig my nails into the implant site and start scratching, tearing, screaming in pain as I try to cut deeper into my flesh with
my blunt claws. "The hormones. I need them out. Get them out
of me. Get them out of me. Out. *Out!*"

Blood and flesh mix with the dirt beneath my nails. They are
just a little farther down. I need a knife. I have my teeth.

As I bend my mouth to my arm, hands wrap around me.
They yank my limbs back, hold my head. I think someone calls
for a medic. The number 10-96 is shouted over and over. I barely
hear it above my screaming as I try to wrest away from the officers and go for my bicep.

I am lifted and strapped onto a gurney. Belts restrain my
arms and tie down my legs. As I writhe on the bed, begging for
someone to remove the needles, a doctor jams something sharp
into my thigh. My eyelashes descend, a fuzzy screen that blurs
the images of the uniforms around me. Then everything goes
black.

*

I wake in a hospital bed in a strange room barely big enough for
the bed and the person slumped in the chair beside it. My vision
is hazy from the dimmed fluorescents and whatever drugs I've
been given. Painkillers, probably. I don't feel a raw burning in my

scraped arm or throbbing in my head. I don't feel sad or anxious, despite the stranger in the chair.

I squint at my visitor's arm, expecting to see a blue shirt and a policeman's badge. Instead, I see a fuzzy navy pullover and a lock of long red hair.

"Chris?" My voice crackles like it's coming from an ancient two-way radio.

She murmurs something, still asleep. I've no idea of the time. The window to my right is covered with a blue film that turns day into evening. It could be five. Could be eight. I scoot up to see better and am surprised to find that I can use my hands for leverage. They are not tied to the bed post as they had been when I got here. I remember how I got here.

"Chris." My voice cracks as I increase my volume.

She opens her eyes slowly and turns to me. "Hey, Lizzie." Her mouth curls in a sad smile. "You're up."

"How long was I out?"

She glances behind her at the window and then, realizing it doesn't hold any clues, looks at a phone on her lap. "It's four. I guess about a day."

She points to my left arm. My bicep is wrapped in thick gauze. I wince as I recall clawing my skin. "You would have been up sooner, but the doctors decided that the hormones were making you hysterical so they removed them. I think the painkillers coupled with whatever they gave you at the police station made you sleep longer."

"Have you been here the whole time?"

She gives me a weak smile. "David's death made the news. I came as soon as I heard. The freaking police didn't want to tell me which hospital you were sent to at first. But I called George. My ex is good for something. He phoned one of the prosecutors he used to work with when he was here, and that guy must have lit a fire under someone, because next thing I knew, the police were offering me a ride."

"Thanks." I force a smile. "Calling George was going above and beyond."

She wrinkles her nose. "He's not all bad, I guess. Emma's having a great time in the wilderness. Apparently, there's cell service." She stands and glances at the open door and the light on in the hallway. Soft voices and monitors whir beyond. "They won't let me close it."

Chris walks toward the top of my bed, squeezing her body in the small space between the mattress and the wall. I press the button to raise the back so I can see her at a better angle. Bags weigh down her eyes. I'm better rested than she is at the moment.

"George's friend said that the prosecutor's office isn't planning to press any charges against you. David was self-defense. People on the street below saw him, the fight for the gun. He would have pushed you over if you hadn't . . ."

She trails off, not wanting to accuse me of murdering my husband. But that's what I did. Charged or not. I know the truth. I killed them both.

"Anyway, since the cops had already charged David with Nick's death, they're considering that case closed too. David killed his boyfriend, probably to keep him from exposing their relationship before he was ready, and then tried to shut you up when you found out." Chris looks up at the ceiling and blinks away a tear. "I'm so sorry, Liza."

"Hey, there's no reason for you to be sorry."

"I shouldn't have told you everything. You weren't ready. It made you want to run to David and try to make things right with him, or something." She twists her hair and then releases it. "He could have killed you." Again, she looks at the tiled ceiling, trying not to cry. "Some friend I am."

I grasp her hand. It feels cold compared to mine, which has been wrapped beneath the hospital blanket. "You are the best friend anyone could ever ask for. You're my family."

"Yeah." She offers a little smirk. "Well, I guess I'll have to stop bitching about George now since you clearly win in the asshole husband department. Like, hands down. No competition."

She's trying to make me laugh, to smile, but I can't. I think it might be a long time before I feel anything.

"I was going to head to my apartment and get some food. A change of clothes." She pulls at her pant legs, expanding them like a striped tent. She's wearing the same pajama bottoms that she had on when I last saw her. I may be imagining it, but I see sand on the thighs. "Can I get you anything?"

What do I still have? My marriage is over. My husband is dead. I won't ever have a baby. After what I did, I won't ever have peace of mind.

I think of an aspirin bottle and how close I came as a teenager to cutting my life short. That's not how I want my story to end. I am a fiction writer. I can imagine a new beginning for me. I have my freedom. I have my family. I have Chris. Trevor. And Beth. I'll always have Beth.

"Would you bring my laptop?" I ask. "I have to finish a chapter."

# Chapter 19

THE STROLLER MAFIA IS OUT in full force on this sunny afternoon. I push my carriage toward the rows of Bugaboos, Stokkes, and City Selects lining the children's playground area. Before I come within shouting distance, I veer onto the lawn with my carriage. I can't run into anyone from my moms' group right now. I must talk to Jake.

He's sitting beneath the cherry tree where we ate sandwiches last spring, months before I'd given birth to Vicky—perhaps before he'd started cheating. The summer sun has turned the tree's leaves bright green. In a few months, they will morph to burnished orange, and come spring, pale-pink petals will again cover the bark as they did during our picnic. The flowers will break free when the wind whips off the water and drift down in a tinted snow of petals. Vicky will get a kick out of that. I'll have to tell Jake to make sure he takes her out and snaps pictures so I can see. If he won't talk to me, I'll ask my mother to do it. She won't cut off contact with me, her only daughter, just because I'm in prison.

Victoria coos at me as I take her from the bassinet and sit down with her beside Jake. The Hudson River sparkles aquamarine in the sunshine. It's a beautiful day to say good-bye to my daughter.

Jake believes I will start talking. Explain myself. I can sense his expectation in his gaze. But what can I say? He has the flip-flops. Somehow, he knows that they're hers. Undoubtedly, Colleen's DNA and mine are embedded in their rubber soles. True, a clever defense attorney might be able to blame the presence of my genetic material on an unwitting transfer from Jake. But I don't see how anyone could convince a jury that there's an innocent explanation as to how the shoes came into my possession.

I lift Vicky up and down, making her eyes flutter and mouth open with excitement, hoping that Jake takes his time calling in reinforcements. He's probably already dialed his police buddies. Undoubtedly, the officers that appear to be lazily patrolling the lawn to make the moms feel secure in their million-dollar apartments are actually here to arrest me.

Jake rubs a hand over his head. "I bought Colleen those flip-flops off a street vendor. She was always complaining that her toes hurt by the end of the night from the high heels she wore. When I saw you shove them in the stroller, I thought they looked familiar, but I also thought that maybe I was imagining things because of my shock that Colleen had been murdered. Still, I followed you to see where you were going that you needed two pairs of shoes. When you tried to hide them in the diaper before throwing them away, I knew."

Tears tumble down my cheeks. I keep focused on Vicky, trying to commit every detail of her little face to memory. I imagine how the nondescript features before me will grow into a combination of Jake's face and my own. Surely she'll come to visit sometimes. My mom will bring her.

"I know why you did it." Jake's voice is as raw as a skinned knee. "You were suffering postpartum depression. You probably followed me, saw us make love in her apartment through the window, and then went to confront her. She mocked you, right? And with the depression and sleep deprivation and all the emotion from the betrayal, you just grabbed something and started hitting her."

Sadness rips through my arms, making it too difficult to keep bouncing my baby while supporting her neck with my fingertips. I hold Vicky close to my breasts and brush my palm on her fuzzy bald head, smell the sour milk on her neck. I must memorize the feel of her in my arms. This is what will carry me through whatever is to come.

Jake wraps his arm around my shoulders. "It's not your fault." His voice is barely more than a whisper. "It's mine. I knew you weren't well, and I pushed you past the breaking point. I am so, so sorry, baby. I am so sorry."

The apology is a sign-off. I stiffen, expecting men to haul me to my feet momentarily. This is the end. I'm almost relieved. "They must be coming for me now, then."

"They?"

I kiss Victoria's head and pass her to her father. "I need you to be better, Jake. For Vicky's sake."

He holds her between his thick hands and brings his nose near her face. "I will. I promise. You'll see. I'll—"

I look at the cop pacing nearby. He seems to be watching us for a signal. "Is it that one?"

"What?"

"Is that the cop coming to arrest me?"

Jake takes a choppy breath. "No one is coming to arrest you. But they will one day soon. This is a cop murder, honey. The NYPD won't let this lie. The best thing for us to do is to talk to a lawyer and prepare an insanity defense. If you turn yourself in, that will count for something. I think I can pull some strings to get the DA's office to accept a plea of not guilty by reason of mental defect."

For a moment, I think I'm filling in Jake's open mouth with words that I want to hear. He can't really be letting me off for murdering his girlfriend. "You didn't call the police?"

He places Victoria in the crook of his elbow and grabs my hand with his free one. His blue eyes remind me of the sky today, clear and bright. I think back to the first time I saw those eyes in the courtroom, the way they lit up when he saw me. "I want us to be a family, baby. You were seeing a shrink for postpartum depression, so we have the record. I think we can win on mental grounds. You'll have to do some time in a hospital, but you'll get out." He smiles weakly. "We can put this whole thing behind us."

Jake and me and baby makes three. Is that really what he wants now? Can I want that again? "I don't know." I'm overwhelmed with emotion, crying so hard that I can barely breathe. "You don't really want me anymore. This is to get me to turn myself in."

"They're going to find evidence. You know it. This is the best way for us to be a family again."

A moan gurgles from my throat. I cover my face with my hands, trying to control myself. In the darkness, I see what I did to Colleen. The picture will always be with me. "I can't forgive myself."

Jake hugs me to his side, still holding Vicky. "I forgive you." Victoria yawns as she rests in her daddy's arm. Jake smiles at her and sniffs. "We made a beautiful baby, didn't we?"

I have no idea what she will look like grown up. Her blue eyes may not stay that way. Her round face will become more angular, square like Jake's or maybe oval like mine. But she is beautiful. She is ours.

My husband stares at me. Tears stream from his big blue eyes, water slipping over the edge of a sparkling dam. "Come on, honey. Let's go to talk to that lawyer."

*

Jake hires Lauren Dayton, one of New York's big-name criminal defense attorneys, to represent me. He's faced her in court and swears that she's the best. Within an hour she's in our living room, arranging with the district attorney's office for me to turn myself in.

Both Lauren and Jake escort me to the precinct while my mom stays with Victoria. Jake's position secures my humane treatment. The police pretend that I'm a run-of-the-mill crazy murderer and not a cop killer. Though I am fingerprinted, made to change clothes, and checked, naked, for contraband, I am not roughed up or left to rot in a holding cell for hours with other criminally insane people.

When I am done being "processed," I enter a musty-smelling room with gray carpet running up the sides and a table in the center. It's cold in my thin orange jumpsuit. Lauren sits on one of two chairs beside a metal table. She smiles at me in an encouraging way, as though I've been through the worst of it.

I slump on the metal stool, feeling as though my life force oozed out of my body at some point during my transformation from wife to inmate. "Where's Jake?" I sound desperate. I've never wanted to see my husband so badly. His determination to stand by me has reignited all the loving feelings that I ever had for him, burning through my apathy and hate. I love him. I need him. He and Victoria are my everything.

Lauren tilts her head and grins. "Jake is outside. I want to talk through my strategy with you first. You're my client. Jake doesn't need to hear everything we discuss."

I straighten up on the stool. She knows something that she believes Jake shouldn't. Has she spoken to Tyler?

"I've interviewed some fertility experts," she says. "They will swear that the hormone withdrawals that you experienced after giving birth likely played a role in destabilizing your brain and made you unable to control your actions."

I breathe. "That's good, I guess."

"We also have an expert on circadian rhythms who will testify that the sleep deprivation you were experiencing from nursing an infant all night might have also contributed to you becoming divorced from reality, kind of putting you in a dream state while you were talking to the deceased."

I think back to Colleen's hand, how it had resembled a spider crawling toward the gun. Was I half asleep when I murdered her? Was I incapable of stopping myself?

"The pipe makes what you did look premeditated, but I think the sleep expert will go a long way toward convincing a jury or judge that you picked it up without being fully aware of your intentions."

She smiles at me. There's something behind the expression. I nod for her to continue, still bracing myself.

"I also spoke with that shrink you were seeing."

My stomach drops to my knees. She'll either tell Jake that I revenge-cheated or it will come out in court. He won't support me then. Right now, he feels as though he's to blame for pushing his vulnerable wife over the edge. But if he feels that I was not weak and helpless, that I, in fact, was ready to leave him . . .

"Dr. Tyler Williams will swear under oath that you were suffering from a very severe type of postpartum depression that made it difficult for you to control your actions and emotions."

"He said that?"

My lawyer smiles, a closed-mouth, knowing expression. There's a glint in her eye. "He did. He also said that your postpartum depression was so severe that you may have also suffered from transference—thinking that you had romantic feelings for your doctor and that they were reciprocated. Given everything you were going through and your discovery of Jake's cheating, it makes sense. He said you might believe that things happened between you that never did. You could have suffered delusions."

I understand the subtext. Tyler is willing to testify that I was crazy when I killed Colleen as long as I don't out him for having a romantic relationship with a patient. "I understand," I say. "Any feelings that I had for him were really just me being desperate and delusional."

She raps the metal table with her fingertips in approval and dips her head toward her briefcase. When she rises, she holds a manila folder, a pen, and a yellow legal pad. She places everything on the table and then pulls the notebook in front of her. She peels back the cover, picks up the pen, and taps the point against the first sheet. "Okay." She inhales and then exhales audibly, as though we have a long night ahead of us. "Let's go over our story from the beginning."

# Acknowledgments

Thank you to all the wonderful family and friends who have encouraged me to continue telling stories. You know who you are. I love you and write with you in mind. Thanks to my amazing agent, Paula Munier, who tells me like it is, and the fantastic team at Crooked Lane. Much thanks to the creative, supportive, and vibrant thriller writing community for your friendship. I am deeply indebted to my husband and daughters, all of whom deal with my distraction and everything that comes with my living between the real world and imaginary ones. You three are my heart. Thanks to the early readers who weighed in on this book before it went to print. Your fresh eyes made me see it better. Last but never least, thanks to the higher power that I'll never believe is fiction.